PRAISE FOR WEST POINT

[*West Point* is] an appealing tale of military service during a very trying time in our national history. —Mike Herbert, CAPTAIN, USN (Ret)

West Point has all the qualities of a good read; it is enjoyable, informative, humorous, and true to life. —L.D. Swift, PhD

Exceptional story! Captivating! .... I could not put it down. —Steve Faustm, MSgt USAF (Ret)

I'm hooked on the trilogy! Serious, humorous, and emotional. Great read. —John Barrett , Chief Master Sergeant, USAF (Ret)

Not only does he capture daily life of a cadet, he details the ethos these institutions instill in young men and women willing to serve. —Greg Graves, Reviewer

His writings are addictive. You won't be able to put them down. An amazing author, mentor, and friend! —J.B. Snipes, Major, U.S. Army

[*West Point*] will leave you excited for further explorations into a unique transitional period in American culture centered around an institution that seemingly holds true to its principles even through cultural shifts. —Trae Wolfe, 1LT U.S.Army, USMA Class of 2016

A young man forms lasting friendships and finds meaning in his life while attending West Point in J.M. Patton's debut novel set in the Vietnam War era. ... A coming-of-age tale about friendship and patriotism. —*Kirkus Reviews*

WEST POINT

Publish Authority
Offices in
Newport Beach, CA and Roswell, GA USA

Raeghan Rebstock, Cover Design Lead
Sandy Lyons, Editor
Frank Eastland, The Publisher

The Library of Congress has established a Cataloging-in-Publication record for this title.
ISBN: 978-1-7325347-7-3
eBook ISBN: 978-1-7325347-6-6

www.PublishAuthority.com

Chief Petty Officer Donald R. Patton, USN- Hospital Corpsman,
3ʳᵈ Marine Division, Vietnam (2) – RIP.
For his service many Marines lived to go home

And

Midshipman First Class Steven O. Coats, United States Naval Academy,
Class of 1973 – RIP.
In our hearts and minds, he will remain forever young

And

Jim Roth, Sr. - RIP
An Exemplary Individual

The long gray line has never failed us. Were you to do so, a million ghosts in olive drab, in brown khaki, in blue and gray, would rise from their white crosses, thundering those magic words: Duty, Honor, Country.

GENERAL DOUGLAS MACARTHUR

FOREWORD

As I start this Forward, I'll first try to answer the question of what qualifies a retired Navy pilot to comment on a book with the, specifically, non-Navy title of West Point. It's a good question, and one that helps me illustrate the point that regardless of branch of service one serves in, all military service is more similar than the reader might assume. The author J. M. Patton, more commonly known as Mike, and I were both college cadets at New Mexico Military Institute (NMMI) in 1967-1969. As roommates, we shared a lot of great and memorable experiences while we were there, but that's a story better told over a beer or two. After leaving NMMI, Mike went on to West Point while I became a Navy pilot. It's a fact that our service was inspired by the same underlying tenets we had learned at NMMI, and because of this, our military experiences were actually more alike than they were different. During my Navy career, I experienced the reality of what the author so accurately portrayed about military service during this time period. I am honored to offer my comments of J. M. Patton's *West Point*, Book I of the trilogy *A Full Measure,* not only as a Navy pilot but as his friend who has walked this path with him.

West Point begins with the engrossing story of a Texas boy who joins West Point's Long Gray Line during the pervasively anti-war, anti-military, anti-establishment, anti-everything Vietnam War Era. For Jake, the book's main character, the 1960s-70s were not "drugs, sex, and rock and roll," but the beginning of a military career based on tenets of Duty, Honor, and Commitment. The book's setting in this era illustrates the disdain that military members faced at the hands of their civilian contemporaries. The author shows us how Jake intellectually matures as a future officer while staying the course despite the appearance of a country that hates him for his desire to serve it. And, when he is exposed to both good and bad role models with respect to ethical leadership, Jake discovers that not all officers are worthy mentors for him to emulate. Jake seeks to honorably serve in his nation's military, and he is quickly revealed in the novel to be an embodiment of the military's underlying and foundational ethics. That's the essence of Patton's *West Point*. It lets the reader see and experience, through Jake's eyes, the realities of military service, and the personal sacrifices that will come as a by-product of that commitment. As the reader is exposed to that reality, one is likely to laugh out loud, be energized by the tale, and perhaps shed a tear or two.

As Jake's story progresses, the reader will discover that the book is much more than a book about his West Point experience. You will read about the bonding, which is commonplace in military service, between Jake, his roommate Patrick McSwain, and Jake's life-long friend at the Naval Academy. And, the author captures the camaraderie that exists between the different branches of our nation's services with his depiction of the Army-Navy football game, made manifest by the traditional pranking that always transpires as part of their inter-service rivalry. This is an accurate depiction of what happens in real life. Whenever you have warriors from different branches of the military rubbing shoulders, you'll always hear the traditional ribbing and put-downs that come with being recognized as a Jarhead, Grunt, Flyboy, or Squid. Patton brings to life on the written page this key facet of military life as these Army-Navy brethren act out their inter-service rivalry. It is not only exhilarating and humorous to read, but it is also real.

This first novel of the trilogy, *A Full Measure*, introduces an insidious antagonist that forebodes the core evil found today in real-world Islamic terrorists who broadcast their ruthless beheadings and other despicable acts of violence against the Western world. Islamic fundamentalism and its Doctrine of Taubid, relevant to targeting unbelievers for jihad, is millennially historical. Yet, the last half-century's steady resurgence of terrorism has redefined the mission of the U.S. military since the latter days of the Vietnam War. The last two decades of escalation has become the most significant threat toward Western civilization in these contemporary times. In Patton's trilogy, the reader will see how the challenges in Jake's career change and multiply as the military mission shifts from Vietnam's cold war to today's threat of extreme Islamic terrorism.

You, the reader, will discover that *West Point* is relevant and entertaining for both the Vietnam and post-Vietnam era. We have a front row seat as the book's characters evolve from boys into warriors who are at the point of the spear. Both military and non-military readers will resonate with Jake's story. The first book in Patton's trilogy, *West Point* provides a great first step into a meaningful insight of the demands of military service and the impact that it has on those that have chosen to love the serviceman, but not necessarily the service itself. Regardless, the profession of arms ultimately requires they share the sacrifices and bruises of this calling.

This book, and the entire trilogy, tells a meaty and emotionally provoking story that will make the reader want to follow Jake and his comrades in arms throughout their careers. I anxiously await the next book in Patton's trilogy.

Mike, from me to you — Mission Accomplished.

Bravo Zulu!
Mike Herbert
CAPTAIN, U. S. NAVY (Ret)

PROLOGUE

I WAS a cadet at West Point (United States Military Academy) in the Class of 1973. Some early readers of the novel West Point, Book I of the trilogy *A Full Measure*, have called it a work of fact-fiction. Unmistakably, the entire trilogy consists of three novels, and therein, fiction. While the framework and settings are factual, the characters and events are fictional, yet presented in a manner that will give the reader a good view of what it is like to be a cadet at West Point during the Vietnam War Era.

While Book I, *West Point*, is intended to bring awareness of the West Point life and mission during that era, the trilogy—*A Full Measure*—takes the reader on a journey through the difficulties of reconstructing the military after Vietnam and the changes that have occurred at the service academies as a result. Controversy abounds as many view the pre-1976 academies as "The Old Corps," a dividing line of change, which has been greatly influenced by political and social changes in America. Are the changes good, and in the best interests of America's military readiness? By way of these novels, you, the reader, may decide for yourself.

J.M. Patton

CHAPTER ONE

1 July 1969
0930 Hours
United States Military Academy
West Point, New York

EIGHTEEN-YEAR-OLD JOHN PAUL JACOBS, better known as Jake, sat next to the window near the rear of the bus as it rumbled smoothly along the road that mimicked the banks of the Hudson River, fifty miles inland from New York City. He had boarded the bus at the New York Port Authority as his letter from the academy had instructed, and he felt dazed by the changes he knew he was about to experience.

In spite of the silence of the passengers on the bus, and partially because of it, Jake knew that all aboard were destined for their first day at West Point. The bus ride had been disturbingly quiet, except for the whine of tires on black asphalt and the muffled roar of the diesel engine. There were a few short, superficial conversations, but for the most part, the passengers were preoccupied with their thoughts, or more likely, their fears.

As the bus rolled along the banks of the Hudson River, Jake marveled at the magnificence of its mighty expanse and felt a

3

sense of his own insignificance next to it. There were rivers around Comanche, Texas, but none as vast and majestic as the Hudson. He thought of how little he really knew about any place except the small county to which he had been born. The extent of his travels had been to neighboring towns for football games and two trips to Austin where he and his father had driven Charley to the airport to begin his first year at West Point, and yesterday.

Jake and Steve Ross had been driven to Austin before daylight by Steve's mother to board an airplane that would take them both to new worlds. Steve had flown once before and needlessly detailed every little movement, sensation, and sound for Jake's benefit.

On the ground in St. Louis, Jake and Steve found a snack bar, gulped down two hot dogs and a cola, then scurried down the long gateway for Steve's connecting flight. Steve was going to Baltimore and Jake to New York City. As Jake's bus snaked along the Hudson, Steve sat on a similar bus with anticipation of setting foot for the first time at the United States Naval Academy, Annapolis, Maryland.

"Good luck, Steve. See you in Philadelphia in November, when Army beats Navy," Jake had said over the female voice announcing the boarding of Steve's flight.

"Fat chance of that! I'll meet you under the Army goal post at halftime. We'll see how cocky you are then."

The boys joined in a firm handshake and looked into each other's eyes. They had planned this moment for years, each with his dream about to be fulfilled separately, yet still inextricably connected and bonded for life. Without another word, Steve turned, picked up his small bag, and headed for the ramp. Just before he stepped inside, he looked over his shoulder, winked at Jake, flipped a wave, and turned to be on his way.

The bus maintained its speed as it passed through the gates of the academy. The scenery changed immediately from the civilian environment he had known to one of impeccability and military propriety. The Thayer Hotel flashed past him, and the roar of the downshifting bus announced that within minutes all life as he had known it was gone forever. Simply gone, yet inexplicably so but for those who had walked the same path. Unconsciously, Jake sat erect in his seat with a surge of adrenaline rushing to meet his increased anticipation. The moment was an odd mixture of new visible reality and old imaginations created in his mind from the stories Charley had told across the dining room table while on Christmas or summer leave. It had been from those mental images that he had grown since the age of thirteen to a deeply rooted desire to follow his older brother's footsteps to West Point and the life of a professional soldier. He thought he knew what to expect for the next four years. Charley had told him. But when the bus came to a stop, all the anticipation of the glory that he had so long imagined turned to fear. The bus driver set the brake, opened the hydraulic door, and looked in his mirror at his passengers. "We're here, boys. Good luck."

Even before Jake could decipher the slight sarcasm in the driver's tone, an upper-class cadet scrambled up the steps and stood for a long moment beside the driver, surveying the forty-odd sets of wide eyes upon him. The cadet looked the model soldier in his gray trousers with a black stripe down the outside seam of both legs, crisply starched short-sleeved white shirt with gray epaulets, white gloves, and white hat with a gold braid, its black visor placed exactly a two-finger distance above his eyebrows. With a perfect dress-off, his heavily starched shirt was absent a single wrinkle around his waist, and his presence embodied the very essence of West Point's superior bearing and military functionality.

"Welcome, gentlemen, and I use that term with some reservation. Your ass is mine. On my command, and only on my command, file off this bus in an orderly fashion with your one bag of gear and form on me per my instructions. Stand tall and keep your mouth shut until you are requested to speak. Do you understand?"

The new arrivals continued to sit wide-eyed and open-mouthed. Not a sound was heard.

"When I ask a question, you will all sound off immediately with a great deal of vigor!" the upperclassman barked. "I say again. Do you understand?" he bellowed out at about 90-decibels.

"Yes, sir," came a weak reply from the newly arrived. The response was neither in unison nor was it from enthusiastically booming voices.

The young men filed off the bus into four lines, following the instructions of the half-dozen cadre members. Now off the bus, Jake had his first clear view of the post. He was almost over-whelmed by the massive granite buildings and the view across the parade ground, known as The Plain, toward the towering marble cylinder of Battle Monument at Trophy Point, backdropped by a vibrantly beautiful view of the Hudson River. His mouth parted slightly in awe at the magnificent beauty of his new home. The environment itself was beyond his wildest imagination.

"What are you gazing at, Mister!" an upperclassman shouted, not more than an inch from his ear. "You thinking about buying this place?"

Jake froze in his tracks as his shoulders tensed, and the hair on his neck immediately began to rise from fear. "No," Jake said, his eyes staring straight ahead into the far distance.

Coming immediately around to address Jake nose-to-nose, the upperclassman, slightly bending at the waist, arms and hands stiff-ened at his side, screamed, "You mean, 'No, sir!' Don't you! You scumbag smack!" going red in the face and spitting a little as he raged.

"Yes, sir!" Jake shouted back, unnerved, heavily emphasizing the "sir." "I mean, No, sir!" he then said meekly. He was suddenly confused about the proper answer, and actually, even the question. Jake was petrified as though his blood had suddenly run cold. He had expected to be yelled at. He had expected to be verbally harassed. But he had not prepared himself for a vicious, panic-producing assault.

"You better not be gazing around, smack! You keep your head and eyes to the front, Mister, at all times," the upperclassman said, still an inch from his ear and with a thoroughly disgusted tone in his voice. "And, Mister, when you respond to a question, I want to hear you pop off with the answer! You know what "pop off" means, you worthless piece of meat?"

"No, sir," Jake replied stiffly.

The upperclassman rose slightly on the balls of his feet to get even closer to Jake's ear as he shouted. "It means that when asked a question, you respond like you have a set of balls, boy! When you pop off, I want you to awaken the dead! If you insist on sounding like a wimp, we'll send your scrawny ass to the Naval Academy. You got that, Mister?"

"Yes, sir!" Jake screamed at the top of his lungs, sweat beading on his forehead and rolling down the sides of his face. Without another word, the upperclassman turned crisply and walked away.

The next half-hour organized the new arrivals into smaller groups ready to be delivered by a cadre member to their respective new cadet companies, and Jake was beginning to feel less personally attacked in his recent encounter with the old cadet. As he stood rigid, he heard others enduring similar verbal attacks from all over the post for other high crimes against the Corps of Cadets. He strained his ears to hear and understand the plight of others in the hope that he would never again bring the wrath of an old cadet upon himself. When ordered to move-out, his group followed an old cadet in single file to the far side of The Plain to a large concrete slab in front of Washington Hall, the five-story gray, granite building that served as a barracks facility and housed the enormous mess hall.

As Jake waited his turn for the old cadet working his way down the line with a clipboard in hand, checking his roster, and issuing instructions, Jake was astonished by the highly organized chaos around him. With eyes staring unflinchingly straight ahead, he was fully aware that the area was hyperactive with squad formations passing in front of his view. Some of the squads were at a march, others at the double-time. Some of the new cadets were still in civilian clothes, others were wearing gray shorts and white T-shirts. Some new cadets had hair, others had absolutely no hair at all. As he watched the chaos from his very narrow field of vision, the thought occurred to him that the one constant in this new and frightening environment was that the air was filled with a great deal of popping off.

"What's your name, Mister?" the upperclassman asked as he stepped in front of Jake.

"John Paul Jacobs, sir."

"Mister Jacobs," the cadet said in a calm but businesslike manner as he checked his roster, "the correct response is, "New Cadet Jacobs." The only one that cares that you have a first name is your mother. For the next eleven months, you may occasionally be addressed as Jacobs, but for the most part, you will appropriately be answering to the names of smack, crot, bean, beanhead, scumbag, or any other descriptive noun the upper class might rightfully assign to you. Do you understand?"

"Yes, sir!"

"Mister Jacobs. When I tell you to do so, you will take your bag and report to the man in the red sash standing in the Sally Port immediately over my right shoulder. Do you understand?"

"Yes, sir!" Jake replied crisply. He was greatly encouraged that there existed an old cadet that appeared to be civil.

"Mister Jacobs. You will double-time to the man in the red sash, stopping at a distance exactly three feet from him, set your bag on the slab, come to the position of attention, and render a salute. You are to hold that salute, and you are to say, "Sir, New Cadet Jacobs reporting to the man in the red sash, as ordered." You are to continue to hold that salute until the man in the red sash returns your salute, after which you will terminate your salute by bringing your right arm crisply to your side in the position of attention. Do you understand, Mister Jacobs?"

"Yes, sir!"

"Move Out, Mister Jacobs," the cadet said as he executed a

precise right-face, took one step, then a left-face to issue instructions to the next new cadet.

Though terrified that he would somehow fail to follow his instructions to the letter, and thereby suffer the wrath of the man in the red sash, Jake survived the task. Prior to returning the salute, the man in the red sash took two steps forward, asked Jake, "May I have permission to touch you?", and with the desired response, adjusted the positioning of Jake's hand in the salute, then stepped back.

"Mister Jacobs. At my command, you are to enter the door to my left and double-time to the fifth floor. At all times, Mister Jacobs, your arms are to be in a position parallel to the ground, and you are otherwise to appear to be physically in the position of attention. You will square all corners and remain to the far right-hand side of the stairwell. If you approach a member of the upper-class, you are to immediately stop, slam your back to the wall in the position of attention, and request permission to pass. You are to say, "Sir, may I pass?" With permission, you may continue your mission. Do you understand, Mister Jacobs?"

"Yes, sir!" Jake replied.

"Mister Jacobs. You have been assigned to the 7th New Cadet Company. Upon your arrival to the fifth floor, you will be escorted to the office of the company first sergeant. When you enter the first sergeant's office, you will stop precisely three steps from the desk, render a perfect salute until returned, and you will say exactly, "Sir, New Cadet Jacobs reporting to the First Sergeant of the 7th New Cadet Company for the first time as ordered." Do you understand, Mister Jacobs?"

"Yes, sir!"

Jake entered the stairwell at a run, remembering his instructions of the protocol as a new cadet. Zigzagging up the stairs toward the fifth floor he alternately mumbled short prayers to himself in the hope that he would remember exactly what he was to say to the first sergeant, would not be too winded to report after running up five flights of stairs, and that he would not encounter any old cadets en route. And, since religious miracles do occasionally occur, Jake did arrive on the fifth floor without significant incident from the old cadets along the way, and he did manage to successfully report to the first sergeant.

Jake was given his room assignment, then lead down the hall to his room. His apprehension grew with each step as he became conscious of the organized chaos that was at an even greater fervor than it had been on the slab. There were old cadets everywhere, an inch or less from some poor soul's ear or nose, discussing with him, in the West Point fashion, his most recent crime against the Corps.

Jake's room was half-way down a long hallway with windows overlooking The Plain and the Hudson River in the distance. When he found and entered it, simply caused by his sudden appearance, two other new cadets jerked their heads in his direction to quickly determine whether he was friend or foe. The room was furnished for necessity only. There was one stacked bunk on the right, a single on the left, three desks with bookshelves, three closets with an assortment of built-in drawers, and one sink. At the moment, the room was in disarray. Jake's new roommates had gear scattered from the large duffel bags on their bunks. The bags contained everything required for one to set up home, as long as one's concept of home is to possess only that which allows one to merely exist. The immediate problem was where to put everything.

With the small bag he had brought from Texas still in his hand, Jake paused just inside the doorway, taking into his already spin-ning mind all that he saw. Almost immediately a tall, handsome young man with blond hair straightened from the single bunk and his scattered gear, grinned widely and quickly moved toward the door with his hand extended as though he had just been reunited with an old friend.

"Welcome, pilgrim," the young man drawled, not unlike a young John Wayne.

I'm Patrick McSwain from Chattanooga, Tennessee."

Jake met Patrick's hand and warm smile enthusiastically. Leon than two hours into the fray, a friendly, Southern accent was most welcome. "I'm John Paul Jacobs from Comanche, Texas. My friends call me, Jake."

His other roommate extended his hand as well and introduced himself as Stephen Hamilton from Boston. Though friendly enough, Jake was aware at once that Stephen was a little disappointed that both his roommates were from culturally barren small towns and spoke with twangy Southern drawls.

"You're on the top bunk," Patrick said. "We haven't the slightest idea what happens next."

Jake glanced at his wristwatch and stared at the dial in disbelief. "It's only eleven o'clock! My God! I thought it was the middle of the afternoon. If time drags like this for the next four years, I'm in big trouble."

"In case you haven't noticed, you are already in trouble," Patrick said chuckling. "By the way, it's eleven hundred hours in Mickey Mouse time. Not eleven o'clock. That "o'clock" business will get you pitched out of a window, or worse. I learned that lesson by getting my ass jumped this morning. You'd of thought I shot a general or something the way they yelled at me. I gotta say, I'm not real crazy about learning the do's and don'ts around here by having some mad dog with rabies slobbering on the bridge of my nose." Confirming Patrick's statement, the enemy was audibly raging up and down the hallway with enough hostility to last them a lifetime.

The door flew open with a quickness that terrified all three of the roommates and immediately vaporized all thoughts, but one. Oh, crap! There, in the doorway, stood an old cadet, immaculate in his uniform, feet spread a shoulder's width apart, hands on his hips. His firm jaw announced his bearing and his cold eyes peered from exactly a two-finger spacing from the shiny black bill of his service hat. His presence told them that the enemy had arrived to claim the victory that was theirs over the Class of 1973 and eleven months in the making.

"Who told you beanheads to close my door?" the old cadet said in a disgusted tone with the corresponding grimace. "This door is never to be closed. If you, ladies, wanted privacy, you should not have joined the United States Army. You should have gone to some Podunk University." He paused again, surveying the three rigid new cadets with their eyes riveted on the wall. "Five minutes. Uniform is as for PT and form up in squad formation against the wall in my hallway." Without another word, he turned and vanished down the hall. The open door brought the sounds of the calamity that awaited them.

With a genuine desire to comply with their instructions, the three scrambled out of their civilian clothes and into the shorts and T-shirts lodged at the bottom of the duffel bags. As they filed out of the room, Jake in the lead and the other two on his heels, the old cadet stared at them as though their timeliness was as big a crime as though they had been late. Others ran from their nearby rooms, twelve in all, and slammed their backs against the wall in a row. Shock and fear were the looks of the day.

"Very good, gentlemen," the old cadet said in an affable tone as he slowly surveyed the twelve and the imprinted names over their academy crested T-shirts. "I am Mister Cantrell. I'm your squad leader for the first detail of New Cadet Barracks, affectionately known as Beast Barracks, should any of you worthless looking beanheads actually manage to survive the next two months."

Jake and the others stood rigid in their best-untrained position of attention with eyes fixed on imaginary spots on the wall. Until an hour ago, the thought of failure to survive the plebe year had never crossed their minds.

"You are the members of the fourth squad, 3rd platoon, 7th New Cadet Company. My job is to assist in teaching you to become a cadet and a future officer in the United States Army. Do what I tell you when I tell you, and you will be well prepared to succeed at West Point. Fail to give me the best that the academy expects from you and you'll find yourself with a one-way trip back to your mother. Men, West Point is serious business because our country at war is serious business."

Cantrell took a long pause and looked at each member of the squad before issuing the command that could only be executed as imperfectly as any untrained group paralyzed with fear might do. "Left-face! At the route step, follow me to the company area." Without looking back, Cantrell headed for the stairwell with his new gang trailing stiffly and silently behind him like a paddling of ducks, each wondering what a route step might be.

On the slab, Cantrell oriented the squad to the company area and identified for each the exact spot he was to stand for every formation over the next two months. The next fifteen minutes were devoted to the squad's initiation to close order drill, which proved to be disastrous, but informative. Cantrell announced to his squad of disbelievers that by the end of the day they would know how to execute these basic maneuvers and that, as the Class of 1973, they would march as a unit of a thousand strong, in full uniform, to Trophy Point to give their oath of allegiance to the United States.

Any observer would have noticed that the chaos on the slab was nonstop. Squads were moving around in every direction, and all the newcomers were suffering the wrath of their squad leaders. Organized chaos captured a frightening and permanent meaning for those of the Class of 1973.

The fourth squad spent thirty minutes more practicing right and left-face, about-face, the proper and correct way to salute, the position of attention, and parade-rest. If Cantrell spotted the slightest error, he was quick to make the corresponding correction. If the right hand was not at the proper angle to the ground in the salute, or the feet were at a forty-six-degree angle instead of the required forty-five degrees at the position of attention, Cantrell would give instruction down to the smallest detail. More than one newcomer stabbed himself in the eye trying to snap his salute to the corner of his eye with untrained reflexes to do so. The movements were all so strange, and Cantrell demanded perfection in their execution.

JAKE and his new associates were marched through a sally port to the backside of Washington Hall and called to a halt at the double doors leading to the barbershop. Cantrell went inside. During his absence, the squad, for a moment at least, lost all its fear. The professional hairstyling of a West Point barber was an experience they all expected, and their first haircut, but only the first, would prove to be a point of amusement as it had to every entering new cadet since 1802.

"Leave the sideburns, please," Jake whispered out of the corner of his mouth, just loud enough for three or four down the line to hear.

"I'll have a mohawk if you don't mind—and blow dry the top," Patrick said as they all started giggling.

"Are you kidding? These guys have never even heard of a blow dryer." Jake muffled again.

Just as the entire squad was about to get their chuckles under control, Cantrell reappeared. "Who gave you girls permission to talk?" Cantrell shouted. "Jacobs! You think something's funny, Mister?"

"No, sir!" Jake popped off.

"Get your scrawny ass in here, Jacobs! You're first. Keep running your mouth off, and I'll run you out of my beloved Corps within a week. And, you'd better realize I can make you so miserable you'd be begging me to let you pack your bags." Without a reply, Jake marched into the barbershop at the double. Jake's eleven classmates of the 4th squad followed close behind, and they were terrified once more by Cantrell's rage. One barber, out of a group of thirty, motioned Jake with the flick of his hand and Jake moved to his chair as quickly as possible without running. The barber draped a striped cloth around Jake's neck, adjusted it properly, just like a real barber, and asked, "How would you like it, son?"

Jake's mouth slightly dropped open as he slowly turned his head with eyes that spoke of total disbelief at the question.

"Just kidding," the barber said as he simultaneously laughed loudly, in an almost evil sort of way, laid a heavy hand on the top of Jake's head, clicked on the barbershop variety of a chainsaw, and began a smooth skull deep cut from the base of the neck to the center top. Jake watched in the mirror, both in horror and fascination, as his immaculately groomed, dark hair of eighteen years fell to the floor in globs. In its place was nothing but an obscenely shaped skull that was white from having never seen a ray of sunlight.

Though highly amused at their most recent humiliation, the members of the squad took their position against the wall with the appearance of complete seriousness. Cantrell's presence, pacing the line with his hands behind his back, ensured it. When all had arrived at the wall looking rather pitiable, had they been asked, none could have argued against the military efficiency involved. There were twelve haircuts in twelve minutes.

"Gentlemen. Now you know why plebes are known as beans or beanheads. You all look lovely. Of course, your girlfriends back home won't have anything to do with you anymore, but fret not. If the Army wanted you to have a girlfriend, they would issue you one," Cantrell said with the best he could do at not breaking a smile. "Mister Jacobs. Since you like to run off at the mouth, which of your classmates do you think is the loveliest?"

Jake bent at the waist, twisted his neck to look down the line at his classmates, returned to the position of attention, and responded, "It's obvious, sir! I am!"

"Oh? I suppose you're a real ladies' man, in addition to grossly overestimating your current physical appearance, huh, Mister Jacobs?"

"No, sir. I'm a one lady's man," Jake replied.

"Ok, Mister Jacobs, why don't you go ahead and tell the squad about this lady of yours, so they don't have to be bored through two months of Beast Barracks listening to you brag. What's her name?"

Regretting now that he had exposed himself to this much conversation with Cantrell, Jake replied, "Sara, sir!"

"And what does this Sara look like, Mister Jacobs?"

"Gorgeous, sir!"

"A ravishing young morsel, I take it," Cantrell said mockingly. "From what I've seen, Miss Sara may have poor taste in men. I'm not sure you are going to make it at West Point, Jacobs. Thirteen hundred of your classmates are here today. By the end of Beast Barracks, three hundred can go back to Podunk USA. Almost twenty-five percent will not last two months. Where are you from, Mister Jacobs?"

"Sir, I'm from Texas," Jake said, struggling to control his anger.

"Well, gentlemen. That explains Mister Jacob's big mouth, his over-evaluation of his personal appearance, and possibly, even the exaggeration of the stunning beauty of one Miss Sara. More important, is that Mister Jacobs did not express one bit of anger while I threw some pretty good insults at him. Never let anyone read your emotions. Stone-faced through hard times and good times. Good job, Jacobs."

Cantrell marched his squad up the steps of the mess hall like a mother goose and a dozen ugly ducklings trailing closely after her. The sunlight made dramatic the white bony heads of the newly sheared. "Gentlemen," Cantrell said. "You will find the food at West Point the best in the world. Even better than mom's. Unfortunately, you won't be eating much of it until next June. Rather than elaborate, I'll allow your table commandant and his two eager assistants to teach you proper etiquette. I can assure you, gentlemen, that sitting down to a meal will never be quite the same again—for the rest of your natural lives."

Cantrell slowly paced down the line with his hands behind his back as he read the terror and dread in each face. The sounds belching from the entry to the mess hall confirmed to the new cadets that Cantrell spoke the truth without exaggeration. Turning sharply at the end of the line he said, "When we enter the mess hall, keep your chins in, your chest out, your head and eyes straight to the front, and your mouth shut. When you are assigned to your table, stand at attention an inch behind your chair, eyes fixed on the center of your plate. You'll be told to take seats by none other than the King of Beast, who dines with his staff on the "poop deck" in the center of the mess hall. Since I'm certain that none of you beauties have any questions, follow me."

Though Jake and Patrick had known each other less than two hours, both made sure they were together. Somehow, the thought of having at least one friend in this unholy place was a comfort, but in reality, it only further proved the old adage that misery loves company.

Jake found entry into the mess hall to be one of the hardest things he had ever done. It took all the concentration he could muster not to gaze around in awe. Through his peripheral vision, Jake saw a ceiling that seemed to tower fifty feet in height with massive chandeliers hanging in the four wings that tabled a thousand cadets in each wing. When entering the massive hall, it looked like a sea of tables for ten. The walls were lined with windows reaching to the ceiling, flags from every State, portraits of the forty-two superintendents of the academy, the names of Thayer and Lee and MacArthur and Taylor and Westmoreland being but a few, and multi-colored battle flags, equally spaced, hung with bullet holes, tears, and scorches. Each flag was original, and each had been carried in battle by units of the United States Army in a nearly two-hundred-year-old history of fighting for freedom around the globe. In one wing that Jake could see, the back wall framed an enormous stained-glass window that spread the entire width of the wall and half its height. From his readings, he knew that the window portrayed the life of George Washington. In the center of the four wings stood a granite structure resembling a small castle; the poop deck, and the table belonging to the King of Beast. As Jake and his squad continued their walk to the south wing, he could hardly avoid staring at the magnificent mural covering the back wall depicting twenty great battles and twenty great generals in world history. For the moment, Jake felt that in his being here, at West Point, he was a part of history, that of the past and that yet to be made. And, indeed he was. However, for the privilege, the price to pay for it had just begun.

Cantrell made sure that all twelve of his squad were at one of two tables adjacent each other in the company area, then took his place on the table commandant's right at the head of the table. Jake had only a quick glance at the table commandant before he riveted his eyes to his plate in front of him. The table commandant wore brass on his epaulets with a black background and four black bars. Jake knew from Charley's days at The Point that the table commandant's brass was that of a first classman or "firstie," whereas Cantrell's gray-blue brass signified that he was a second classman or "cow." The four black bars were anyone's guess as far as Jake was concerned, but if nothing else, they probably meant that this firstie was high on the list of upperclassmen to avoid making mad.

The table was quiet but for the three upperclassmen talking in normal tones at the end of the table. It certainly was not so at many tables around them. The sounds of furious upperclassmen and new cadets popping off were enough to make the seven new cadets at the table stand like statues with eyes glued to their plates.

"Battalion. Atten shun!" came an ominous command over the loudspeaker system from the poop deck. The mess hall immediately grew quiet. Following a few short announcements, that made no sense to the new cadets, and the saying of Grace over the meal, the command was given, "Take seats!" And with that command from the King of Beast, the cadet commander of Beast Barracks, the protocol for mealtime announcements and correct military commands—with their long, drawn-out enunciation—set the pattern for the Class of 1973's next four thousand meals in the mess hall.

"All right, smacks!" the table commandant barked. "Mount your chairs. You will sit at attention on the last three inches of your chair. Arms to your sides. Eyes fixed on the academy crest at the top of your plate."

The new cadets scrambled to the sitting position, none wishing to hesitate at the slightest command. Jake sat at the end of the table, directly facing the table commandant and felt envious of Patrick, on his right. He thought that being the most visible was bound to mean trouble. The others, on the sides of the table, seemed less conspicuous.

"Pass the food around clockwise. Everyone takes a serving. Mister McSwain, you are the Gunner. Mister Jacobs, you are the Beverage Corporal. Mister Lamont, you are the Dessert Cutter."

While the food was served around the table, Cantrell said, "McSwain. As Gunner, your job is to ensure that there is always sufficient food on this table. You will be served each dish last. When the dish comes to you, and you've served yourself, you will determine how many servings remain in the dish. Then you will say, "Sir, there are four-and-a-butt servings of mashed potatoes, or whatever it is, remaining. Would anyone care for an additional serving of mashed potatoes, sir?" Then, you are to glance down the table to determine how many cadets have stuck their arm out, thereby indicating their desire for an additional serving. It's simple, McSwain. If there are more arms than servings remaining in the dish, you are to hold the dish with your left hand over your head until a waiter comes to take it from you. If there's no interest in additional servings of mashed potatoes, then set the dish on the table. You are to do this with every dish. Do I make myself clear, Mister McSwain?"

"Yes, sir!" Patrick popped off, totally confused.

"Mister Jacobs," the table commandant said. "Your job as Beverage Corporal is to serve everyone their beverage. Tonight, before taps, you are to ping, meaning to scramble like your pants are on fire, around to the rooms of the upperclassmen at this table and determine their beverage preference for each meal. Bring a notebook. In addition, Mister Jacobs, it's your duty to request permission for your classmates to eat. When each of your class-mates has his food, and when all duties at the table have been completed, you are to say, "Sir, the fourth classmen at this table have properly completed their duties and are now prepared to eat." And, in preparation, each new cadet is to tear off one small piece of bread and place it on the corner of his plate. When I give the command to eat, each new cadet is to quickly snatch his piece of bread into his mouth before preceding further with the meal. Do you understand, Mister Jacobs?"

"Yes, sir!" Jake popped off, looking even more confused than Patrick.

"Mister Lamont," the table commandant barked again. "You are the Dessert Cutter. You see that apple pie on the table?"

"Yes, sir!"

"Your job is," the table commandant continued, "to hold the pie up with both hands in front of you and say, "Sir, the dessert for this meal is apple pie. Would anyone at this table care for a serving of apple pie, please, sir?" Those that want dessert will stick out their hand. Those that don't won't. Count carefully, Mister Lamont. When you have the count, cut the pie accordingly. Have you ever cut a pie into ten precisely equal portions before, Mister Lamont?"

"No, sir!" Lamont popped off with fear in his voice.

"After you've cut the pie, Mister Lamont, you'll again hold it in front of you and say, "sir, the dessert has been cut. Apple pie to the head of the table for inspection, please, sir." After I've inspected your excellent work and made whatever comments it deserves, you will have completed your duties. Do you understand, Mister Lamont?"

"Yes, sir!" Lamont said as he reached for the pie.

"Sir! There are four servings of cream corn on the table. Would anyone care for more cream corn, sir?" Patrick screamed.

"What did you say, McSwain?" the third upperclassman at the table yelled. "Start over, McSwain. You screwed it up!"

As Patrick searched his memory for the proper words and fought off the distraction from the sweat rolling down the middle of his back, Lamont announced the apple pie and screwed that up as well. Jake did not have the slightest idea what to pour into the glasses, so he alternately poured from the two large containers. Some of the glasses had ice. Some had none. Within moments, all three upperclassmen were yelling at the three new cadets at the end of the table while the other four new cadets sat in silent terror, forever thankful that they had been blessed with a chair out of the war zone.

"Did I tell you I wanted this yuk green juice, Mister Jacobs?" the table commandant shouted. "And who told you I wanted two ice cubes? Do it over, Jacobs —and get it right!"

"Cut the pie, smack! Ten equal pieces," the third old cadet snarled in a tone that hinted of demon possession.

"There are exactly four servings, huh, McSwain?" Cantrell ridiculed. "If there aren't exactly four, you better say "four and a butt." You got that, Mister? Do it over, McSwain!" Lamont cut the pie as though he had a vibrator strapped to his wrist and managed to get it to the head of the table after a half dozen corrections to his assigned verbiage.

"What the hell is this, Lamont?" the table commandant said, staring at the apple pie in disbelief. "Eyes up here. All you, smacks, look at this!" The new cadets reluctantly looked to the head of the table as the old cadet held the pie at an angle for them to see. There may have been ten pieces. But then again, there might have been more or less. One piece was the size of a full third and others were cut so thin they would not make for a single bite. "I'm not believing this, Lamont! This is pitiful! Fix it!"

The pie was shuffled back down the table toward Lamont, handled by the new cadets along the way as though it were a live grenade. Everyone at the table had the same thought. How does one recut an already cut pie? The question was terrifying because it was apparent that the table commandant fully expected the pie to be fixed. The beads of sweat were no longer confined to the back of Lamont's neck. The pressure. His face suddenly glistened as though he had just walked in from a heavy rain.

"Well, fix it, Lamont!" the demon-possessed old cadet shouted.

Following two or three minutes of silence at the table with all three upperclassmen staring at Lamont, as he in turn, helplessly stared at the pie in front of him while praying for a miracle, Cantrell said, "Mister Jacobs!"

"Yes, sir!" Jake replied, wondering what this God-awful dilemma had to do with him.

"Since you claim to be the most handsome among your classmates, and since you are from Texas, I'm sure you'll have no problem helping your classmate. Take the pie from Mister Lamont. You fix it!"

Jake hesitated. Lamont's fear was contagious. After a moment, he took the pie and placed it next to his plate as ordered. A reasonable solution to the problem seemed to escape him because of the distracting thought of wanting to reach out with both hands and strangle Lamont.

"Well, Jacobs," Cantrell said. "We're waiting. Surely a Texan can do something as simple as fix a broken pie."

Without a moment's hesitation, Jake picked up his spoon, and viciously attacked the pie. He decimated it into a thousand tiny pieces and vented his anger at Cantrell's flippant insults toward the State of Texas. As he slashed at the pie with wild swings, bits and pieces took to the air and splattered both Patrick and Lamont.

In less than ten seconds, Jake dropped the spoon with a loud clatter, picked up the pie in both hands, and announced in a military manner, "Sir! Apple cobbler to the head of the table for inspection, please sir!"

Silence followed for a full minute. All three of the upperclassmen sat stunned, mouths slightly open, eyes staring at Jake in disbelief as he sat with the recently acquired cobbler extended in front of him. Upperclassmen at adjacent tables had heard the pie problem as it developed and its solution. They now came over to the table with the same unbelieving stare. In that silent minute, the table was surrounded by upperclassmen who came to get a closer look at the bold before June plebe and to see how Cadet Captain Jonathan Scott, the company commander of the 7th New Cadet Company, was going to handle the situation. Or, possibly, to try to prevent the murder of a new cadet in front of so many witnesses.

Without moving the pie, or his eyes, Jake was very much aware of the mob gathering. A single bead of sweat slowly rolled down his back, an excruciating sensation adding misery to an already hopeless situation.

"Mister Jacobs," Cadet Captain Scott said calmly. "Put the cobbler on the table."

Jake did as he was told without flinching his eyes in the least.

"Congratulations, Mister Jacobs. You are to be commended on solving a difficult problem, under pressure, with some creative thinking. I think I recall a similar solution from years ago. You may survive Beast Barracks. Or not. If it turns out that you're nothing more than a smart-ass, I'll personally break you. Do you understand, Mister Jacobs?"

"Yes, sir!" Jake popped off. Relief poured over him. He would be permitted to live awhile longer.

As the mob of old cadets returned to their tables satisfied that the shedding of blood would be postponed, Scott asked, "Mister Jacobs, do you know why Mister Cantrell has an irritating grin on his face and looks so smug?"

"No, sir!" Jake responded, afraid to look up from his plate.

"Because Mister Cantrell, like you, is from Texas. Amarillo, Texas. And, like you, he thinks that all Texans are smarter, tougher, and better looking than the rest of the human race. We failed to teach him otherwise when he was a plebe, but we'll succeed with you. When you come around to my room this evening for beverage preferences, plan on staying awhile for a little chit-chat."

"Battalions Rise!" was heard from the poop deck. Jake could hardly believe his ears. In front of him, completely untouched, was an inviting meal of round steak grilled in onions and brown gravy, cream corn, mashed potatoes dripping in melted butter, stewed carrots, hot apple cobbler, and of course, one tiny bite of bread. Seven plates at the table were untouched. Three plates were in stark contrast. They were empty. Only the three upperclassmen were fed and content.

CHAPTER TWO

1300 Hours
1 July 1969
United States Military Academy
West Point, New York

THE MEMBERS of the fourth squad took their disbelief, and their hunger, to the company area on the slab, which was characterized by uncontrollable anxiety. Cantrell, again with hands behind his back, walked down the line looking at each member of his squad. "Gentlemen. Let's cover a few items of interest while we wait our turn to get uniforms. First, unless asked a direct question that calls for elaboration on your part, a cadet has four basic answers to any question. They are "Yes, sir", "No, sir", "Sir, I do not know", and "No excuse, sir"." Cantrell paused before walking up to within inches of Patrick's face. "Mister McSwain. If you were late to one of my fascinating formations because a truck ran over you and broke both your legs—what would your response be when I asked you why you were late?"

Quickly, Patrick mentally processed the data. Before he answered, he went through the pros and cons for an answer that would not put him on the wrong side of Cantrell for the next year.

In the blink of an eye, he thought, *The reasonable answer would be that I was hit by a truck, and I had broken both legs, and therefore late. However, there is the conflicting data that nothing at West Point, so far, seemed to fit the criteria of being reasonable. It is likely that there is only one place in the world where getting run over by a truck, resulting in two broken legs, is not a reasonable excuse for tardiness. And, that place is West Point.* Therefore, from this process of rapid deduction, Patrick was able to deliver the correct response to Cantrell. "No excuse, sir!" he popped off.

"That's correct, Mister McSwain, though I know you don't really believe it. But, that's ok because no one around here gives a hoot what you believe, nor think. What we do give a hoot about is that cadets don't give excuses for failure."

Cantrell took one step and a modified left-face to stand nose to nose with Jake as he shouted, "Jacobs, are you hungry?"

"Yes, sir!" Jake shouted back.

"Why are you hungry, Mister Jacobs?"

"Sir, I do not know!"

"It's because you and your dipshit classmates screwed up. Isn't it, Mister Jacobs?"

"Yes, sir!"

"Why did you screw up, Mister Jacobs?"

"No excuse, sir!" Jake said. Though his eyes were unflinching while Cantrell screamed in his face, the sweat rolling down his back more truthfully told of the stress he felt.

Cantrell backed away from Jake expressionless. Following another nerve-racking silence of sixty seconds, Cantrell said, "Secondly, gentlemen, there's a great deal of poop, or memorized information, you are expected to know. At any time, an upperclassman can ask you what we are having for any meal during the entire week. Be prepared. The week's menu is posted on the company bulletin board every Sunday. You're expected to know what we are having for every meal, for the entire week. That's twenty-one meals. Tonight, in the barracks, we'll go over all the other plebe poop you're required to know."

Without further comment or hesitation, Cantrell gave his squad the appropriate commands and marched them away from the company area for a frantic afternoon. The fourth squad stood in multiple lines for gear and uniforms, then ran up the five flights of stairs to dump the load on their bunks, only to immediately run back down the stairs for more lines, more gear, and more uniforms. An army of tailors measured every inch of their bodies a dozen times until a perfect fit was matched. They were issued gray trousers with black stripes down the legs, white short-sleeved shirts, dress-gray coats, full-dress coats complete with Frankenstein buttons at the neck and tails, full-dress whites, white trousers, black class shirts, long overcoat, short overcoat, raincoat, light jacket, gray hat, white hat, shorts, sweats, T-shirts, handkerchiefs, and socks. Each trip brought a new experience from the upperclassmen in the hall and stairwell as the new cadets slammed their backs against the walls, with piles of gear to the tip of their noses shouting, "Sir, may I pass!" More often than not, the request was met by demands to know what was for dinner at some date in the distant future, or some other poop totally foreign. Yet, in each of these situations, strict reliance on the standard four answers resulted in a quick session of belittlement, and a command to get out of sight before the old cadet got sick from having to look at a scrawny-good-for-nothing smack. As the afternoon progressed, sweat dripping new cadets watched the mounds of chaos grow in their rooms. Enlightenment spread like smallpox that the days of mom's nagging to clean their room would be but sweet memories of past tranquility.

In Mickey Mouse time, 1600 hours, with rooms a disaster, Cantrell snarled, "Five minutes! Uniform is as for showers. Squad formation against my wall." Disorientation to reality was the look of the day. It was written in bold letters on every face. "Bathrobes, smacks! Get in your bathrobes, shower thongs, white towel folded in thirds draped over your left arm and soap dish in your left hand. Move it, girl!"

The new cadets scattered at a run to their rooms to rip their clothes off and frantically try to find the required equipment. Neither as individuals nor as a military unit was this formation even remotely considered successful. The very second the five minutes had elapsed, Cantrell paced the hall screaming at the top of his lungs for the fourth squad to form up immediately. Out of the rooms scrambled twelve horrified new cadets. Half the squad did not have a towel or a soap dish, two came without shower thongs, and four were wrapped naked in a towel for the absence of their bathrobes. Cantrell was livid. For the next ten minutes, the back of twelve necks were flat against the wall with chins pulled in so tightly that multiple wrinkles could be counted at the jaw. Cantrell yelled at them as a group. Then he yelled at them individually. Finally, he yelled at them as a group again.

"When I give you the command," Cantrell said breathlessly, "you hopelessly worthless scumbags get in the shower, then form up again on my wall! Five minutes! Move it!"

Within three minutes, the squad had showered without a word to each other. They waited rigidly against the wall for the appearance of the squad leader from hell, Mister Cantrell.

"All right, smacks!" Cantrell said as he rounded the corner from his room. "You have twenty minutes to get ready for the next formation. Dress-up time. Put on gray trousers, white shirt with epaulets, white hat, and white gloves. Special inspection against my wall—in twenty minutes. You scumbags better not be late. Move-out!"

Again, the squad scrambled to their rooms. After an initial five minutes of digging through piles for the correct articles of clothing, there was at least some relief to the new cadets that the simple act of putting on a pair of slacks and a shirt was probably one order they could carry out today without disaster. How difficult could that be?

Cantrell came to each room to give instructions on how to trim the size forty-two belt to fit precisely. He could have let nature take its course, but he still had vivid nightmares of coming to this formation two years earlier with the tongue of his belt hanging down to his knee.

A full minute before formation, the new cadets filed out of their rooms and took their positions against the wall. Cantrell again approached the squad with his eyes seeking errors in the wearing of the uniform. Unlike the members of the fourth squad, Cantrell was dressed in full-dress whites, which consisted of stiffly starched trousers, a high collared starched white coat extending to mid-thigh, white gloves, gold buttons, and a three-inch white waist belt connected with a brilliantly polished brass buckle. Though his hat was the same, the black bill had been polished to reflect like a mirror.

"Gentlemen," he said, "It looks like everyone has managed to get into the right uniform. Now let's see if we can make you look like cadets." As he motioned Hamilton to the front of the squad, he began making the corrections. "Your hat is to be centered on your head—not cockeyed like a sailor, or a Zoomie at the Air Force Academy. The space from your eyebrows to the sweatband is exactly a two-finger distance." Cantrell demonstrated the proper position of the hat on Hamilton, then helped each of the others with theirs until he was satisfied that the hats were properly mounted.

"Next gentlemen, is the dress off." As he started his explanation, Cantrell began transforming Hamilton's shirt from one worn by a civilian to one of a West Point cadet. "A dress-off gathers the loose material at the side seams and folds over against the back, giving both the front and back of the shirt a wrinkle-free, tight fit. Until you learn how to do this by yourself, you're to help each other. In fact, if one man comes out of a room to formation looking less than perfect, I'm gonna be all over the other two roommates like hair on a hippie. Check each other before every formation. Work as a unit."

At Cantrell's command, the new cadets took turns unfastening their trousers while another tightened the shirt and folded back the excess material from the sides. When satisfied with the results, Cantrell said, "You're looking better, girls. Alignment. The edge of your shirt, coming down the row of buttons, the left edge of your belt buckle, and the fly of your trousers should be aligned exactly, at all times. Do it now." The squad shuffled their shirts, trousers, and belts until they felt they were acceptable, then returned stiffly to the position of attention. Cantrell walked the length of the squad looking for the slightest problem in the way his men looked. "Mister McSwain!"

"Yes, sir!" Patrick popped off.

"What are you doing with a rope on your shirt?" Cantrell stood in front of Patrick and pointed accusingly at a little string that hung from the buttonhole on the right pocket.

"No excuse, sir!"

"Gentlemen. We don't do ropes on our uniforms at West Point. Don't ever come to one of my formations with ropes hanging on your uniform. Check for ropes. Get them off. Now!"

Frantically, the new cadets started trying to find any tiny strings on their shirts or trousers that might be classified as a rope. In doing so, Hamilton bumped his hat, toppling it to the floor. It rolled like a frisbee on its edge to the other side of the hall. Hamilton popped to attention, afraid to move.

Cantrell glared at the hatless new cadet. "Mister Hamilton, do you know what will happen to you if you lose your cover in a company formation, or worse yet, on the parade ground?"

"No, sir!" Hamilton thundered.

"You'll be on the area and on confinement for the rest of your natural life. The Area is where you will walk back and forth, in full-dress uniform under arms, during all your free time. And, confinement means that you have the privilege of staying in your room—except for classes, meals, the library, and the latrine. Get your hat, Hamilton. Drop it again, and you'll find out exactly what I'm talking about."

"Yes, sir!" Hamilton said, quickly crossing the hall to retrieve his hat.

"Company formation. Move it," Cantrell said as he turned toward the stairs.

Upon reaching the slab, the fourth squad was somewhat in awe to see seven other companies forming. It was a real formation. A thousand new cadets were scrambling to find their personal slice of the slab. In the distance, toward the river, the West Point Band in Dress Blues could be seen on The Plain near Battle Monument at Trophy Point. Already they were playing military marches as a crowd of civilians gathered nearby. The trials of the day were put aside as each new cadet absorbed the excitement of marching as the Class of 1973 for the first time. Within the next hour, they would march to Trophy Point and give their oath of allegiance to the United States of America.

The 7th New Cadet Company formed three platoons. The platoon leaders, the company commander, who was Cadet Captain Jonathan Scott, and his staff took their positions dressed in whites with gold handled swords. Then, as the sound of the band floated over The Plain, the squad leaders and cadet officers passed through the ranks, looking for uniform corrections.

"Where are you from, Mister McSwain?" Scott asked as he stepped in front of Patrick.

"Tennessee, sir! The great Volunteer State, sir!"

"I see," Scott said calmly. "I think we'll break you of that volunteer crap over the next few weeks. What do you think, McSwain?"

"Sir, I do not know!" Patrick popped off, wishing his mouth had not dribbled out anything about being a volunteer. The term meant one thing back home, but it probably meant something entirely different in the army.

"I'll try to remember that you're a volunteer in the future, McSwain. Thank you for that useful piece of information." Scott smiled as he turned to face Jake.

"Mister Jacobs." Scott paused just long enough to make Jake squirm. "So, Cadet Jacobs, is your surname of Jewish descent or English?"

"Sir, I do not know!"

"You don't know your ancestry?"

"Just Texan, sir."

"Well, I suppose some of us would just as soon Texas be a country all on its own," Scott said with a grin. How do you like it here at John Wayne University so far, Mister Jacobs?"

"Fine, sir!"

"Are you ready to give your oath and your commitment to Uncle Sam for the next nine years?"

"Yes, sir!" Jake popped off, enthused that his long-awaited dream of being at West Point had become a reality.

"What's your favorite military march, Mister Jacobs? I'll ask the bandmaster to play it, especially for you."

"Anchors Aweigh, sir!" Jake said before realizing what he had said. The phrase "Beat Navy" at West Point was more common than air. Stating his musical preference definitely fell in the category of gross lack of judgment. "Are you kidding me, Mister!" Scott barked and flushed red in the face. "I'm not believing you actually said that!"

It was true. In a flash, Jake realized his assessment at lunch that the four bars on Cadet Captain Scott's epaulets meant that he was not the right person to make mad was absolutely correct. Scott was an inch from his face, red with anger, purple veins on his forehead and neck expanded. And then, Cantrell appeared. Scott made room for him so that both could get in Jake's face. Within seconds, Jake could not distinguish what was being yelled.

"You better get yourself together!" Cantrell shouted. "Anchors Aweigh, my ass!" Scott screamed. Jake stared off into space, his neck pulled back so tight he thought it would break. Fortunately, the King of Beast saved him from further abuse, temporarily, by calling the battalion to attention. Scott and Cantrell immediately went to their posts without another word, and by doing so, they left Jake with the dread that the incident was far from being finished.

In company formations, the battalion marched from the slab down Thayer Road toward Trophy Point and formed in companies abreast around Battle Monument. To an untrained eye, the one thousand new cadets appeared to march perfectly. Little did the spectators know that surrounding upperclassmen muttered instructions under their breath for the new cadets to align to the right, change step, swing arms forty-five degrees to the front with semi-closed fist and thumbs pointed to the ground, and a hundred other instructions that made the group appear that it had marched together for years. Though the new cadets knew they were novices, it was exciting nonetheless that in a mere seven hours, they had been uniformed and taught enough of the basics to march respectfully as a thousand-man unit.

A crowd of civilians were on hand for the ceremony. Parents, relatives, and girlfriends of those new cadets who had been driven to the academy were standing to one side, watching proudly. To them, it was a moment of pride, pageantry, and glory. Little did they know of what had occurred over the past seven hours to Little Johnny. To be sure, Little Johnny was not feeling the pride, the pageantry, and the glory in quite the same way he had before he entered the gates a few hours earlier. Some fathers would not have been affected by the truth, in fact, some smiled because they did know the truth. But truth known to the mothers and to the girlfriends probably would have brought tears to their eyes rather than smiles of pride.

The West Point Band played marches and songs that brought forth feelings of patriotism and love of country. One such medley, much to Jake's satisfaction and possibly his survival, was composed of songs of all the branches of service. The sound of Anchors Aweigh was sweet music to his ears in more ways than one, and he had visions of Captain Jonathan Scott and Mister Cantrell gritting their teeth. Jake could not stop himself from humming along as the band played.

When the band stopped, the superintendent, a major general, stepped to the microphone. For thirty minutes, the general delivered an introductory welcome to the United States Military Academy and the Oath of Allegiance. With their right hands upward, the Class of 1973 swore allegiance to the Constitution and swore to maintain and defend the sovereignty of the United States. The oath and ceremony, as they all knew, represented a commitment to four years at West Point and five years as a combat officer in the service of their country.

When the general had delivered his final remarks, the band began playing, and commands were given to set the formation in motion. The battalion was marched to the opposite side of The Plain near the superintendent's and commandant's residences, down the slab, and to the mess hall. Again, the reality of West Point was upon the new cadets.

LIFE in the mess hall had changed little since lunch. During the forty-five-minute meal, the fourth squad was allowed almost a full five minutes to eat. Yet, five minutes of eating at attention and squaring every rise of the fork were somewhat different than shoveling food into one's mouth for five minutes. Jake surveyed his plate before requesting permission from Captain Scott for his classmates to eat. It was becoming evident that a plebe's choice for the next eleven months in the mess hall was not concerning quantity or quality, but rather what would serve the body best to make it to the next meager meal.

As at lunch, properly performing the fourth class duties to the satisfaction of the old cadets was difficult and time-consuming. Patrick was harassed as Gunner for not having an accurate feel for how many servings remained in each dish. Jake was harassed for not having the slightest idea what beverage to serve. And, Lamont was harassed over the apple pie at lunch since the dessert for dinner was considered a no-brainer because it was tapioca pudding. The upperclassmen were disappointed that a cake or another pie was not served to test Lamont's skills as a master cutter. Even after the duties were performed, the opportunity to taste food was delayed. Taking turns, the upperclassmen asked questions of each new cadet that were impossible to answer, and in each instance, the four standard answers were their only defense against the attacks. What's for breakfast Tuesday morning? The Days? What's Schofield's definition of discipline? How's the Cow? What's the definition of leather? What are the six points of the Code of Conduct? What's the Sunday night poop? When did the cadets at West Point cheer for Navy at an Army-Navy football game? Who was Pyrene? Finally, after glancing at his watch, Captain Scott threw his hands up in disgust, called the new cadets worthless and hopeless, then snarled a command to eat.

At dismissal from dinner and back in their rooms, the new cadets felt that the day was surely over, less cramming all their gear and uniforms into the closet. Though still two hours before sunset, a twelve-hour nap seemed a reasonable request. Not only was the body hungry and exhausted, but the mind was in shock.

"What the hell are we supposed to do with all this stuff?" Patrick asked.

"Beats me," Hamilton replied more to himself than as an answer to Patrick. "But I'll bet money that you know who will be around to tell us."

"Shove it under the bed. That's my vote." Jake said.

Jake had no sooner gotten the words out of his mouth when Cantrell walked through the door. "Under the bed, Mister Jacobs? I think not, girls. This room will look spiffy in two hours."

The other members of the squad filed into the room and Mister Cantrell immediately started giving instructions and demonstrating where everything went and exactly how it was supposed to look. Every article of clothing had its proper place and was to be folded a certain way. The bed was to be made with hospital corners, the blanket and top sheet folded to the exact specifications of a dollar bill, and the blankets pulled so tight that a quarter would bounce from its surface. Cantrell gave a quick demonstration on the art and science of spit-shining shoes and on the necessity of removing the lacquer from all brass. An immaculate shine on shoes and brass was an immediate expectation. Bugle Notes, a small three-hundred-page book affectionately known as the Plebe Bible, was introduced as a literary work of art to be memorized from cover to cover by a preferred date of yesterday. Leaving the new cadets stunned from information overload, Cantrell exited the room as quickly as he had entered.

For the next three hours, the members of the fourth squad worked on putting their rooms in order as instructed. Closets, drawers, and desks were organized. Beds were made. Cantrell traveled from room to room, making corrections where needed, and giving one-on-one instructions when a fold in a sheet or underwear was not perfect. As the evening wore on, the piles of chaos diminished, and the rooms became more livable, in the West Point sense of the word.

"What made you decide to come to the academy?" Hamilton asked Jake as they made a bed together.

"My brother, Charley, was in the Class of '66. I was only twelve when he started here, but I've wanted to come to West Point ever since."

"Well, it can't hurt to have a big brother in the Army ahead of you. Maybe someday the two of you will get to serve together in the same unit. That'd be great to have your brother as your battalion commander, or something. Wouldn't it?"

"Hey, Patrick," Jake said, dodging Hammel's question, "what's a suave talking Tennessee boy doing in a place like this? I mean besides the fact that you're a volunteer?"

"That volunteer business is going to be the death of me. I've been here less than one day, and I've been tagged with a nickname I'll probably live to regret. Give it to Patrick to do. He's a volunteer. But, to answer your question. It's all about girls. West Point. Yeah, the girls dig it."

"Well, I'm sure they all appreciate your sacrifice." Jake said, laughing.

"I came here for the academics," Hamilton announced.

Both Patrick and Jake looked at him and grinned. Patrick

muttered, "If it's academics you want, you're gonna get all you can handle."

"Well," Hamilton said smugly. "I was in the top five percent of my class in high school, and I scored a combined fourteen hundred on the SAT. I was accepted at MIT and Stanford."

"Is that a fact? You're just smarter'n a whip, ain't ya, Hamilton?" Patrick said. "Hey, Jake. Were you in the top five percent of your class?"

"Yep," Jake replied, smiling with his head turned away from the conversation.

"And tell me—you cow crap, lowlife Texas boy—did you score in the fourteen hundreds on the SAT?"

"Yep," Jake said again. "Ain't that interesting! Guess we got us a room plum full of smart sum-ma-bitches," Patrick said, digging into Hamilton with his down-south routine. "Hamilton, I think when you have a chance to snoop around a bit, you're gonna find the academic competition here steeper than a vertical wall. And, not every smart sum-ma-bitch is gonna make it. This ain't Boston High no more."

Hamilton stood with a semi-stunned look on his face. Somehow, the thought had never crossed his mind that he might not be known any longer for his academic excellence. His past identity as a person was rapidly fading, and he felt uneasy at having his only area of confidence at West Point stripped away.

"Don't worry about it, Hamilton," Jake said. "You'll do great. In a few months, I'll have you helping me with plebe math. Most of that stuff is black magic to me."

Hamilton smiled. He didn't necessarily believe Jake, but he did appreciate the attempt to pick his confidence up from the floor and hand it back to him.

"That's right," Patrick said, some embarrassed about shaking Hamilton's identity. "It's going to get tough on the books. We're all going to need help from each other in one way or another."

"Mister McGwain. That's about the sweetest thing I ever heard," Cantrell said, leaning against the doorjamb.

Jake called the room to attention at the sound of Cantrell's voice. Having the door open all the time, potentially put an upperclassman in the room at any time without a whisper of notice.

Cantrell walked further into the room, his eyes looking for items out of place. "You're absolutely right, McSwain. An army wins wars with leadership and with teamwork. You're here to learn both. You'll be found—meaning we'll throw your ass out of here—if you don't develop individually as a leader, or if you can't operate effectively in a team to accomplish the mission. You'll be graded at everything you do here. And not just in academics. Make below a "C" in academics, and you'll be found. Fail to develop leadership characteristics, and you'll be found. Fail to work as a team member, and you'll be found."

"Taps and lights out in one hour. Mister Jacobs, report to the company commander and get your beverage preferences."

As Cantrell turned his back and stepped quickly out of the room, Jake pulled a notebook and pen from his desk drawer, then was on his way down the hall. He covered space as quickly as he could, stopping every twenty feet to turn his back to the wall so he could see the nameplates on the doors without having to turn his head. Being accosted for gazing around again was worth avoiding, if possible. When he found Captain Scott's room, he stepped to the doorjamb, knocked twice on the open door, and waited for a response from the company commander.

"Enter!" Captain Scott said firmly.

"Sir, New Cadet Jacobs reporting to Captain Scott as ordered!" Suddenly Jake remembered Scott's desire for a little chit-chat and realized he was not standing here just for the beverage preference. *Which was it? The apple pie or Anchors Aweigh?* Jake felt the muscles in his neck tighten.

"Well, Jacobs. Don't just stand out in the hall. Start over."

Jake again knocked on the door, and the entire procedure was repeated with him marching stiffly into the room five paces to report after being told to enter. To Jake, the hallway seemed safer than this room, and there was nothing safe about a hallway full of upperclassmen.

"At ease, Mister Jacobs. Do you know why you're here?"

"Yes, sir!"

"So, why are you here?"

"Sir, you wish to discuss with me the incident at the table today, or sir, possibly my unpardonable preferences in music." "Mister Jacobs," Scott said in a normal tone, "I already told you what I thought of your action at lunch. As far as that Anchors Aweigh business goes, the band saved your ass on that one." Jake felt uncomfortable with Scott's pause because he now had no idea what the ordered "chit-chat" was about. He did not know whether it was his turn to say something, or to stand silent, or to do an about-face and get the hell out of Dodge.

"The reason I ordered you to my quarters, Mister Jacobs, is to talk to you about your brother— First Lieutenant Charles E. Jacobs. The tactical officer of the company, Major Ellis, notified me that your brother was killed in action on Hamburger Hill in Vietnam less than two months ago."

Jake stood silent as Scott slowly walked back to his desk, sat on the edge, then again looked at him. "Were you close to your brother?"

"Yes, sir," Jake replied in an even tone. "I miss him a lot, sir."

Scott lowered his eyes for a brief moment, then raised them to meet Jake's. "The Corps wishes to express our condolences to you and your family. Lieutenant Jacobs was one of us, and we are a part of him. We are The Long Gray Line. I think as you go through your years at West Point, you'll become even closer to your brother. Mister Jacobs, I think you'll come to really understand how and why your brother performed his duty in Vietnam and served his country, though he personally may have disagreed with the political decisions that made it necessary for him to be there. I'm sure I speak for the entire Corps, and all its graduates, when I say that we've lost a brother as well. During Beast Barracks, if you feel that you'd like to talk to someone, just let me know. Either I, the chaplain, or Major Ellis are available. Your life at West Point will be no different from the thousands that have preceded you. We owe that to you. And Charley. And the Corps, and the country. I just want you to know that we're here to help you if you need it. Do you have any questions?"

"No, sir."

"Very well, Mister Jacobs. If you want to talk, just let me know. You're dismissed."

Jake did an about-face and marched out of the room much relieved that the little chit-chat had nothing to do with his misdeeds of the day.

"Mister Jacobs!" Jake slammed his back against the wall directly across the hall from Scott's room. "What's my beverage preference, crot!" the demon-possessed old cadet from the mess hall yelled.

"Sir, I do not know!"

"Well, I'm here to give it to you. Write this down and don't screw it up!" Mister Mitchell impatiently gave Jake a moment to get his notebook and pen at the ready. "For breakfast, I'll have milk with two ice cubes and a cup of coffee. For lunch, if it's above ninety degrees and not raining, I'll have iced tea with three ice cubes. Otherwise, I'll have the juice of the day with two ice cubes. For dinner, I'll have exactly the opposite of my preference for lunch. You got that, Mister?"

"Yes, sir!" Jake said, already horrified at how complicated his life was going to be as Beverage Corporal. With three upper-classmen at the table, the task was bad. Real bad would be when the entire Corps was together in the fall, and seven upperclassmen sat at the table. Twenty-one beverage preferences to memorize. Twenty-one preferences, totally distorted by the temperature, precipitation, which day of the week it was, and in some cases, whether or not the old cadet got a letter from his girlfriend that day.

"Pass!" Mitchell said indignantly, as he walked away.

Though Jake was sure that Mitchell was, in fact, demon-possessed, he was thankful that he had reminded him of the need to get the beverage preferences. All he needed was to go back to the mess hall, not having the slightest idea what to serve the three at the end of the table. Jake immediately crossed the hall to Captain Scott's quarters, then down the hall for Mister Cantrell's preference.

With fifteen minutes remaining before taps, Hamilton and Patrick helped him memorize what was to be served at breakfast as he reluctantly put on the official-looking pajamas that were issued.

"I haven't worn pajamas since I was ten years old," Jake grumbled. "These are really cute."

"Yep." Patrick agreed. "It's ninety degrees in this room. But, Cantrell came in here while you were off visiting with the captain and there's no mistake about it. We have to wear this junk until the end of Beast."

Jake looked at the baggy legs of the pajamas. "I wonder if Cantrell would throw a fit if I cut the legs off? I can stand to be a little embarrassed. Hell, I don't look nearly as silly as you do, Patrick, but I can't stand being hot when I'm trying to go to sleep."

"Sweat, buddy. You look like a lean, mean, killin' machine in your little gray pajamas with the academy crest on the pocket." Patrick threw himself on his bunk, laughing.

The lights in the hallway dimmed, and the sound of taps was heard from across The Plain. Jake picked up his picture of Sara from the desk for a longing look before climbing to the top bunk. A solo bugler played as a thousand new cadets reclined on their bunks in the dark after their first day of Beast Barracks.

CHAPTER THREE

0700 Hours
28 November 1969
Philadelphia, Pennsylvania

FOR THE FIRST time in five months, Jake and his classmates were seeing the real world. Though the sun was barely new for the day, the early light brought back vivid memories of people doing conventional things with their routine lives, like going to grocery stores and gas stations, living in homes, playing with dogs and children, and wearing blue jeans. The bus trip to Philadelphia would take all morning. An army of coaches snaked along the banks of the Hudson River with four thousand from the Corps of Cadets to collectively meet, in battle, the Brigade of Midshipmen from the Naval Academy.

It was not just a football game. The Corps had yelled Beat Navy at the dismissal of every formation since the first day of Beast Barracks, and Army-Navy week had the entire Corps worked into a frenzy. Nightly rallies in the mess hall made the week festive and peaked anticipation for the game, though daily academics droned on as usual. The band would strike up a magnificent old Viking song, and the beverage corporal at each table would leap onto the end of the table as he donned the emptied, stainless ice bucket on his head. With each beat of the song, hundreds of plebes clashed knives against metal dish lids, held like shields. The table commandants stood like a ship's captain while the eight cadets on the sides of each table raised it with one knee, made rowing motions with their arms, and pushed the table forward in unison; hundreds of tables circled the mess hall like Viking warships at sea.

Throughout the week, the cadets were much amused to see the naval tactical officer, Commander Jenkins, sit on the slab at his desk in the snow. His office was complete with file cabinets and all. Each day he huddled over his desk preparing daily reports or counseling a cadet, bound warmly in his long overcoat and scarf as snowflakes covered him and his work throughout the day. Cadets on their way to class would snap a salute in passing. "Good morning, sir. Have a nice day, sir." Of course, he rarely replied. The sign he had taped to the side of his filing cabinet, depicting a goat with a smoking pistol and a dead mule, was ignored by the cadets.

On the night of the bonfire, dressed in his full-dress Navy Blues and ceremonial sword, Commander Jenkins drove to the sight in his ten-year-old VW Bug. He was stunned, and later completely speechless when he had to stand before the Corps of Cadets to make the traditional speech about how Army would be defeated two days hence in Philadelphia. The reason for his incapacity to speak was that a horde of cadets grabbed the commander as he proudly stepped out of his car, to keep him from hurting himself lest he faint or have a heart attack, while an M-60 tank rounded the corner and ran squarely over the top of his car. It looked like a press conference as hundreds of cadets tried to preserve Commander Jenkins's face on film as he stared in disbelief at his flattened and mangled automobile. The mission was accomplished. Commander Jenkins stood before the Corps, in the light of the bonfire, unable to say a word. He recovered his ability to speak later in the evening when the commandant informed him that all four thousand cadets had pitched in a dollar to replace his two-hundred-dollar car.

Patrick was already asleep in the seat beside him. Missing a single moment of semi-freedom in the outside world was not on Jake's agenda. He could sleep later. None of his classmates had yet been off post since that first day in July, but his circumstances had been a special kind of fun. He had just gotten off the area and confinement four days ago. For four months he had spent his Saturday afternoons and Sundays walking back and forth on the area wearing out shoe leather. Though walking the area was not amusing, confinement was worse. Watching Patrick and his other roommate, Wayne, leave the room on Saturday nights for the weekly hop and a hamburger, or the movie in North Auditorium, while he attempted to maintain his sanity in his little gray cell, was much harder than walking tours. Jake knew that those four months of punishment was not necessary because the lesson was immediately learned when he had failed to use the standard four answers. A month of tours and confinement had occurred when he had replied, "I'd punt, sir," when the old cadet in the hallway asked what I'd do if it were third down and ten on my opponent's thirty-yard line. A smart plebe would have said, " I'd pass, sir," and that would have been the end of it. Jake was convinced that one not only lost his freedom upon entering the main gate at West Point, but he also lost his sense of humor.

Of course, that was minor compared to the three months added to the sentence. Near the end of first month on the area, the Officer of the Day, Major Duncan, a burly airborne Infantry officer with qualification badges and ribbons galore, had stepped in front of him during a customary inspection, extended his right foot a few inches, and asked, "Your shine, or mine, Mister?" The approved solution for this scenario was to reply, "Yours, sir!", whereby the officer makes a few derogatory remarks about one's lousy shine, then moves on. But, the major had even less of a sense of humor than did the old cadet who put him on the area in the first place. Jake's reply of, "Mine, sir, but yours are coming along!", was not considered the least bit funny by this particular 82nd Airborne Division Ranger.

As the bus rolled along, Jake thought of how lucky he and Patrick had been to find themselves in the same company and as roommates after Beast Barracks. They were friends for life. Patrick gave him an occasional teasing about his daily half-hour habit of studying the Bible and taking notes, and even more frequently about his love for Sara. It was not uncommon for him to pick up her picture from the desk and go into a drooling skit dramatizing how he would go about romancing her to the point that she would forget all about Jake. These skits would always end the same. Jake would curse Patrick for blaspheming a saint and a laugh at Patrick's never-ending dramatics.

They were an unlikely pair, but inseparable. Patrick had blond hair and a thin, six-two frame, and Jake, at five-foot-eight, stocky build, and jet-black hair. Even in athletics, they had different interests. Patrick loved lacrosse, an unheard-of sport in Tennessee, yet he planned to try out for the varsity team in the spring. His long arms and aggressive play made him a natural and deadly with the stick. Jake, on the other hand, had taken a liking to boxing and also had been recruited for the pistol team. Though plebe boxing had been a disgusting ordeal at zero-seven-hundred hours every morning for nine weeks, Jake found the daily lingering headaches a worthwhile price to pay for the fun it gave him. When the sign-up sheets came around for winter intramural sports, Jake was the only one in the company to volunteer for boxing. The boxing team was normally involuntarily composed of those poor souls on the tactical officer's current hate list, but since Jake liked boxing, the tactical officer would have to dream up some other good deal for him.

Patrick shifted in his seat, the journey not affecting his sleep in the least, while Jake continued to stare out the window thinking alternately of a ten-day Christmas leave at home with Sara, and how he might make the best of the few hours of freedom they would have in Philly after the game. At midnight their magic pumpkin would turn back into a bus, and they would return to being neck-bracing plebes. At the thought of the bus ride back to West Point, he recalled the plebe's only rule of protocol for the trip. The upperclassmen had made a big "to-do" about plebes not getting carried away in Philadelphia with booze. Getting sick on the bus was very bad. He could see the headlines in the New York Times, "Plebe at West Point Found Hanging from Battle Monument for Puking on Old Cadet."

With the continued drone of the bus rumbling toward Philadelphia, Jake wondered how many of his classmates would survive the first round of finals in January. Academics were grim. The cadets had classes on Monday through Saturday noon, week after week, and survival always at issue one day at a time. Who would have thought one would really find themselves in an environment that demanded twenty-hour days for a twenty-four hour course load with a test every day in every class, year-round athletics, the trials and tribulations of being a plebe, punishment tours on the area, full-dress parades twice a week, and the antics of a goofy roommate from the hills of Tennessee.

ANY COMPLAINTS JAKE had imagined while gazing out the window of the bus now evaporated in the excitement of being a uniformed participant at this annual event. One hundred thousand had come to witness the sixty-ninth battle between the United States Military Academy and the United States Naval Academy, with both four thousand strong. With Navy already seated in the East, Jake marched proudly with the Corps of Cadets as they entered the north end of the stadium in long overcoats, capes buttoned back in traditional fashion. Life as a boy in little Comanche, Texas had not prepared him for the enormity of the crowd, the pageantry of the event, nor the rush of adrenaline he felt from being a part of it.

Following a precision salute to the colors and officers in the East, and the West, a rabble yell was given to cheer on an Army victory, and then the Corps was marched into the stands on the west side of the stadium. The noise level increased to a deafening pitch. Both sides yelled cheers for their team, and both bands played their traditional tunes loudly. Eight thousand cadets and midshipmen shouted and sang with all their emotional being for the victory they hoped they could claim at the day's end.

War began immediately. The midshipmen, with a massive catapult, slung water balloons across the width of the field to crash among the cadets, but their volleys fell short, and the cadets quickly coordinated an ear-splitting chorus of feet-stomping laughter that rocked the stadium. Aimed directly at the Brigade of Midshipmen, Army fired dummy rounds from a 155mm howitzer as if to say, "We wish the shells were live!", then a float manned by midshipmen, likened to a PT boat, began a journey to the west side. Within minutes, an Army Armored Personnel Carrier entered the field from the ramp leading to the locker rooms, dashed forward with dual fifty caliber machine guns blazing blanks and penned the PT boat against the inner wall. The sailors stood on the deck of their defeated warrior ship brandishing swords with indignation. From the East came a deafening blast from four thousand freon horns. From the West, four thousand Dress-Gray coats were shed and twirled overhead exposing white sweatshirts with the number "12" emblazoned on the front. "Twelfth Man! Twelfth Man! Twelfth Man!" the cadets shouted in unison, indicating that the entire Corps of Cadets was on the field in spirit with the Army team. As the Navy team entered the stadium, the noise from the midshipmen increased. From the West came, "Big deal!, So what!, Who cares!". The army team took the field, and the intensity of the noise in the stadium doubled while the four thousand in the East turned their backs as if to deny the cadet's existence. The Army-Navy game was underway.

AT HALFTIME, Army was ahead by a score of 20-17. Though better-executed football is found almost anywhere, close Army-Navy games are emotionally exhausting for both those on the field and all those somehow connected to the military uniforms of America, past or present, direct or indirect. Rivalry and brotherhood clash dramatically for a few short hours at duty stations around the world, and for millions of veterans and their families.

As Jake rounded the corner of the north end of the field, he saw Steve doing the same coming from the East and was proud to see his friend in his Dress Blues and white hat. Their eyes met at a distance of twenty yards, and their broad smiles told each other that they were again in touch with a little bit of home.

"Jake, it's great to see you," Steve said, grabbing Jake in a bear hug.

"You, too, sailor! You look spiffy in your little blue outfit. When is the Navy going to come up with a real uniform?"

Steve laughed. "Now, don't you start giving me any lip about the score. This game's not over yet."

"I wish it were over," Jake said. "I'm about to have a stroke. I'd feel a whole lot better if we were a couple of touchdowns ahead."

Steve smiled. "Say, Jake, I want us to trade cufflinks. Right here. Right now. You wear mine from Annapolis, and I'll wear yours from West Point. We'll wear them to graduation in four years. This way we will have a part of each other with us all the way through."

Jake started unfastening his cufflinks for the trade. "I'll be proud to wear yours. But, I want your Naval Academy bathrobe also."

"You what?"

A mischievous grin crossed Jake's face. "If Navy loses today, you send me your B-robe. If Army loses, I'll send you mine. We'll do it every year."

"Good idea. But what in the world am I going to do with all those Army B-robes hanging in my closet?"

"We'll see. Don't go counting them yet."

"How are you doing on the Hudson?"

"No real complaints, but I'm having a pretty rough time with math. I need you explaining that black magic to me like you did back in Comanche."

Steve winced. "Believe it or not, pal, I am having trouble with it at Annapolis. They take it a lot more serious than ole lady Hancock."

"Well," Jake said, "I don't know why. All you swabbies gotta do is be able to count how many boats ya got—one, two, three. I figure if a sailor can count to twenty without taking his shoes off, that's all the math he needs. "And, does it really take four years to teach you, sailors, how to tread water?"

"Very funny. Since you're so disrespectful toward the pride of America, you can buy me dinner tonight."

"My pleasure," Jake said as he affectionately patted Steve's shoulder. "We'll find a nice restaurant and try something new. We'll eat like human beings."

"CAN YOU BELIEVE THIS?" Jake commented to Patrick and Steve over his shoulder as they were escorted to their table. "Real food. Real table. I think I'll slouch through the whole meal. And Patrick, don't forget where you are. It won't be necessary for you to hold up a platter and shout, "Sir, there are two-and-a-butt servings remaining."

"Ha!" Patrick snorted. "I'll have you know we Tennessee folk are downright sophisticated when compared to you Texas hicks."

"See what I have to put up with day-in and day-out?" Jake said to Steve as they sat at a table for four with a white linen table cloth and a bouquet of fresh flowers in the center. "I know this will shock you, but this guy's favorite color is orange. Have you ever known anyone who loved orange? I swear, if they'd let him, he'd dye his uniform and wear an orange University of Tennessee baseball cap. No class. None. Zip.

Steve laughed and shook his head as the waitress approached the table. A beautiful young girl with long blonde hair and a full figure highlighted in a low-cut blouse and tight miniskirt welcomed them to The Steakhouse, gave each a menu, and explained the specials for the day. "Hi, gentlemen, I'm Rosemary. Would you like something to drink while you look over the menu?" she asked.

All three sat semi-stunned. Finally, Jake managed to order iced tea around the table, and Rosemary walked away teasingly. Their eyes opened wider, and their mouths dropped open.

"Jeez!" Steve observed. "We've been cooped up way too long, guys."

"The way we're drooling, she'll probably just think we're starving to death for one of these steaks," Jake said. "Speaking of steaks, let's eat."

"How can you think of food at a time like this?" Patrick barked. "Didn't you see what I just saw? Talk about leadership qualities! Man, I'd follow her anywhere. Lead me right off the edge of a cliff. I'd go in a heartbeat."

"So, ask her out. I'm sure she'd be thrilled to take a bus ride. Really impressed with your wheels, ya know what I mean?" Jake retorted.

"Oh yeah. Well, maybe she'll be here in four years when I get my car," Patrick said sadly. "Besides, I know why you'd rather have a greasy ole steak. If it ain't Sara, it ain't nothing. Right?"

"You got that right, hillbilly."

"Steve, you gotta help me out here," Patrick said mockingly. "I have to hear this, Jake and Sara yuk every day. Believe me, it's tough. Our first squad leader, Cantrell, named her the "Ravishing Young Morsel." I just call her Morsel."

Jake leaned back in his chair, shaking his head, knowing that Patrick was now initiating one of his dramatic skits. Steve sensed it, too, but laughed because he had seen Jake and Sara together for too many years to doubt one word.

"I walk into the room," Patrick continued, "and Jake's eyes are all glassed-over. Oh! We got mail from the Morsel today, huh? Nothing new. This guy gets more letters and care packages than anyone in the entire Corps of Cadets. This guy is so much in love with the Morsel, and faithful, it makes me sick. He won't even talk to another girl, much less allow himself to have a thought about carnal knowledge. I swear, Steve, if Lil' Miss Rosemary came prancing up to the table begging ole Jake to take her out, he'd say, "No thank you, ma'am, I'm saving myself for my ravishing young morsel back in Comanche, Texas." Yuk! Ya know what I mean? He says he's up studying until three every morning. Bull. He's up slobbering on Morsel's picture while Wayne and I are sleeping. He ain't got me fooled! You oughta hear it. "Here's a picture of Morsel and me at the lake. Here's a picture of Morsel and me at the prom. Here's a picture of Morsel and me holding hands. Here's a picture of Morsel and me eating, swimming, talking, looking, sitting, being". Yuk! It makes me sick."

Immediately, Jake and Steve clapped at the performance, and heads at other tables turned at the sound of the commotion. With his face a dark shade of red, Patrick stood and took a bow.

"Well, you're lucky," Steve said, still laughing. "You'd have to see them together to know just how bad it really is. They've been together since nursery school. If there was ever a couple made for each other, it's Jake and Sara. They've been living in their little world for as long as I can remember."

"Sickening, ain't it?" Patrick noted as Jake savored his slouch with a smile on his face.

"You guys are just jealous, that's all," Jake said.

"Looks like that will never happen to me. I met this girl at a hop at Annapolis, and I thought I had found the girl of my dreams. I was head over heels. But you know what happened?"

"You caught a social disease?" Patrick quipped.

"Worse! After three months of thinking I had found the woman of my life, I get this letter saying that she loves me but can't see me anymore. It seems her sorority sisters convinced her that it was immoral for her to see a guy in the military—Vietnam and all."

"Ouch!" Jake winced. "She was a real independent thinker, wasn't she?"

"Don't mean nothin'," Steve said.

Jake frowned at the apparent hurt in Steve's voice. "Friends. Sara is my best friend. That's why it works."

Patrick looked as if he were trying to relate to a difficult calculus problem, concentration apparent. "The Friend Factor, huh? "Sounds like a religious thing to me," Patrick said with skepticism."

"Well, simple emotion won't take you far."

"You're telling me!" Patrick exclaimed. "That's how I got to West Point. Pure emotion. No rational thought. Otherwise, I'd be a fraternity man, a man about campus."

All three laughed at Patrick's comment. There was an element of truth to being at the academies based on an emotional decision rather than full knowledge of the facts.

Realizing that Steve and Patrick were resident in their private thoughts, Jake said, "The right girl will come along for you someday. Meanwhile, let's eat the biggest steak in the house."

CHAPTER FOUR

2000 Hours
28 November 1969
Philadelphia, Pennsylvania

ROSEMARY BROUGHT coffee to the table and took the dessert orders. "I hope you gentlemen enjoyed your meal. The couple sitting three tables over have arranged for your check. I'll be right back with the dessert."

"You're kidding," Jake said as he strained to get a look at the couple. "Let's go thank them."

All three rose from the table and introduced themselves to the attractive middle-aged couple. The gentleman stood as they approached the table. He was attired in an immaculately tailored, gray suit and had salt and pepper hair to match. By appearances, he might have been a successful businessman, perhaps an investment banker or a high-level executive. His wife equally matched his physical presence. She was elegant and charming and had a look of comfort in any social setting.

"We appreciate your gesture, sir. Ma'am. That was very kind of you," Jake said.

"I'm John Field, and this is my wife Suzanne," Mr. Field said.

"The pleasure is ours. Will you gentlemen join us for dessert and coffee?"

The boys sat at the table. Steve was nervous, but he could not quite put his finger on the reason his instincts were warning him. Jake and Patrick were fine. Their instincts told them nothing. Steve passed the feeling off.

"It's refreshing to see a couple of cadets and a midshipman having dinner together," Suzanne said. "How did that happen? I mean, isn't this the day you are supposed to be arch enemies?"

"Yes, Ma'am," Patrick said. "But since Army won the game, we can afford to be a little gracious to the likes of him. I mean, him being a lowlife swabbie and all. We don't usually stoop so low. We're truly embarrassed to be seen with him."

"You'll have to excuse my roommate, Mrs. Field," Jake said apologetically. "Steve and I are from the same town back in Texas. We grew up together and have been friends since we were kids. Having dinner together is going to be our Army-Navy tradition until we graduate. Army and Navy, we are like squabbling siblings, but we're still brothers."

"What do you do, Mr. Field?" Steve asked, trying to figure out why this couple seemed familiar.

"Oh, I'm in government service. Nothing nearly as exciting as the life you live, I'm sure. We live down in the Washington- Maryland area and are in Philly for a social event. Tell me, since you're in the service academies, what opinions do you have about the war in Vietnam? I mean, how do you feel about it? Most of your peers are out protesting the war, and I suspect, like all the military, you're not very popular these days."

"Wow! That's a loaded question, sir," Patrick said.

"Just curious. But I really would like to know," Field said with no indication of retreating from the question.

"Well, sir," Jake said, "I suppose we all have a different opinion to some degree. Personally, I've chosen to be at West Point and a career in the Army for reasons beyond the specific issues on Vietnam, but Vietnam certainly does have a way of stereotyping us, doesn't it, sir?" Jake looked Patrick and Steve in the eyes, hoping that his comment was not contradictory to their opinion. Their non-verbal response told him that they would prefer that he follow through with Mr. Field's question. Being in the military was not popular, and it was not uncommon for some unknown civilian to draw a serviceman into a conversation about Vietnam with the intention of belittling him for the wearing of a uniform.

"What do you mean?" Field pressed.

"Well sir, I don't think any of us would sit here and tell you we necessarily agree with all that's happening in Vietnam. I think, if you took a survey at all the academies, you would not find the opinions so very different from those at universities. I mean, sir, the political issues that got us into Vietnam are far from clear-cut, and the fact that the military has been given the mission to be there, but not a directive to fight the war to conclusive victory, is not rational. Disgraceful is more like it. In theory, we are there to assist the South Vietnamese so that they can defend their country for themselves, but, that's not happening. The political policy concerning Vietnam is self-defeating. I suspect that sooner or later, the U.S. will leave Vietnam in the hands of the South Vietnamese only to have them drop the ball. If that turns out to be the case, it seems we will all be asking ourselves why we were there in the first place, and why so many men had to die for no gain."

"I don't disagree with that," Field said. His eyes narrowed as he pressed Jake further. "But you are being vague. Why are you at West Point, instead of in Washington carrying a sign?"

Jake did not like the conversation. Field was trying to tie him down to a fixed position. He had one, but why was Field trying to get him to commit himself? What kind of counter-argument would Field expose? Had they been asked to sit with the Fields just so he could entertain himself in a philosophical debate, or even worse, to get his chuckles by ridiculing two young soldiers and a sailor? Patrick and Steve were not oblivious to Field's probes either. Steve nodded his head at Jake to continue.

"I'm at West Point because I believe in the preservation of the

United States. Wars don't just pop-up two days after an incident, or after a political decision is made. Wars come twenty or thirty years after political decisions are made. Vietnam comes from the days of Eisenhower and Kennedy. The wars and problems my children and grandchildren will face come from decisions and policies made today. While the world exists, there will be wars, Mr. Field, because there will always be people who lust for power and wealth. Vietnam, I suspect, is in one way or another a product of some jerk's career development on Capitol Hill. And, it continues for the same reason. On our side and theirs."

"So, you think Vietnam is just a political fiasco initiated a long time ago that no one wants to correct?" Field asked.

"Well, sir," Jake replied, "I think it's a lot more complicated than that, but essentially, no one in the political arena wants to admit it's a fiasco and take the heat to do what's necessary to win the war or send the boys home. Vietnam is a fiasco. Going back to the 1950's, all they wanted was autonomy, that is, to not be occupied by the French. Ho Chi Minh approached us for help, and we turned him down. So, he went to the Soviets for help, and here we are. We made our own war because we denied Vietnam the right to do exactly what we did with the British in 1776. For the most part, we have some very career-minded folks in Washington. There are too many involved whose career is either built on the sufferings of the Vietnam War or they fear to take an honorable stand against it because it would damage their career."

"But, don't you think you have a part in all this? You're part of the establishment that created the war and is directly involved in its continuation. The majority of your peers think you are a disgrace to this country."

"I hesitate to quibble, sir," Jake said with determination and conviction, "but the military is a servant to the people. When I'm twenty-one, I'll get to vote. One vote. Other than that, I have no power to direct political events. My peers? I can respect a man who is against the war in Vietnam and is willing to go to jail for his beliefs. He is not so different from the man who puts on the uniform to serve his country and is willing to die for what he believes. But, Mr. Field, the majority of my peers protesting the war and hating soldiers do not have a committed belief. Woodstock was a three-day orgy of sex, rock, getting stoned, and burning the flag that my brother, Charley, died for last May. For most of my peers, the anti-war movement is nothing more than a social definition, for which their forefathers would be greatly embarrassed and ashamed. For many, it's cowardice. They protest the war and belittle soldiers with arrogance and self-righteousness to mask their guilt. They plot and plan and pay for their deferments out of cowardice, convincing themselves that by superiority they have a long-term, worthwhile contribution to make to America while poor Americans march off to do the fighting and dying in their place. College enrollment is up, the number of marriages is increasing for those of military age, the baby boom is back, and before too long we will have more preachers in this country than lawyers. Peace? Love? These people sure have a violent and unloving way of getting their point across. I"ve been spit on, cursed at, and assaulted by these paragons of peace and love, and that is on post at West Point. I can imagine what it is going to be like on Christmas leave. And, Mr. Field, there is also that brave group that is afraid to identify themselves with the anti-war movement outright or to take a stand that might put them in the fight. They don't stand anywhere. If one has the right political pull, the National Guard is the perfect solution. The waiting list is incredible. Can you imagine what would happen if Washington called some of these units to Vietnam? It would be a disaster. These guys would throw down their rifles and swim home as soon as it got dark, and you can't blame them for that. There is a big difference between a soldier that is active duty training for war every day, and a soldier that trains a few hours one weekend a month. A young stud can hardly get in the guard today because it's full, but you let this war come to an end, and the ranks of our National Guard will be empty for years to come. Yes, Mr. Field, I'm a part of the establishment. If my peers want to think I'm a disgrace, then so be it. When people hate the military for Vietnam, to me, that's ludicrous."

"So, you think the military is not responsible for Vietnam, huh?" Field asked mockingly.

"I'm not saying there aren't some unethical military careers being enhanced from the war, but generally, I think we are all responsible, sir. We are all collectively responsible for the policies and perseverance of our country. You asked me what I thought about Vietnam, and I told you. I think it's either a war we shouldn't be involved in, or it's a war we should be fighting to win. And, sir, I'm not in a position to know whether we should be committed in Southeast Asia or not, but I do know that this country, through its political system, needs to make that decision and do something about it. Real men are dying every day with a solid commitment not made one way or the other. Real men, real blood, real death."

"I agree with you," Field said convincingly. The tension at the table was almost overpowering for everyone. "But since you think the political system is in error, why are you at West Point? Why are you, by choice, a part of this establishment?"

Jake was now committed. He couldn't stop. "The United States is not perfect," he said. "We, as a Nation, aren't going down the road of history without making mistakes. We are trailblazing. Mistakes? Sure. But this is still a great country, and this country is worth preserving. Vietnam is only one piece in our history. I think the military is a noble profession. As I said, I don't think my life will have a major impact on history, but what I think I can do is to recognize the reality of history and to try to have a small impact on this country by just simply being a good soldier. Mr. Field, West Point, isn't training me specifically for Vietnam. The mission of the academy is to prepare men for the war twenty or thirty years from now. There are events in the world today that will produce that war. Maybe you've never thought about it, but when war does come, it's the civilian soldiers that fight it. That's true in every war we've ever fought, right or wrong. So, what's the role of a professional soldier? What's the purpose of a West Point or an Annapolis? Sir, I submit to you that it is to provide professional officers for the next war. The one twenty years from now. Our purpose, the three of us, is to be prepared to buy the time necessary to fight that war, to train those civilians that will have to fight it, to provide professional leadership in those battles, to win them, and to conserve, as best we can, the lives of those fighting that war. West Point and Annapolis have provided a steady flow of professional officers for nearly two hundred years. We, sir, are here for preservation, for continuity in future years. Frankly, sir, Vietnam is goofy. But that doesn't change our mission or our duty when the country calls."

"That's an interesting perspective. Do you agree with that?" Field asked of Steve.

Steve sat forward, glanced momentarily at Mrs. Field as she waited with interest for his reply, then made firm eye contact with Mr. Field. It was no longer vital that he could not recall why this couple seemed familiar. He would answer the question truthfully. "Yes, sir, I agree. Jake and I have talked about it often. We didn't just show up at the academies without a lot of thought. I went to the Naval Academy with conviction."

"So, you feel that being a good career naval officer is, more or less, your contribution to society. Is that it?" Field asked sincerely.

"Yes, sir. That's about it," Steve said confidently, continuing his direct eye contact with Mr. Field. "The nation will survive Vietnam. When I'm old and used up, there will still be fresh new plebes at the academies, ready to carry on."

"What about you, Mister McSwain?"

"I feel the same, sir. But I don't think the three of us will see that war twenty years from now. I think we'll graduate. Go to Vietnam. And die. We will never see our thirtieth birthday. The life expectancy of an infantry platoon leader is a week. Vietnam started when I was ten years old. As far as I can tell, it will never end. Some of us are willing to go for our country, but most are willing that others go."

John and Suzanne Field sat staring at Patrick, reflecting on what he had said. For a full minute, silence hung over the table. The boys sat fully expecting a lengthy rebuttal to their openness.

"John," Mrs. Field said, her eyes visibly filling with tears, "you found out what you wanted to know. Why don't you go ahead and tell these young men who you are?"

Suzanne's plea immediately brought apprehension to the table. For Steve, it merely intensified his paranoia.

"All right," Mr. Field said seriously. "But first I'd like to say something," He paused, glanced at the ring that had been on his finger for twenty-four years, then met the anticipating looks in front of him. "I'm some surprised at the responses you've given. I guess I didn't expect such serious thought to have accompanied your decisions to enter the academies. I thought I'd hear about how you were getting a free education, or maybe some reason like excitement or challenge. Maybe it's the times we live in, Vietnam and all. I have to tell you, it's refreshing to know that young men are entering military service today with the kind of values and principles and convictions I've seen in you. It's not an easy thing to do when your friends and peers ridicule your choice."

Steve felt the tension in his neck, knowing now that somehow, he should know who this man was, and that he should not be sitting with him at this table.

"I owe you an apology," Field continued. "I've misled you. I am not Mr. Field. I am Vice Admiral John Hollifield, superintendent of the United States Naval Academy."

All three of the plebes began to stiffen in the presence of the three-star naval officer as though they were back on the tables in the mess hall. Steve turned ashen and felt faint. He had seen the Admiral a hundred times, but only at a distance and always in uniform. Jake's arms went to his sides as though at the position of attention and he quickly reflected on how uncustomary it was for star rank to socially mix company with plebes. Meanwhile, Patrick frantically tried to recall precisely his initial comment about lowlife swabbies and wondered if five years of duty in Iceland was as bad as he had heard it was.

Mrs. Hollifield began to laugh, though she tried to avoid it. Her hand covered her mouth as if to push it away, but the look on the faces of the three plebes was more than she could handle. Her laugh was infectious. Within moments, the Admiral was laughing as well, and then the plebes themselves. When composure finally returned, Hollifield went on to explain how difficult it was for him to get a feel for what was going on in the lower ranks of his command, as people tend to tell an admiral what they think the Admiral wants to hear. He had seized the opportunity at hand to find out what two plebes at West Point and one at Annapolis thought. Again, laughter returned to the table. They laughed at Patrick and his blind remarks about sailors. Though an unusual social group by rank, a bond had been formed. With more coffee poured, the conversation light and jovial, Jake was caught off balance by the all too familiar, "Good evening, Mister Jacobs."

Jake and Patrick rose speechless as Cantrell approached the table. "You and McSwain out for a night on the town with a sailor, huh? What does a plebe rank, Mister Jacobs?" he demanded, amusing himself.

Jake's eyes widened. He glanced at the Admiral, then Steve before returning to Cantrell's expecting face. He did not want to comply with the request.

"Well?" Cantrell said smugly. "What does a plebe rank, Mister?"

After momentarily closing his eyes and swallowing the large lump in his throat, he popped off above the din of conversation in the crowded restaurant, better than he ever had, in a loud, clear, and impressive military fashion. "Sir the Superintendent's dog, the Commandant's cat, the waiters in the mess hall, the Hell Cats, the Generals in the Air Force, and all the Admirals in the whole damn Navy!"

"Outstanding, Mister Jacobs," Cantrell said as he noticed the humorless stares at him from everyone at the table. The long silence began to feel uncomfortable. "Ahh, I hope you all are enjoying your dinner. Ahhh, why don't you introduce me to your guests, Mister Jacobs?"

Jake looked at each of his guests as their irritated stares turned to mischievous grins. "Mister Cantrell, sir, I'd be delighted to introduce you to my friends."

CHAPTER FIVE

1830 Hours
10 December 1969
United States Military Academy
West Point, New York

"Sir, there are two and a butt minutes remaining for dinner formation. The uniform is Dress-Gray with Short Overcoats. For dinner, we are having steak and lobster, country potatoes, corn on the cob, stewed tomatoes, and chocolate pudding. This is the last call for this formation. Two minutes, sir!" Jake left his post as the minute caller, and the residents of the 50th division scrambled down the stairs. With hats cocked on the back of their heads, upperclassmen slipped their arms into their overcoats and wrapped their scarves around their necks. Plebes squared corners and slammed backs against the wall.

Jake hated being the minute caller. Not only did he have to start the routine fifteen minutes before every formation, he was also highly exposed to verbal abuse from the old cadets, especially for reveille-breakfast at zero-six-hundred. For one, if he was just ten seconds off schedule, some grump was all over him. He had begun to wonder if it were in some upper class handbook that they use early to just sit around staring at their watches, waiting for the minute caller to screw up. Then, after surviving this duty, Jake would run down the stairs at attention to join his classmates in the customary pre-dinner harassment.

Since being late to any formation, for any reason, was an unpardonable sin, Jake had learned over a period of months how to shave seconds off every task he needed to perform. For example, he was proud that he could be fully dressed in forty-five seconds flat at the sound of the reveille cannon. To achieve this small feat, each night before taps he would dress for the morning, then he would only unbutton the top button on his shirt and leave his light gray jacket partially unzipped before taking them off by pulling them both over his head and setting them aside for the next day. He would also leave his shoes loosely laced so he could slide into them as though they were loafers. When reveille sounded the next morning, he was nearly dressed already. He would pull the shirt, tie, and jacket over his head like a sweater and slip into his trousers and shoes. It was a pre-fab wardrobe. For months, he and Patrick raced to see who could be out the door first. Making the bed was yet another concern. Since the bed had to be made properly before formation, the solution was simple. Never sleep in it. On cold winter nights, a set of sweats a size too long and the issued comforter made sleeping on top of a scratchy wool blanket more acceptable than the hassle of making the bed under extreme time constraints. Jake had reached the conclusion that he might never sleep between sheets again.

As Jake trotted to the company formation, the upperclassmen were still visiting each other, occasionally stopping in front of a plebe when the conversation dulled. Jake took his place in the squad next to Patrick. After nearly six months of the great life at The School for Wayward Boys on the Hudson, the plebes of Company C-4, 1st Battalion, 4th Regiment were accustomed to standing like statues for hours at a time.

"Mister McSwain," the squad leader said. "You're a mail carrier, aren't you?"

"Yes, sir!" Patrick popped off.

"You been stealing my mail, Mister?"

"No, sir!" Patrick said, knowing that Mister Bean was about to again bitch about not having any mail for the day. Bean was a typical squad leader. He had to find something to yell at every plebe about, every day. If it were not shoes, brass, or plebe knowledge, he would invent a reason. Properly trained, he had a 'Misery is my job.' type philosophy as an old cadet.

"Then how come I didn't get a letter from my girl today?" Bean asked, in all seriousness.

Patrick's first thought was 'Because the wench has class and she's too smart to write to you. That's why!' But, with reason prevailing, he responded with the tried and true, "Sir, I do not know!"

"Well. You ping around to my room after dinner and get her address. You write her a letter and tell her I'm gonna give you unmitigated grief unless I get in a better humor. And, don't hack her off. You got that, Mister?"

"Yes, sir!" Patrick replied, thinking that an artfully drafted letter to the future Mrs. Bean might have interesting possibilities.

"Mister Jacobs," Bean said as he stepped in front of Jake. "You're a floater tonight. Go find yourself a nice relaxing table over in the 1st Regiment area. You'd like eating with the 1st Regiment, wouldn't you, Jacobs?"

"No, sir!" Jake immediately said with emphasis.

"Why not?"

"Sir, because they're meaner'n hell over there."

"That's right, Jacobs. They should have assigned you to 1st Regiment in the first place. Make a warpo and a killer out of you. The plebe system over there would make you think twice about that big mouth of yours. Have fun at dinner, Jacobs."

As the company entered the mess hall, Jake tried to decide which direction he should float. Anywhere would be acceptable except in a first regiment area. He was not looking forward to wandering up to a strange table and asking permission to sit for the meal with seven upperclassmen bored with torturing their own plebes.

"Sir, may I have permission to sit at this table?" Jake asked of the table commandant. He had wandered to the far south side of the mess hall, which was totally unknown territory.

"Sit," the table commandant said with disgust after looking at Jake from top to bottom. "Welcome to Company H, 1st Regiment."

Jake took his position behind an empty chair on the side of the table, silently swearing at himself for his poor, blind luck.

"Where you from?" the table commandant asked when the order to take seats had been given.

"Sir, I'm from Company C-4!"

"You're from 4th Regiment? Nothing but a bunch of wimps and girlie-men in 4th Regiment. Which are you, smack?

"Sir, I do not know!" Jake popped-off, fearing that the standard answer sounded as dumb to the old cadet as it did to him.

"You look like you're both. No hair at all. That's what I think," the old cadet said, much amused with his first regiment sense of humor.

"Where's Podunk, smack?"

"Sir, I'm from Comanche, Texas," Jake replied.

"Texas, huh?" the old cadet asked. "Injuns and wetbacks, ain't that right, Mister?"

"Sir, I do not know!"

"You speak any Mexican, smack?"

"Yes, sir!" Jake said without thinking and instant regret. The only Spanish he actually knew was the very little he had learned one summer working on a hay baling crew.

"Well," the old cadet continued, "I've been taking Spanish for three years. It's my area of concentration. Speak me a little of that Tex-Mex, smack!"

Jake paused. His mind scrambled through the brain cells,

currently paralyzed by fear at being at a 1st Regiment table, trying to recall a Spanish word, or phrase, or something that would satisfy the old cadet.

"Well, smack. I'm waiting. Speak me some Español," the table commandant barked, much to the amusement of the other 1st Regiment types at the table.

"Besame el culo, hijo de puta!" Jake popped off. Immediately after the words came out of his mouth, he felt nauseated and faint.

"Damn, son!" the old cadet said with a baffled look on his face. "Is that Spanish? I don't recognize any of that. What did you say?"

Jake knew there was no escape from answering, and that a lie would be an honor offense. Finally, with resignation in his voice, and knowledge that all the wild dogs of the first regiment were about to be unleashed because words had preceded thought, Jake said, "Sir! I said, 'Kiss my ass, you son of a bitch!'"

There was silence at the table. It was a deafening silence. It hung over the table just as deep, dark, life-threatening clouds hang low just before a tornado reaches down with its wand of destruction. Still, it was not long until sounds were heard. First, it sounded like someone choking. Then, pitiful growling noises came from the table commandant's end of the table. And finally, a roaring noise was heard, which might have been the old cadet's initial attempt at making a sentence. It was hard to tell. The words were all run together.

Over the course of the next thirty minutes, Jake did not eat. When one upperclassman had yelled obscenities all he could, the next would take over. With his ears ringing, Jake said to himself, 'So much for the wimps and girlie-men theory for the 4th Regiment. Back to the area, I suppose."

2100 Hours
15 December 1969
New York, New York

SUKARNO BANGJAR SAT ALONE in the darkness of his penthouse apartment watching snow fall on the city. The lights of Manhattan contrasted against the darkness of Central Park provided a spectacular view. But for Sukarno the view was merely a backdrop for his thoughts. He slumped in a black leather recliner, his thoughts consumed with himself and possible options he might have regarding his father, the Indonesian government, and Darul Islam's jihad. Since meeting with his father and learning of the plans made for him, he had isolated himself. No longer was he concerned with the frivolity of student life at Princeton and seeking a trade, at least not in the traditional sense. His studies in finance at Princeton had taken on new meaning. Each course now gave him insight into the patterns and trends and predictabilities of the American people in their political and economic history. With great interest, he now studied to acquire the tools of manipulation against a nation and its people. The studies now had purpose and direction, and more than ever before, the studies delighted him.

Sukarno rose from the recliner and walked slowly to the desk. Standing, he stared beyond the glass windows into the black void that covered the never resting New York City, and after a long pause, he walked slowly back across the room to the coat closet and slid his arms into a heavy leather jacket and put on a wide-brimmed, suede hat. With slow deliberation, he strolled back to the desk, opened the top drawer, and gently removed a Beretta 9mm pistol. After chambering a round, he put the pistol in his coat pocket and swiftly made his way to the dark streets of New York.

The snow fell in large flakes as Sukarno walked four blocks away from his apartment building and hailed a cab to take him to Times Square. A Yellow Cab pulled close curbside allowing him to step into the taxi without soiling his shoes. The driver began his friendly chatter before Sukarno had closed the door and paid no attention to the fact that his passenger said nothing after identifying his destination. As the yellow car swerved through traffic, a half-dozen near misses and a surge of acceleration at traffic lights just turned yellow, Sukarno silently watched the blocks pass and the people on the streets bundled warmly against the falling snow. On such a night, most people were in their homes, leaving the streets to those who were either in route to a warmer place or forced to be on the streets because they had no place to go. Times Square and the surrounding blocks of the old theater district were but one area of New York City considered home by the homeless. There were other neighborhoods where transients were in abundance, but Times Square had its fair share of men and women that had found their life ending in a cheap bottle of wine and a bed made of trash in a dark alley.

Sukarno flipped a twenty-dollar bill into the front seat of the cab as he exited without a word.

"Damn foreigner," the driver mumbled as he slid across the seat to retrieve the twenty that had floated to the floor on the passenger side.

Sukarno walked briskly away from the bright lights and businesses to the darker and near lifeless surrounding area. Within a three blocks distance, he found himself only one of a few pedestrians on a dimly lit street with old buildings neglected over the years. As he approached the alley, he put his hand in his pocket and caressed the Berreta into a firing grip, then flipped the safety off with his thumb.

The alley was dark. Moving slowly forward, Sukarno's eyes adjusted to the change in light. He could see all he needed to see. Never before had he been in a place so damp, so dirty, so littered with trash and garbage. The odor of rotting food permeated his nostrils, and for a moment, he almost turned to reenter the world more real to him. But, instead, he continued to walk. With each step, he felt he had stepped out of civilization and was walking deeper into a world of chaos where death lingered and desperation ruled. He was the hunter in a jungle, and the darkness ahead held his prey.

"Hey, Mister," an old man said with slurred speech as he rustled the newspapers that covered him.

Sukarno was startled. He jumped backwards, his hand clutching the pistol in his pocket. He strained to see in the darkness, staring toward the voice coming from the rubbish stacked against a dumpster. His heart raced with a rush of adrenaline as the old man uncovered himself from his bed of trash.

"You got some spare change, Mister?" the old man asked, unable to raise his body. "I could use a place to spend the night. Too cold to sleep in this here alley. You got some spare change for a poor ole man? Do ya, Mister?"

"Why would I want to waste good money on you?" Sukarno said in a disgusted tone, staring down into the pleading eyes of the old man. "You are nothing but a drunk. You are worthless. Worthless."

"Now Mister, don't be like that," the old man said, trying to prop himself against the dumpster. "I'm just a bit down on my luck. That's all."

As the old man struggled to sit upright, Sukarno took the pistol from his pocket. When the old man looked at Sukarno again, he was looking into the barrel of the 9mm less than three feet from his face. At his recognition of the gun, his eyes grew wide and fear froze his expression.

"It's time for you to die, old man," Sukarno said coldly. Just as the old man started to speak, Sukarno fired the pistol. The impact of the bullet entering the old man's chest slammed him hard against the dumpster, blood quickly soaking his tattered overcoat. Again Sukarno fired into his chest, the noise reverberating against the walls of the narrow alley. As life ebbed from the old man's eyes, Sukarno fired a third time, the barrel of the pistol pressed snugly against the forehead.

Sukarno stepped back to the center of the alley, consciously dropped the untraceable pistol to the ground, and admired the power of the weapon. In a flash, three pulls on the trigger, and a man was dead. The old man's eyes still had a look of terror as blood flowed from the gaping hole, his face now covered with blood. Without further hesitation, Sukarno turned and hurried back down the alley toward the street. "I can be all that I am meant to be." Sukarno said to himself aloud.

CHAPTER SIX

22 December 1969
Comanche, Texas

SARA MET Jake's plane at Love Field in Dallas and they spent the afternoon driving southwest to Comanche. Simply being together again was a familiar joy for both. After wrestling his B-4 bag from the trunk of Sara's car, they stood for a moment and absorbed the fact that he was home. Though everything between Sara and him was the same, the rest of his life in Comanche somehow seemed different. The house looked the same, but it felt different. The little town looked the same as they drove down the wide residential streets, but it felt like a place far in his past. Suddenly, it occurred to him that the only thing that had changed was himself.

"Jake!" Mrs. Jacobs squealed as she flung open the screen door. Mr. Jacobs and the Lowells, Sara's parents, were on her heels out the door. The excitement on their faces was evident and Jake automatically broadened his smile only seconds before his mother squeezed him and smeared lipstick on his cheek. Simultaneously, his father pumped his right arm up and down enthusiastically.

"You look like the Army agrees with you, son," Mr. Lowell said as they went into the house. Mrs. Jacobs immediately rolled a cart into the den loaded with a feast of snacks, maintaining her long-standing philosophy that food, and plenty of it, guaranteed the success of any social gathering.

"It's ok," Jake said. "I'm just glad to be home. It's great seeing you all. Especially this gorgeous thing right here." With that, he grabbed Sara and gave her a deep backwards dip, kissing her on the neck. She let out a girlish giggle and everyone laughed at the familiar sight of Jake and Sara grabbing each other.

"I know what you mean. I was out on leave from the Army once, too, you know?" Oliver Jacobs said teasingly.

"You never bent me over and kissed me like that," Jake's mother said.

"Sure I did, honey. Least I think it was you."

"It better had been me!" she replied with her hands on her hips.

"Oh yeah. It was you. I remember now," Oliver agreed, winking at the others.

"You two just remember to keep the hanky-panky at bay," Bob Lowell said clumsily. "Only three-plus years to graduation and a wedding. You can hanky-panky all you want then. It will be here before you know it."

"Here Bob, have some more of these little sandwiches," Laura Jacobs said as she stuck the platter in his lap. Somehow, thoughts of Charley and Margie and how little time they had together bothered her. Life seemed so unfair, and every minute so very important.

Tenderly holding Sara's hand, Jake had to wonder exactly when simply living what you feel begins and dutiful compliance to honor and trust ends. "It never ends.", Jake said to himself."

2200 Hours
1 February 1970
United States Military Academy
West Point, New York

"THE BOARDS WERE HORRIBLE TODAY," Patrick said in a depressed tone.

"You've got that right!" Jake immediately replied as he snapped his head around in recognition of Patrick's statement. "I was deficient for the day five minutes after I got to class."

"Green Death," Wayne passively pitched into the conversation. Wayne Barnes was from Venice, California and had become a good roommate for the two inseparable Southern boys. He was more interested in the beach than anything else, and the army barbers were the only ones who could disguise the "surfer" in him. His biggest complaint at West Point was how difficult it was to maintain a tan.

"How'd you like to be General Green?" Jake asked jokingly. "Just think about it. With his grandson on his knee, the general has to fess up and tell him that during the war, instead of fighting bad guys in the name of Old Glory, he sat on the Hudson writing twenty-four gawd-awful training manuals for calculus. And, not only are they gawd-awful, but they've tortured and terrorized plebes at West Point for decades. The Green Death. Smallpox brings less misery."

"Yeah," Patrick agreed. "On the boards today, I got slaughtered. The professor made me recite on my problem and I blew it. I stood there, all proper and stiff, at attention with the pointer for twenty minutes trying to fake my way through my problem. Major Edwards just left me up there banging my gums and suffering. Finally, he chewed me out for not being properly prepared and announced to the class that I had just gone .3 out of 3.0 for the day. Man, that's serious deficient!"

Jake laughed at Patrick for going deficient. It did not happen often. To attest to this, Patrick was currently in the third seat of the first section. No class had more than fifteen cadets, and once each month the roughly eight hundred remaining plebes taking the Green Death were reshuffled based on academic standing. The cadet with the top grade average sat in the first seat, first section. Patrick had the third highest grade in plebe mathematics. A part of Jake's laugh was at himself. Going deficient for the day was not an unusual experience for him. He sat in the fifth seat, fifty-second section. Considering there were fifty-three sections, Jake felt some degree of comfort knowing that he had twenty-five of his classmates envious of his skills as a master of the Green Death.

The entire Corps of Cadets had returned to West Point the first week of January, and to the man with the same look of depression on their face. The Gloom Period had arrived, finals started immediately, and summer leave seemed an eternity away. The physical environment was gruesome. For three months, the weather is gray, the uniforms are gray, the buildings are gray, and the mood is gray. Jake and Patrick agreed that it was the Gloom Period from which Edgar Allen Poe derived his settings of horror. As a cadet, Poe had known the Gloom. The only consolation to a plebe during this period was the hope of surviving to be an old cadet for next year's Gloom. And there, Jake and Patrick concluded, lies God's purpose and reason for the plebe system in the first place. After all, being an old cadet in the Gloom Period without plebes is like being an axe murderer without a victim. It simply makes the Gloom Period more tolerable.

"Only a month left of winter sports," Patrick stated. "Looks like I'm gonna get to play lacrosse and sit on a Corps squad table for the spring. Sure will be nice to get away from the company tables."

"Yeah," Jake replied as he flipped the page in the Green Death. "I'm looking forward to the tables for the pistol team. Can you imagine what it will be like not having to eat at attention for three months? Jake paused as he closed the book and walked to the window. He stared into the darkness, seeing nothing. "Got a question for you, hillbilly."

"What's that, hick!" Patrick asked, returning the slur.

"What would you think about me signing up for the Brigade Boxing Championship? I mean, do you think I'd have a chance?"

"I figured you'd get around to that," Patrick said as he turned around in his chair grinning. "You really are a pugilist, aren't you? Beats me how a guy can get a kick out of having his head battered till it bleeds, but I never did consider having to introduce you to my friends as the smartest guy I know."

"But, yeah, I think you should sign up," Patrick responded with enthusiasm. "I don't think you should be shy about signing up. You're undefeated in the company competition. Course the only reason you win is that the other guys are smart enough to quit doing something that hurts. But, at 167 pounds, you know who you'll fight if you make it to the finals, don't you?"

"Yeah, I know," Jake said, looking Patrick in the eyes. "Our illustrious regimental commander, Captain Jonathan Scott, undefeated brigade champion three years in a row."

"That's a fak, Jak!" Patrick said, raising his eyebrows and pursing his lips. "Hell, if he wasn't in the army, he could go pro. Rumor has it that he will go to the Olympics in '76 and win the gold. I mean, he's seriously good as a middleweight. Do you have some kind of delusion that you can actually whip him?"

Jake walked slowly back to his desk, re-analyzing the risks in his mind and searching for objective commitment. Taking on Scott was, in their microcosmic world, a big decision, especially for a plebe. If he lost to Scott, it was really no big deal, other than maybe spending a week in the infirmary for face repair, but if he beat Scott, having defeated the regimental commander and a Corps hero could move the level of plebe misery up a notch.

"I can win," Jake said with as serious a tone in his voice as Patrick had ever heard. The only time he had heard Jake sound that serious was when it was time for him to cease and desist in a morsel skit. That was serious.

"Ok. What can I do to help?" Patrick asked. He had learned to admire Jake's tenacity. When Jake set his mind to overcome the odds, there was nothing that could stop him. Beating Scott in the ring would be a sight to see, but if Jake did beat him, it would not be because he was more skilled than Scott. Scott was a superior boxer. Jake would have to beat Scott with something else.

"I'll need some help training on weekends and at night after study hall. And more importantly, I want you in my corner at ringside. I want you to help me mentally."

As Jake stared at him, Patrick knew that Jake was committed to giving this fight everything he had, and he sensed that Jake might actually do it. He might actually defeat the legend, the man known throughout the Corps for his unbeatable skills in the ring.

1830 Hours
22 March 1970
United States Military Academy
West Point, New York

"Sɪʀ, the 4th classmen at the table have properly completed their duties and are now prepared to eat!" Jake announced. "Sir, the 4th classmen at this table request a fall-out." The firsties of Company C-4 were letting the plebes fall-out, or eat at rest, two or three times a week now, so long as they had a skit or some interesting trivia for the upperclassmen's entertainment. The skit for tonight was an altered version of a scene from *Gone With the Wind*. Greg Patterson, an Ohio native, weighing in at a smooth two hundred pounds and only slightly less hairy than a grizzly bear, was acting the part of the lovely Miss Scarlet O'Hara. Jake portrayed a dashing Rhett Butler with a mustache made from a plume off a full-dress tar bucket parade hat, and Patrick quickly parted his short blond hair down the middle to provide a convincing rendition of a very sweet Ashley.

After ten minutes of hilarity, Jake, Patrick, and Greg sat to eat while cadets within a ten-yard radius tried to get their laughter under control. The skit successfully entertained the old cadets sufficiently for a well-earned fall-out.

"Great skit!" the table commandant said. "You guys are going to spoil us. We may have to keep you as plebes so we can enjoy dinner every night."

Jake smiled at the old cadet. Eleven months were more than enough. Still, coping with the plebe system was easier now since the fear was gone. The plebes were getting bolder by the day, coming into their own. The upperclassmen knew it. They knew it because they had been plebes, too, and had experienced the process of maturity. They knew every plebe was now without fear and perfectly capable of telling an old cadet to kiss-off in any given situation. But as part of the process, these last few months of the year was designed to teach the principles of self- enforced humility. One such principle being obedience to authority with cognizance and confidence. In many ways, these last months were the hardest.

"Mister Jacobs," the table commandant said, interrupting Jake's thoughts, and his meal.

"Yes, sir!" Jake popped-off.

"Are you ready for Scott tomorrow?" the old cadet asked sincerely.

Jake was well aware of the mixed emotions within the company. Scott had been a hero in the 4th Regiment for the past three years, and they were proud to be represented by him. Yet, Jake had earned their support, too. He had gone undefeated in company competition for three months and he had fought his way to the finals in five grueling battles in as many days. He had won the fights, one at a time, each with no special skill, but on a tenacious spirit and a desire to win.

Jake sat at the end of the table with his cheeks slightly swollen under the eyes and a red lip, distorted on one side. The week had started with ridicule and with an expectation that he would never make it to the finals, but as the week progressed and he stacked up the wins, the support he had received from the company at ringside had gone from the cheering of only his classmates to an increasing number of old cadets as well.

Tomorrow afternoon was the Brigade Boxing Championship finals. The gym would be packed with the entire Corps of Cadets and as many civilians and officers. Next to the Army-Navy game, it was the event of the year. Though Jake was gaining support within the company, everyone, except Patrick and Wayne, thought he would be embarrassingly whipped. Scott was not only a fast and skilled technician at the sport, but he was also deadly. He seldom fought into the third round. Most of his opponents were on the canvas, unconscious and bleeding by then.

"Yes, sir," Jake replied to the table commandant. "I'm ready. I... "

"Sir." Patrick interrupted. "Jake, I mean Mister Jacobs, is gonna kick Captain Scott's ass tomorrow. Scott ain't gotta prayer against my man here."

Silence fell on the table. All eyes were diverted from Jake and Patrick. It was an unconscious gesture indicating that they did not believe Patrick's hype. At the moment, Jake felt very alone.

Following dinner, study hall was routine in preparation for Saturday's classes, and the normal Saturday morning room inspection. Jake, Patrick, and Wayne finished on the books then spent two hours getting the room ready. The room was immaculate with no dust, no spots in water glasses, rifles clean, brass polished, and drawers fine-tuned perfectly. Conversation had been light throughout the evening. All three of the roommates felt the presence of tomorrow's fight. It was one o'clock in the morning and the time for words and talk was finished. In the past month, the three had trained and prepared for tomorrow as one. Jake would be in the ring, but Patrick was his right hand, Wayne his left. Patrick and Wayne had spent hours working with Jake. The three roommates did five-mile runs every morning at zero- five-hundred, thousands of sit-ups and pushups, and weekends spent on the bags in the gym. Win or lose, the three had stood together.

In the quiet of the early morning hours, a rumbling noise rose from the first floor of the 50th division barracks, which in five floors of four rooms each and a latrine, and continued to mount as it resounded up the stairs toward the fifth floor. Puzzled at the noise, Jake and his roommates came out of their room into the hallway. They stood there dumbfounded at the sound of a hundred and twenty cadets climbing the stairs en masse, chanting "Jacobs! Jacobs! Jacobs!" The chanting grew louder and louder as the company ascended the stairs, adding strength to their numbers as they passed each floor. "Jacobs! Jacobs! Jacobs!"

Jake, Patrick, and Wayne were stunned at the sight as the entire company streamed onto the fifth floor. Though the company was less formally dressed in sweats, bathrobes, or shorts than they would be for a rally in the mess hall, a rally it was. It was a rally for one plebe and his two roommates. Desk chairs were pulled out of the room and Brad Steele, the company commander, ordered the three to stand on them so that their heads were above the screaming cadets for all to see. In the ensuing chaos, stimulated by bodies shoulder-to-shoulder chattering and bantering in a space designed for twelve cadets rather than one hundred and twenty, Jake and his roommates stood on the chairs, well above the hullabaloo.

When the company quietened, Steele said, "Mister Jacobs, we all came up here tonight to let you know we are behind you tomorrow. None of us have given you much support but we're with you now. You've done good, kid. No matter what happens tomorrow, you and your roommates have done C-4 proud. Kick Scott's ass!"

"Speech! Speech!" the frenzied company yelled. Steele extended a hand toward Jake, palm upward as if to introduce him to the mob. Jake shuffled on the chair and looked at Patrick and Wayne. Their smiles and nods told him to kick the lump out of his throat and say something reasonably intelligent.

"Well," Jake said, embarrassed, "I don't know what to say." He was overwhelmed by the company's demonstration of encouragement. So much so that he had difficulty finding appropriate words to express his thanks and to respond to the speech they were expecting. "Thanks for your support. I know in many ways it's out of place for me to be fighting Captain Scott tomorrow, and I know I have no right to expect to beat him. But I will win tomorrow."

A stunned silence fell upon the hallway, As revealing as words spoken, the silence of the upperclassmen of Company C-4 declared their true thoughts. Many in the crowd looked at him as though to say, "You poor, dumb beanhead. We're supporting your effort, but you're gonna get killed".

"Captain Scott is a champion," Jake continued. "He's a better boxer than I am. But, gentlemen, I'll take the title from him tomorrow. It won't make him less of a champion, nor me a better boxer, but I will win the match. Scott assumes he'll win. He assumes he'll win because he's done it three years in a row, because I'm a plebe, and because I'm just a cow lot scrapper from Texas. Fact is, I'll win because I want it more than he does."

A fog of silence permeated the hallway. But this silence was now different. Jake's statement of resolve hit the upperclassmen like a thunderbolt. The upperclassmen were not foreign to the power of desire and determination and personal courage. They had been at West Point long enough to know that they, too, had become overcomers of adversity. Jake stepped down from the chair and backed into his room. Within the span of a few minutes the company had climbed the stairs in a show of support, and all would have cheered for Jake but would have bet their hard-earned money on Scott. But now! Now, they were not so sure that an upset was not in the making. The set of Jake's jaw and the determination in his eyes told them that Scott was in for a very long three rounds.

CHAPTER SEVEN

1400 Hours
23 March 1970
United States Military Academy
West Point, New York

JAKE ENTERED THE RING. Glancing around, he noticed for the first
time that the main gymnasium was packed. The stands were full to
capacity and the upper level, used as an indoor running track, had
cadets and guests along the railing. Banners hung from the walls
with company emblems and homemade signs to cheer on a
favorite cadet. Being a Saturday afternoon, many cadets escorted
dates, most post officers with their families, and other civilians that
had traveled for miles to enjoy the annual event. In the locker
room, he and Patrick had been so focused on warming up and
discussing—for the one-hundredth time—their strategy for the
fight, the noise and screaming from inside the gym had hardly
been noticeable. But now, the impact of being in the center of this
crowd made him feel conspicuous, and indeed, he was. Scott had
not yet entered the ring as it was customary for the defending
champion to enter last.

Patrick motioned him to the corner, and with Wayne, they

began giving instructions, not only to cover the strategy for the opening round but also to keep Jake from being distracted by the crowd. Company C-4 was in mass behind his corner. They had raised the roof with their shouts and cheers when he exited the dressing room and approached the ring with Patrick on one side, Wayne on the other. Brad Steele was a one-man cheerleader and, surprisingly, it was the first classmen of the company who were setting the tone for the crowd. They were yelling encouragement nonstop. Jake waved to the company with a smile and noticed a familiar, nonresident face in the cheering mass. Cantrell stood when he saw that Jake was looking at him. He smiled, shook his right fist in the air, and winked.

The noise level suddenly increased to a deafening pitch. Jake turned to see Captain Jonathan Scott climb through the ropes into the ring. Scott wore black silk trunks, a gold T-shirt with "#1" imprinted in black, and real boxing shoes. His appearance was in major contrast to Jake's. Jake did not look nearly so dashing in his gray PE shorts, C-4 T-shirt, and black hightop, Converse basketball shoes. If personal appearance was to be a factor in the outcome of the fight, he was a dead man. Not only was Scott dressed better than Jake, but he also entered the ring dancing around like the champion he was, playing to the crowd that cheered him. He was the Corps favorite. As Scott danced around the ring, punching the air with style, Jake stood in his corner motionless, arms draped over the top rope. He watched and admired Scott's pre-fight performance just as much as the crowd did.

"Now remember, hick," Patrick said, stepping in front of Jake, "the name of the game is to work his ribcage till he cries and make the captain fight the third round. Then, he'll be plum tuckered out, and you can go to work on him. We've practiced that damn combination of yours till you can do it in your sleep. Hang tough, buddy. The third round will get here."

"Third round," Jake said. "Third round."

The bell rang. The referee motioned Jake and Scott to the center of the ring and the crowd increased its fervor. The referee quickly gave instructions for the fight and the two pugilists put their fists together.

"Good luck, kid," Scott said. "This shouldn't take too long."

Jake just smiled at him through his mouthpiece and turned for his corner. There was no question about Scott's presumption. When he got to the corner, Patrick and Wayne were all smiles. "Ok Jake, this is it. You wanted it, you got it. You can do this. Just do it like you planned." The bell rang.

As they approached the center of the ring, Scott danced high on his toes and immediately began circling Jake with long floating steps, his arms down as an invitation for a careless attack. Jake followed him through his first full circle, standing almost flat-footed. Scott jumped in smoothly for a light left jab on Jake's cheek then jumped back quickly, still on the move. A half-circle again around Jake, and again he moved for a left jab, connecting with the cheek. As he backed off the one-punch attack, Jake followed him, cut off his circling movement to the right, and stung him with a right hook to the jaw. Jake had his weight in the hook, and it set Scott on the ground flat-footed. He pressed Scott's confusion with a left jab and two quick right hooks. Scott hit the ropes, was off guard and puzzled at the power in Jake's fist.

The crowd went temporarily silent with the indication that perhaps Scott was in the ring for a real fight. With only one minute into the first round, Scott was scrambling to change his attitude about the fight and the smart-ass plebe hitting him.

Scott ducked to his left and escaped Jake's trap against the ropes. Again he rose to the balls of his feet and began his circling dance. As he circled, Jake persistently pursued. For the first time in four years, the Corps was seeing Scott on the defensive. To recover his offensive posture, he moved toward Jake with a barrage of right and left punches to the head, one of which jerked Jake's head back hard. But when he began his retreat, Jake again followed and ended the exchange with a solid punch to the ribs that bent Scott sideways in pain. Scott recovered quickly and attacked with the same barrage, backing Jake into his corner while guarding his head the best he could. Ten, twelve hard blows, each doing its damage. The crowd found its previous confidence in Scott, and the roar increased to peak level.

Jake ducked under Scott and back-stepped to the center of the ring. Scott pursued with yet another set of quick combinations, most of them scoring solid points in his favor, and one to Jake's left eye that brought blood to its corner. Again, as Scott did his damage and retreated, Jake pursued the exchange with a right to the ribs that brought Scott slightly off his feet and a visible wince of pain to his face.

The last minute of the first round continued in this pattern. Scott scored punches ten to Jake's one, and Jake finished each exchange with a blow to Scott's ribs that rocked him in pain. Jake was bleeding from the corner of his left eye, with the blood blurring his vision and trickling down his cheek, while Scott was less on his toes and obviously hyper-aware of the sharp pain in his ribcage with every move. The bell rang.

"Dang!" Patrick shouted. "Just like you said. He's hurting. You must have broken a rib or two. He's hurting bad." Jake said nothing as Wayne swabbed the cut over his eye and Patrick gave him water. "What now?"

"More of the same," Jake said. "I have to take the risk, and let him get me in the corners. If he keeps swinging, he'll be dead tired in the third round."

"Yeah. Well," Patrick said jokingly, "don't you go and hit him with your face too much. You take too much risk and he'll knock you into next week. He can do it, ya know?"

"I know," Jake agreed. "How about points? What do you think?"

"Oh, he has you on points. Big time," Wayne said. "But you knew he was going to do that. It's the third round that's yours. Simple, Jakey Boy, stay alive until the third round, then knock his head off!"

"Right!" Jake snickered. "Why don't one of you guys do this second round so I'll be fresh for the third. I'll say one thing. I know why the guy will go to the Olympics. He's faster than lightning, and I'd sooner get hit with a hammer than one of his fists.

The second round bell rang and Jake lunged from his stool. Before Scott could get to the center of the ring, Jake was all over him with an onslaught of punches. Scott tried to move to his right to get away from him, but Jake stayed with him step-for-step, pounding his right fist into his ribcage. Finally, Scott sensed the futility and grabbed Jake in a hug. As the referee split them apart, Scott danced away in an attempt to control his kind of fight. As far as he was concerned, Jake was not a real boxer. He was a bold and dangerous street fighter.

Following Jake's initial second-round charge, Scott went to work on him like a skilled surgeon. The first minute of the round was uneventful with Scott on the move and Jake in pursuit. Though the bounce was out of his step, Scott was still quicker than Jake. Then, with two and three punch combinations, Scott moved in, landing solid scoring punches. The cut on Jake's eye opened again, his nose began to trickle blood, and by the end of the second minute, his lip was split deep. Jake's blood spattered the canvas as Scott did what he did so well. As the clock rolled into the third minute, Jake backed into the corner under a fierce Scott attack. Scott went for the knockout. Jake covered his head with his gloves as Scott pounded him with everything he could throw. Each blow rocked Jake's head and body as though he was being hit with a baseball bat. For nearly sixty seconds, Scott hit Jake with his most and his best. In those seconds prior to the bell, Jake did not hit Scott a single time. But, just when Jake thought he absolutely could not take one more devastating blow, the bell miraculously sounded.

"Man! You're a mess!" Patrick said as Jake slumped on the stool.

"I've never seen anything like that," Wayne said as he mopped the blood off Jake's face with a wet towel. "What in the world were you doing out there?"

"I was trading the biggest headache for a minute's worth of rest," Jake said calmly. "Look at him over there."

Both Patrick and Wayne followed Jake's eyes to Scott's corner. Scott was visibly exhausted. A full minute of pounding Jake as hard as he could had drained him.

The crowd was wild. Their interpretation of the fight, so far, was that Scott would slaughter the plebe on points, and after what they had seen in the last minute of fighting, Scott would probably knock Jacobs out cold shortly after the bell rang for the third round.

"Ok, hick," Patrick said seriously. "You know what you have to do from here. There's only one way. If it comes down to a decision, you lose."

"Right, hillbilly," Jake said, still staring at Scott. "Are we on target?"

"On target," Wayne said. "He's hurt in the ribs bad. His legs are tired. And, he's one pooped puppy after having thrown some mega-thousand punches into your skull."

"Just remember," Patrick warned, "he knows what condition he's in. He'll either try to stay away from you because he knows he has the points, or he'll come early to put you out because he thinks he can't make the round. You've got him scared, Jake. He doesn't want to lose this fight. It's his last round of boxing at West Point, and he wants to finish a winner. Do your thing, but be careful. Scott will give you the best he has in this last round."

The bell for the third and final round rang, and the roar in the large gymnasium was deafening. Jake walked slowly to the center of the ring. Scott did the same. Their gloves and their eyes met, just as they had done at the start of the fight.

"Apple cobbler, my ass," Scott said, his eyes piercing and cold.

"Anchors Aweigh, sir," Jake countered.

They slowly backed off from each other. Then after a pause of four or five seconds, each staring the other dead in the eyes, it was as though another signal was given for the main charge in full-scale combat like gladiators to the death. Simultaneously, Scott and Jake charged each other, swinging their arms with all the force they could muster. There was no longer any doubt about the decision Captain Scott had made. He was going for a knockout.

Scott was no longer dancing and circling. He was slugging, trying to back Jake again into the corners, but Jake held him to the center of the ring. Scott scored quickly and often while Jake returned fire and solidly scored with power punches of his own. Scott was taking as much as he was giving. Jake's cuts opened immediately and blood flowed freely. Scott, too, was decorating the mat in red with a broken nose and a deep cut at the corner of his lip. Through the first two minutes, there was no maneuvering, there was no finesse. There was only up close, toe-to-toe combat. The crowd responded with emotion. Everyone in the gymnasium were on their feet, yelling and screaming. The intensity of emotion in the large arena came close to matching that in the gladiators' ring.

As the second minute of the third round passed, both Scott and Jake backed off. Both were flowing blood. Both were exhausted from the nonstop two-minute exchange of blows. They circled each other, still in the center of the ring. Precious seconds ticked away in this last short minute as each man sought a way to attack and win.

With forty seconds remaining, Jake charged. Scott met the charge with a defensive flurry of blows to Jake's face and head. Jake ignored the crushing blows and slammed his right fist into Scott's ribcage. And, Scott hesitated. He hesitated from the pain that shot through his chest like fire. With the hesitation, Jake took one step forward and again slammed his fist into the ribs. Another step forward, with feet firmly planted, again he dealt a crunching blow of pain to Scott. With this third ramming punch, Scott dropped his arms instinctively to protect himself. As if in slow motion, Jake saw the opportunity he had practiced a thousand times on the bags in the gym. Without further thought, he jumped back a full step, planted his feet firmly on the mat, and swung with his left. It caught Scott squarely on the jaw, and before he could recover, Jake followed it with another identical left hook, then rhythmically brought a right uppercut, loaded with all his body weight and power, to Scott's chin. Scott's feet rose from the mat, his legs lifeless, his back and head arched backwards as though he were attempting a backflip. Scott was unconscious before his limp body crumpled to the canvas.

With twenty seconds remaining, pandemonium hit West Point. While Scott was counted out, the ring overflowed with the cadets of Company C-4. An exhausted and bloody plebe was mounted on Greg Patterson's shoulders and held up like a trophy for all to see. Moments later, Patrick and Wayne were elevated as well. Jake and his team had done it. The impossible was defeated.

The vision was made real.

CHAPTER EIGHT

1300 Hours
2 June 1970
United States Military Academy
West Point, New York

BEADS OF SWEAT trickled down the back of Jake's leg. The desire to bend over and scratch his leg was overpowering. The tingling sensation of drops of sweat crawling down the tender skin was an excruciating torture, demanding either the cursings of anger or the whimpering of helplessness. Unable to move in the slightest, least he suffer the consequences for extraneous movement on the parade ground, there was nothing to do but suffer the course of each drop and await the next. His full-dress tunic with its high collar and fine wool was soaked with perspiration. His face and neck glistened with sweat in the ninety-degree heat, and his head hurt from the tight fitting shaker with its long black plume. "Pass in review." The Corps had stood motionless for just short of an hour on The Plain.

It was June Week. It was time for the Class of 1970 to have its week of festivities and graduate, and, for the plebes, this parade was as important to them as graduation day was for the firsties.

This was the Recognition Parade. Jake and all his classmates had written their first names on the back side of their white cross belts so that at the parade's end the upperclassmen could pass through the ranks, shake hands with each surviving plebe, and call him by his first name. In less than an hour plebe year would come to an end for the Class of 1973 and Jake and his classmates would be old cadets.

"Mister McSwain," an upperclassman whispered through gritted teeth that held the chin strap to his tight-fitting shaker. "Give me the days, Mister."

"Sir, The Days!" Patrick whispered to the unseen old cadet behind him. "The events for the week are as follows: at approximately 1330 hours, at the company area, there will be a recognition ceremony whereby you will have the privilege to call me Patrick for the rest of your life and I, sir, will have the privilege to call you whatever fits you, and ... "

"I ain't believing you said that, Mister," the old cadet said with mock anger. "I guess you think plebe year is history, huh?"

"Yes, sir!" Patrick said.

"Mister Jacobs," another old cadet whispered. "What's for dinner tonight?"

"Sir, I do not know!"

"Why don't you know, smack?" the old cadet asked, not at all surprised that he would have to find the company bulletin board if he wanted to know. There was not a plebe at West Point that would tell him. Not today. Not now.

"No excuse, sir!" Jake responded.

"You figure you'll slough off today. Huh, Jacobs?"

"No, sir!"

"Then how come you don't know your poop, Jacobs?" the old cadet asked with a grin on his face.

"No excuse, sir!" In the past month, the plebe system had been more irritating to the old cadets than to the plebes. The plebes had come into their own. They played the game, but they were cocky, exactly as they should be. They had survived all that West Point could do to discourage, ridicule, and dishearten them. The plebes remaining had risen above it and had remained focused on the mission when the desire to surrender had been with them every day for eleven long months. They were cocky, and for good reason. West Point was now their's. Forever.

Jake stood at rigid attention, miserable in the heat, as the brigade commander barked the order for the Corps to pass in review. At the sound, Jake shifted his weight to release the pressure of the dress bayonet wedged in the corner of his armpit. Being five-foot-eight had few advantages, but one being that the height of his M-14 rifle and dress bayonet allowed him to lean on it during parades. Only once had this position of rest proven dangerous. He had fallen asleep at attention, his neck propped up by the high stiff collar of his tunic, and when his knees had buckled the sharp point of the bayonet punctured both the underarm of his uniform and his armpit. Although it was a wound inflicted by means of a deadly combat weapon while in the uniform of his country, it was hardly a legitimate justification for the purple heart.

With orders resonant across The Plain through regimental, battalion, and company levels of command, the Corps began to move in the precision march it had performed hundreds of times in the past year. Several hundred spectators were in attendance. The reviewing stands were packed with the bright colors of spring dresses and casual shirts. Jake wondered what the visitors felt as they watched the Corps in parade. Unless one had seen it many times over, as he had, it had to be inspiring. Not only was West Point beautiful in the spring, but for most observers, there was a sense of history felt in viewing the Corps of Cadets. For those that love America, one could hardly dismiss thoughts concerning the history of national adversities, battles and wars fought, freedom gained or preserved, and the yet unrecorded history of the future. All in attendance knew that the young men marching with precision today would be the ones who would fight battles yet unknown.

As they passed the reviewing stand, eyes right, Jake felt himself to be in tune with the world at large. He felt himself to be exactly who and what providence destined him to be. Thoughts of Charley came to mind. The mental image of Charley lying on the jungle floor, mangled and dying, brought a film of tears to his eyes as the visitors passed out of view, and the company marched toward the slab. Jake marched with resolve and pride, believing that while Charley died so young, he lived his destiny. Relative to history, he passed this way with insignificant impact on the consciousness of men's minds, but being what he was, Charley is our history, and he became a part of our day-to-day lives.

"Stand at ease," the company commander said as Company C-4 came to a halt on the slab and responded with a crisp left-face command. The cadets were soaked in sweat, their hair wet as they removed their shakers. Immediately, the plebes turned their cross belt to reveal a first name printed in bold black letters, and the upperclassmen walked through the ranks with smiles on their faces as they pumped the hand of each plebe and called him by his first name. The game was over. Upperclassmen and plebes alike laughed at each other and recalled situations of the past with humor that might have been of crisis proportion only weeks or months ago.

"McSwain," Bean said with sincerity, "I want you to meet my girl this afternoon. I can't believe the letter you sent to her. I have to let her see that you're an ordinary scumbag in real life and not some oppressed victim. I've never been in so much trouble. She has been on my case ever since you wrote her that damn letter."

Patrick's laugh was infectious. "I don't know, Jerry. I think if you introduce us, that'll be the last time you'll see Darlene. She kinda likes the gentle and sensitive types, ya know?"

"Maybe you're right," Jerry said grinning. "I'll just tell her you died today from heat exhaustion and that she's stuck with me."

"Yeah!" Jake said. "Patrick is untrustworthy around women. When he comes to Comanche this month, I'm going to send my Labrador retriever to the kennel and my ninety-year-old grandma to Florida."

"Well!" Patrick said with mocking indignation. "I'm not interested in your dog or your grandma. I was thinking more along the lines of sheep and your little sister."

"I ain't got any sheep, and I ain't got a sister either."

"Damn. Maybe I should take leave with Carl Strake. They've got good looking sheep in Montana. I know because Carl showed me pictures. They were standing around naked, batting those eyelashes, and waiting for Carl to get back home."

"You're disgusting," Jerry Bean said. "I can hardly wait to tell Darlene about you and the sheep."

"Hey, Jake!" Cantrell yelled as he came through the company area to formally recognize his two friends. "I hate to admit it, but I'm glad you two have lived to see Recognition Day. Back in Beast Barracks, I would have given anything to be rid of both of you."

Jake extended his hand. "You have to be kidding. We were the life of the party. Just think how long the summer would have been if you hadn't had us to make things interesting."

"Sure, Jake," Cantrell said, laughing. "You don't know how close to a heart attack I came the day you popped-off with that mouth of yours about why you hadn't shined your brass. With all the suicide attempts, your answer was a real shocker."

"Oh," Patrick said. "You mean when he said, 'Sir, I would have polished my brass, but my roommate drank the Brasso'."

"Like I said, I'm glad you're alive and well, but I am surprised." Cantrell shook Patrick's hand as well. "When you get to Camp Buckner in July, I reckon we'll have another go at it. I'll be the company commander of 5th Company, and you guys are on the roster. I hope this isn't some kind of curse on my military career. Somehow, the thought of you two being in my command for the next twenty or thirty years is depressing as hell."

CHAPTER NINE

2130 Hours
7 June 1970
Comanche, Texas

JOHN TRAINER, a U.S. Senator from Texas, had arranged for an Air Force high altitude reconnaissance aircraft to transport the Texas cadets from Stewart Air Force Base to Carson in Fort Worth, and Jake was on it. Not all the Texans at West Point were aboard. Many, like Cantrell, had duty at the academy during June. They stayed to train for Camp Buckner in July, while others trained to instruct the new incoming plebes. Jake and his classmates were to report to Buckner on 7 July for two months. The old cadets had often referred to Buckner as the best summer of their life, but as Jake sat in a web seat staring at a computer console, he had a hard time imagining how two months of sleeping in tents and eating C-rations were going to be all that great. Either the old cadets were trying to cover-up the truth about a miserable summer, or there was something about Camp Buckner he did not know.

The ordeal to come was not all that important at the moment. All that was important was that he had thirty full days to wear blue jeans, let his hair grow to an inch, and spend every possible moment with Sara. He thought it horrible that as time passed the ache he felt from missing Sara grew worse. He had not seen her in five months. The ache was never less, nor even constant. It grew more intense each day. Though his plebe year was behind him, the three more years ahead of him seemed an eternity in terms of his need to be with her. He smiled in the dim lighting of the plane at his acceptance that Sara was as much a part of his life as breathing or eating. It was as though he were not a whole person without her.

The Air Force crew of three had received a fifth of bourbon by the cadets in appreciation for their efforts, and in hopes they would deliver a smooth flight. In keeping with their wishes, the huge plane revved its engines, lumbered smoothly down the long runway, rotated beautifully, and made a steep climb for a four-hour flight to Fort Worth. However, the plane was noisy. It was cold. It was uncomfortable. Yet, even with its lack of stylish comfort, the price of the flight was perfect. It was free. Approaching Fort Worth, a near miss with a commercial airliner educated the cadets to the fact that Zoomies should be thanked with a bottle of bourbon after the flight, not before it.

As Jake deplaned, he saw Steve and his father waiting for him by the door. A year ago, they had begun their new adventure together, and it seemed appropriate that they return to Comanche the same way. Steve was still in uniform and had arrived on a like flight an hour before him. Cadets and midshipmen milled around the building waiting for transportation to whatever part of the state they were going, and as he approached, Steve's mouth turned up in a broad smile.

"Well, the Air Force managed to get us here in one piece," Jake said, his smile meeting Steve's.

"Yep," Steve replied. "It feels great having my feet back in the Lone Star State. I've missed Texas almost as much as I've missed everything else about my past life as a normal person."

"Then I guess the only thing you've missed is Texas, because you never were normal," Jake said laughing.

95

Watch it, "Kadet." We'll leave you stranded here with the Zoomies." He and Jake had been picking on each other all their lives. With every conceivable insult thrown, not once had they gotten angry with each other. The insults had become a part of their friendship years back and it was, in an odd way, their private way of saying how much they cared for each other.

Steve thought it interesting that he and Jake had shared so much in common over the years. Even now, though in a different uniform, their experiences were so parallel. Jake understood him. He understood the life Steve had lived these past eleven months. He lived with competitive pressure, long hours of study, harassment, and a determination to survive. Only Jake really knew him anymore. No one else in Comanche could understand because one has to experience it to know it. As he walked to the car with Jake at his side, it occurred to him that one Naval Academy graduate knows another, though they have never met and are years apart in age and rank. They know things about the man inside the outer shell. And, it was to always be the same between Jake and him. They each had a knowledge of the man that others will never know.

You two don't realize how different you are, do you?" Steve's father said as the car sped down I-35 toward Comanche. "What do you mean, Pop?" Steve asked with a puzzled look on his face. A quick glance to Jake in the back seat recognized the same curiosity.

"Well," Mr. Ross said, gathering his thoughts, "you look different. You act different. It's not so much in the way you act. It's more in the way you are. You stand, walk, and talk different than you did a year ago. Your facial features are different—tighter—you know? There's a kind of confidence in the way you talk and in your eyes. I don't know exactly. You're different. That's all."

Steve's eyes met Jakes. It was a look denoting mutual acknowledgment that Mr. Ross was right. There was no way to explain the subtle changes in them. Forever, they would be different to the world around them. "Don't worry, Pop," Steve said with a laugh, still meeting Jake's knowing eyes. "As soon as Jake gets home, throws Sara on the sofa, messes up the kitchen, and throws his clothes on the floor, he'll be back to the same ole Jake."

June 1970
Comanche, Texas

SUMMER LEAVE PASSED MORE QUICKLY than Jake could imagine. The time was gone, and the anticipation of going back to West Point was with him before he felt comfortable with the change in routine. Sara worked at the downtown drugstore, which left Jake restless and awaiting five o'clock, Monday through Friday. Though he enjoyed sleeping late and spending time with Steve, Sara remained the purpose of his day. He waited daily on the street outside the drugstore a half-hour before closing. Sara came to the window like clockwork at four-thirty to wave at him and blow a kiss. She, too, was anxious to begin the important part of her day. They were both aware of their few precious moments and the long six months ahead of them before they could meet again.

Sara had graduated from Comanche High three days before Jake left West Point, and she was glad to have her senior year in the past. It had been a disappointment without Jake to share it with her. Though intrigued by the thought of being on her own and living life differently than she had ever known, Sara was not excited about going to the University of Texas in September. Marrying Jake and settling into a cozy little house in Comanche was her ambition if she had a choice. But, like Jake, the practicalities of life as taught by their parents dictated that college and careers were, for the moment, more important than the burning desire they felt for each other and their need to be together. They both accepted that time would pass and that all the little proposed preliminaries to their lifelong happiness together would end, and their dreams of marriage would come into being.

It was Thursday afternoon, Sara's last shift at the drugstore before the Fourth of July holiday and only three days before Jake would leave again. Christmas seemed an eternity away. For the third time, she went to the store window to wave at him, anxious for the last ten minutes of her shift to end. Jake stood by the curb with Steve, waiting for her to finish work so they could make the drive together to pick up Patrick at Love Field in Dallas. She had to chuckle to herself as she saw him through the window in his customary summer attire. Jake temporarily lived in yesteryear by wearing an old pair of faded blue jeans, a bright yellow pocket T-shirt, an old Dodger's baseball cap that set on the back of his head, a pair of white sneakers she knew his mother had tried to throw away at least a dozen times, and gold rimmed military sunglasses. He was in some kind of animated conversation with Steve, hands flaying about, and Steve was laughing. She assumed that he was telling some story, interesting and funny by way of exaggeration, and when he spied her from the corner of his eye, he performed a smooth left-face and a deep bow in old Southern fashion from the waist, hat in hand. Sara laughed, shook her head, and turned toward the back of the store.

Minutes later, Sara walked out the front door all smiles. "Let's go. I'm free at last!" Before Jake could turn and respond, she grabbed him by the back of the shirt, pulled him off balance and dipped him backwards for a kiss. Unfortunately, Jake's weight was a bit too much and both went to the sidewalk, right in the middle of downtown Comanche. All three were stunned for a moment, as were the four elderly gentlemen sitting outside the barbershop next door. It was not until one observing old man said, "That's just Jake and Sara, "so matter-of-factly, like seeing a woman attack a man on the street in broad daylight was normal, that everyone burst into laughter. "Ya better watch out, Jake," one old man giggled. "A woman like that can ruin your back, son. I use to have one that ruint my back." All four of the old men laughed, and Sara, too, though she turned red at the inference.

Jake got to his feet and helped Sara to hers. "Yeah, Mr. Higgins, my daddy tells me that in the old days you got your back ruint pretty often."

"Been a bachelor all my life," Mr. Higgins said, tickled that Jake had mentioned the one thing he had been well known for, at least known for thirty years ago. Since then, he was more known for rocking on his front porch or sitting with his friends at the barbershop discussing the price of farm commodities. But like everyone else, Mr. Higgins was more inclined to hang on to the more exciting and romantic identity of a fading past. "Ya got yourself a feisty one there, son. Hang on to her."

"I intend to, Mr. Higgins. You gentlemen have a nice day," Jake tipped his hat with one hand and opened the door for the feisty one with the other.

Steve's '56 Buick Century hardtop sped past the city limits sign with Sara between the two camouflaged future warriors. The radio ignited the large rear-mounted speakers and the three sang and swayed to the tune of "Crystal Blue Persuasion" as the Buick devoured the road's white lines. For at least a few more days the three were carefree and happy teenagers, nothing more, nothing less, and they were anxious to get Patrick in Dallas. Jake missed his partner, and Steve liked the tall Tennessee boy because Patrick was genuinely down to earth. Sara had heard so much about him from Jake over the past year that she felt like she was going to see a friend of many years, though Jake had warned her that she might expect Patrick to say anything or do anything, whether appropriate and in good taste or not.

After a four-hour drive, a serving of airport hotdogs, and an hour wait at the gate, Patrick marched down the ramp with a dead giveaway military walk. Even to a casual observer, the kid was military, no matter what clothes he wore. His face was smeared with a smile.

"My God!" Jake said. "That's Patrick all right." As Patrick walked the hundred feet toward them, Jake had to admire his roommate's courage, or lack of concern, at how funny he looked. Patrick had on a pair of flowered Bermuda shorts of bright yellows and reds and greens, a white T-shirt, and more orange than one could imagine. He was wearing an orange University of Tennessee baseball cap and windbreaker, an orange UT carryon bag, and a pair of wingtip leather shoes, that might have been brown once, but somehow had made it to a definite shade of bright orange, and no socks. There was more clash in his wardrobe than a freeway accident.

Following sincere handshakes with Jake and Steve, Patrick grabbed Sara by the shoulders and looked into her smiling eyes. "So. You're the ravishing young morsel. You're too beautiful to be with scum like Jake. But, since you love my little buddy, I love you. Glad to meet you after all this time. God knows I've heard enough about you."

STEVE'S BUICK ROCK-N'-ROLLED back to Comanche with only a few hours remaining before dawn. At Jake's house, the four finally gave way to sleep. With only two days of summer leave remaining, the only thing planned was to be together and not to think much about going back. For Jake and Sara, the only way they could handle the upcoming separation for another six months was to ignore its reality.

The following two days were fun as they bounced between Jake's, Sara's, and Steve's house for swimming, barbecues in the backyard, and midnight card games. Patrick was a fountain of information concerning Jake's winning the brigade championship from Captain Scott. The way Jake had reported it, he had won some little boxing match. So, Sara and their parents were astonished to hear the true tale of the now-legendary fight.

On the last night, Jake and Sara walked down the street to the small municipal park a block away. They strolled hand in hand, very much in love, silently knowing their time together was again at an end—for a while.

CHAPTER TEN

1600 Hours
3 August 1970
Camp Buckner
United States Military Academy
West Point, New York

JAKE LAY on the lower bunk in the dark, Patrick above him snoring lightly, with the heavy dew of the early morning hours dripping from the top of the canvas tent to the grass. The tent was large enough for ten bunk beds and had a wooden floor laid with rough one-by-sixes, open flap entrances at both ends, and mosquito netting on the sides for ventilation. It was comfortable enough, and even enjoyable once the smell of damp musty canvas was accepted as a matter of permanence.

Of the seven companies at Camp Buckner, only one, the 5th, had the pleasure of residing in tents. The other companies bunked in Quonset huts, and their facilities were not any harsher than normal barracks life. Though teased by the other six companies, the 5th felt a cut above the rest by living in "Tent City." Their class-mates may have done Buckner, but only the 5th could claim panache to the ordeal.

The upperclassmen had been right. Camp Buckner was the best summer of their lives. The days claimed hard experiences and hard work, but Buckner proved to be a wonderful place. The camp itself was fifteen miles from the main post, deep in the Catskill Mountains, and the facilities were wrapped around a one hundred-forty-nine acre lake, Lake Popolopen, in the midst of a forest of pines. After a day of training and on weekends, the yearlings were free to swim or water-ski or paddle the lake in canoes or lounge on the white sand of the man-made beach. A nightly option was to take in a new-release movie at the camp's theater or simply to sit under tall pines trees and shoot the bull with classmates. Guests were allowed during free time, so it was common to see cadets with their dates at any of the activities, including a stroll on Flirtation Walk along the banks of Lake Popolopen. There was no reasonable limitation on what the cadets might do for fun and relaxation. The optimal word for life at Camp Buckner was "Freedom." They were free from plebe harassment and free to be themselves.

For most, the environment at Buckner was almost too good to be true. Most held slight anticipation for the other shoe to fall and for this good deal to end. The transition from being a plebe to an upperclassman was a period of adjustment. Walking around acting almost like a normal human being at West Point took some getting used to, and Camp Buckner was the perfect place to bury one's memories of plebe year in the past.

However, as great as it was, the relaxation aspect of Camp Buckner was secondary as far as the Army was concerned. It used the two months to orient the yearling to his role as a soldier. The combat branches of Infantry, Artillery, Armor, Engineers, and Signal were all introduced in phases, and for the first time, Jake and his classmates had an opportunity to learn practical soldiering skills. The instructors were first rate, and many were from active troop units returning with experience in Vietnam. They knew the value of intense training under live combat situations and made the training realistic and demanding.

The infantry weapons and tactics enthralled Jake, while Patrick found his calling when the entire class was flown to Fort Knox, Kentucky for a week of intensive training in mechanized warfare and basic tactics of tanks, mechanized infantry, and reconnaissance platoons. It was there that he became enamored with the applications of air mobile operations with the use of helicopters. Specifically, Patrick found the Cobra Gunship to be the most captivating. The Cobra's ability to fly low to the landscape at one hundred and seventy-five miles per hour and maneuver like a hotrod to destroy enemy targets and support troops on the ground tickled his imagination. As opposed to dropping ordinance at thirty thousand feet and calling it a day, the Cobra, armed with a 20mm, 3-barreled Gatling Cannon with 750 rounds, fourteen 2.75 inch rockets, eight 5 inch Zuni Rockets, and Aim-9 Sidewinder anti-aircraft missiles made the gunship a flying, up-close, see-the-whites-of-their-eyes killing machine. The Cobra Gunship was a relatively new concept and being used in Vietnam. It was an offensive weapon, and Patrick knew immediately that flying the Cobra was in his blood.

Meanwhile, each having found his niche, they found the other phases of the Buckner training interesting, to a lesser extent, but key to their total understanding of their future in the army. In the field, they learned how Fire Direction protocols and tactical placement of artillery units could support infantry and armor units. Days spent with the Signal Corps instructors taught the cadets how to establish field communications and how important this was to the support of tactical operations. Engineer training taught them basic land navigation, equipment, and techniques for working with fixed and floating bridges, mine warfare, and demolitions. And a condensed week of Recondo added infantry tactics, long-range patrols, establishing an ambush, hand-to-hand combat, and application of skills supporting the infantry unit. The summer was pleasant.

Camp Buckner was a beautiful place, a reasonable workday, and more recreation than West Point had previously allowed.

Lying awake on his bunk, Jake was excited about the possibility of the 5th Company being roused from sleep to begin Recondo. They had been on alert for the past three nights, and Jake felt sure that tonight was the night. Recondo was a full week in the field and a firsthand look at simulated combat under realistic conditions. During the week, the opportunity to sleep would be almost nonexistent. Jake was excited about applying the skills they had learned, and the opportunity to learn new skills in military mountaineering, survival techniques, and the Confidence Course. Recondo was the kind of experience he enjoyed and he knew that his next taste of it would be Ranger School after graduation in three years. A few were allowed to go to Ranger School while they were still cadets, but Jake did not plan to request it because it would mean sacrificing one of his summer leaves. There was no chance he would voluntarily miss spending every minute he could with Sara. Ranger School could wait.

Cantrell entered the tent with a flashlight as Jake thought of how long it seemed until Christmas leave. "Fall out in fifteen minutes!" Cantrell said with a booming voice. "Recondo gentlemen! Recondo!" Cantrell didn't slow his pace as he passed the bunks and exited the opposite flap to move to the next tent. Jake scrambled into his fatigues, battle dress uniform, and boots as Patrick swung his legs over the bunk, rubbed his eyes and said, "Is this a nightmare? Why can't they take you gung-ho infantry types on this deal and leave us future fly-boys alone? I hate Recondo already, good grief, Do ya know what time it is?"

"Yeah, it's zero-two-thirty," Jake said, yanking on Patrick's leg, pulling him off the top bunk. "Recondo will be great. You'll love eating frogs and snakes. Besides, you have to know what to do when that helicopter bucks you off in the jungle, and you have a hundred mad gooks chasing your ass."

"Well, if it happens at two-thirty in the morning, those gooks can just have my ass."

"Now is that any way for a Tennessee Volunteer to act? Here, saddle up, cowboy." Jake handed Patrick his pants and hoisted the steel helmet to his head.

Within twenty minutes, 5th Company was marching down the road in the dark toward the theater in company formation for the initial briefing. Each cadet was laden with a patrol combat load. Most of the company carried M-14 rifles, some carried M-60 machine guns, and a few carried M-79 grenade launchers. The exercise was to be as realistic as possible, but certainly less than being experienced in Vietnam under live combat conditions.

As Jake and Patrick entered the theater and filed into their seats, they were astonished at the commotion already initiated by the Recondo instructors. Face camouflaged, an Airborne Ranger sergeant swooped down from the rafters on a rope with an assault knife between his teeth. He swung from one side of the theater to the other, pushing hard against the walls with his feet. Instructors were yelling and screaming, their voices at a high pitch, their words incomprehensible. The moment the company was seated, a major, who looked the part of a deranged and dangerous warrior, extended a live chicken by the neck, kicking and squawking frantically as though it knew its imminent fate. The major yelled words almost incoherent in the increasing chaos. He was yelling something about death to the enemy and the blood of victory. With eyes wide and jaws dropped in disbelief, the cadets watched as the major quickly spun the frantic chicken twice over his head, breaking its neck, then ripped the head of the chicken from its body, tilted it skyward, and poured the gushing blood from the open neck on the top of his hat. Blood flowed down the major's throat and splattered his face before he threw the blood spurting chicken into the crowd of cadets. Other instructors did the same. Dead and blood-soaked chickens were thrown to the cadets, and each was expected to take his turn for a dose of blood. The lifeless chickens were passed from cadet to cadet, blood covering every face and throat. Another Ranger yelled words of survival, of living off the land, of the price of victory in war. Before the cadets had fully understood his point, a sergeant, who was stripped to the waist and camouflaged with green and black grease paints, walked up next to the major holding a white rabbit by its ears. The sergeant performed a swift chopping motion to the back of the rabbit's neck, and the rabbit immediately ceased its frantic kicks. The sergeant held the rabbit above his head with both hands then brought it to his mouth and began to gnaw through the rabbit's fur and strip away the skin with his teeth. In a matter of seconds, the rabbit's skin was peeled from its body, exposing only muscle and blood and guts. The sergeant screamed in delight with the rabbit extended, blotches of its fur stuck to his blood-soaked face. Recondo had begun.

Jake laughed at Patrick. For a simple, civilized future flyboy, Patrick was having a great time with the antics of the queen of battle, the infantry. The emotional antics of the chicken blood repulsed him not in the least. Jake was looking forward to reminding Patrick of his enthusiasm the next time they heatedly debated branch choices.

After a thirty-minute briefing on the objectives for the next seven days, the yearlings exited the theater for a forced march to Outpost Charlie, or OP Charlie. Their destination being five miles into the mountains, 5th Company began a march at a pace only slightly less than a run and a great deal faster than a stroll through the park. Daily reveille runs at zero- five-hundred with rifles had conditioned the company for Recondo, but the thirty-five-plus pound loads of a patrol pack and weapons brought heavy breathing within minutes. Those who only a few days earlier thought it wonderful to be assigned to carry an M-60 machine gun, weighing twenty-three pounds compared to a skosh over nine pounds for an M-14 rifle, now bordered on panic as the reality of the extra weight brought pain with every step. Even those with lighter loads winced at the pack straps digging into their shoulders, the handles of entrenching tools unmercifully slapping and rubbing their legs raw, and the weight of helmets bringing strain to their necks.

Three miles. Up the hill in the dark. Sweat drenched. Leg muscles screaming for relief. Excruciating dry mouth. Heart pounding like a racehorse. Burning lungs expanding to their outer limits. Boom! Shattering explosions burst around them, violently jerking them out of their self-absorbed thoughts of fatigue. The aggressors, regulars from the 101st Airborne back from Vietnam, pitched grenades of tear gas from concealed positions and opened with small arms fire. The cadets slammed their bodies into the dirt, and each struggled frantically in his exhaustion to remove the gas mask strapped to his leg and get it on before the gas had its effect. For most cadets, they were too slow. The tear gas burned their faces and eyes, and worse, beyond pain, for it caused the cadets to vomit. Vomit in their masks. Foul fluid filled them and choked their owners. The slow jerked the masks from their faces for a breath of air, only to inhale more gas. More burning pain, more vomit. The aggressors disappeared as quickly as they had attacked and the company was again on the move. Those sick, ran sick.

Fifty-five minutes after departure, the company arrived at OP Charlie. The only smiles were on the faces of the instructors. In fatigues pants, boots, soft covers, and black T-shirts with gold lettered RANGER on the front, the instructors surveyed the cadets who were sweating from every pore, stained by their vomit, and near hyperventilation. As one cadet dropped his pack and sunk to his knees, an instructor rushed to his side.

"Who told you to unload, Mister?" he screamed.

The cadet did not reply. He simply raised his head and looked at the instructor with disbelieving eyes.

"You don't unload till you're told to unload. Report to Major Rock. Now! Move it!"

The company watched as the instructor led the cadet to a nearby rock painted bright red, explained that this is Major Rock, and ordered the cadet to execute fifty perfect pushups with his feet on the rock. The cadet, with his feet elevated higher than his head, counted each pushup loudly while the instructor stood over him, hands on his hips, feet a shoulder-width apart. The company stood silent, still trying to regain normal breathing and wondering exactly what kind of, and how many, sins might qualify one for fifty pushups with Major Rock.

Responding to orders barked by the same instructor, 5th Company walked fifty yards down the trail to a clearing, dropped their packs, stripped to the waist, and moved to the entrance of The Pit. A circle with a one-hundred-foot diameter had dozens of red-painted Major Rocks around the outer edge. Inside the circle, a six-inch layer of water-soaked sawdust covered the ground, and at the entrance, a rope tied six inches from the top of the sawdust stretched across the six-foot wide space. Standing inside The Pit near the entrance was an instructor whose mere physical presence was intimidating. Goliath would have been intimidated. First Sergeant Amos Jackson stood six-foot-four and carried two hundred-sixty pounds of solid rippling muscle. The jagged half-inch wide scar curving downward from an inch above his left eyebrow to his chin gave the impression that the sergeant was no stranger to killing, with or without provocation. As the sun rose, the yearlings stared at Jackson wide-eyed, anticipating their next good deal for the day.

"I'm First Sergeant Amos Jackson, 101st Airborne," Jackson said in a booming voice. "I'm the meanest son-of-a-bitch in the valley. For three hours a day, for the next seven days, your ass is mine. I'll teach you how to kill with your bare hands. I'll teach you to kill with the knife. I'll teach you to kill. Do what I tell you when I tell you, and we'll get along fine. Screw with me, and I'll snap your ass like a twig. Any questions?"

After the cadets looked around at each other to see if anyone was stupid enough to ask a question, First Sergeant Jackson ordered the sweating cadets to enter The Pit in mass, under the rope, not over it. Chaos ensued as one hundred and fifty shirtless cadets simultaneously tried to get under the rope. After fifteen minutes of total disorder, 5th Company surfaced on the interior of The Pit. Every man was covered head to toe with sticky, itchy sawdust.

The hours passed quickly. Jackson paired the yearlings by size and taught his skill. After demonstrating a particular technique, he would search for those who needed help or additional instruction.

Repeatedly, drills were run on approaching a target from the front or rear to snap the neck, or to block a punch and splinter the nose, driving bone into the brain, or blocking an attacking thrust, breaking the elbow, rupturing the kidney, crushing the ribs to puncture a lung, and a final break of the neck. During a short break, Jackson promised the week to provide skills in offensive and defensive uses of the combat knife, and where to place a blade when swift and silent death is required. The red rocks were put to use, and everyone had several chances to get acquainted with pushups, feet elevated and faces deep into the mushy sawdust on every count. By 0800 hours, 5th Company had finished The Pit for the day and exited in the same manner they had entered. It was a free-for-all struggle once again. Mist still rising from the dew-covered grass, the cadets went to their gear exhausted, covered with sweat, vomit, and itching sawdust.

Squad patrols, in every direction, filled the remaining hours of daylight. They walked, and walked, and walked. Up the hills, down the hills, and through the swamps. By nightfall, Jake and Patrick were exhausted, as were all their classmates. The day had been nonstop, hot, and without food. On arrival at OP Charlie, they had an hour to eat before night patrols began. Jake and Patrick dropped their gear, and their bodies, on the jagged rocks and pulled a box of C-rations from their packs.

Jake opened a can labeled "Ham and Eggs" with his P-38 can opener, his hands and arms near black from the dirt gathered during the day. "Should've gone to Annapolis," he mumbled as he stared into the can of pea-green liquid with tiny yellow and brown chunks floating on top. "Bet Steve is eating real ham and eggs. Not this fake, whatever it is. Musta mislabeled this. Looks like a can of intestinal bile to me."

"Wanna trade?" Patrick asked. "Mine didn't even have a label. Some kinda stew, I think. Smells like raccoon meat or, some other dead critter. Who knows?"

The two fell silent as they eagerly scooped the contents of the cans into their mouths and washed it down with warm water from their canteens. The off-colored peanut butter and stale crackers were the highlights of the meal.

"I wish I'd counted the number of times I got myself killed today," Jake said. "Those aggressors must have ambushed us a hundred times. If this were the real thing, you and I wouldn't be sitting here enjoying this slop."

"Yeah," Patrick replied solemnly. "You know, this is hard. I've never been this tired and dirty and hungry in my life. Kinda makes you think about the guys that are doing this sort of thing for real. Humping the hills in Vietnam, I mean. Add real bullets and thirteen months in the field doing this, and you've got one miserable way to live. We got killed a lot today with blanks. We made mistakes. In three years, we won't get to make that mistake but once. I don't know, I guess I admire the dogface a little more than I did yesterday."

Without a word, Jake leaned his head on his pack and was asleep. Patrick glanced at Jake, then closed his eyes to do the same. In less than an hour they would start another patrol that would last until dawn. Their mission was to patrol an area six miles to the southeast of OP Charlie and establish an ambush along a known trail. The fact that it was a deer trail lacked relevance. If a deer pranced down the trail tonight, he was in for a possible heart attack. A hundred rounds of blank ammunition would be fired at him from all sides in a matter of seconds.

Jake awoke with a tap to his foot and the sound of Cantrell's voice announcing that they would move out in five minutes. He was surprised at how black and dark the forest had become during his brief sleep, but he was not surprised at the pain in his lower back from the jagged rock pressing against his kidney. As he rose to his feet, the muscles in his legs attempted to communicate to his brain that any movement at all for the next six to eight hours was not a good idea. Jake shook it off, hoisted his web gear to his shoulders, and prepared to ignore his aching legs.

The six miles through the hills in total darkness to the ambush point proved to be yet another good deal. The stinging camouflage grease covering the squad seemed a waste. The squad members could not see a hand in front of their faces, much less a person, friend or foe, five feet in front of them. Like the hours previous, if this were live combat, there would be twelve pine boxes in a row at Arlington Cemetery. Every few feet someone would stumble or step into a deep hole, crashing to the ground with considerable noise, including a string of profanities heard for miles in the quietness of the night. More than once screams of agony and fright were heard out of the darkness as a cadet unknowingly stepped off a ledge, falling freely through what was immediately imagined to be the deadly space between the top of an enormous cliff and the bottom a hundred feet below him. Since the cliff was only three feet in height, it was both a relief and embarrassing. Cantrell berated the squad each time the laughter from the eleven still on their feet exceeded the noise created by the scream of the victim, lying on his back at the bottom of a three-foot ravine trying to get his heart rate back to normal. The loose straps on web gear and the swivels on rifles had been taped for silence with the objective of covering the six miles without detection. But an hour into the patrol it was obvious it would have been as effective had they radioed the aggressors as to their whereabouts and worn cowbells around their necks. Silent they were not.

Once the ambush was positionally set and fields of fire were properly established to cover the trail, the squad settled in for hours of waiting for the enemy to stroll down the trail. Much to everyone's surprise, the aggressors did not come down the trail. They slipped into each position of the ambush with more silence than the night itself and "cut" each man's throat with a bright red Magic Marker. Again, the squad was dead. It was embarrassing. The Ranger aggressors were on them to cut off any sound they might have made and marked their throats before the cadets knew they were there.

Though the aggressors had already killed the entire squad without firing a single round in the simulated ambush, the exercise continued until it was time to stumble back the six miles to OP

Charlie. There were no aggressors killed, nor deer, but at least one raccoon and an owl theoretically lost their lives to several hundred rounds of blank ammunition. Patrick was the only member of the squad to get killed twice. After hours of lying in the prone position covered with brush above the trail, he decided that no one would be the wiser if he stood to urinate in the total darkness. No sooner had the sound of the urine hitting the ground than the squad opened fire on him. As far as Jake was concerned, Patrick would forevermore be remembered as the man who was killed by his own men with his pecker in his hand.

As THE WEEK of Recondo progressed, the routine continued. There was no sleep for more than an hour or two on the jagged rocks at OP Charlie. The C-rations were gone by the third day, and the cadets had the opportunity to relish Ranger stew. A large black kettle boiled water and whatever the cadets could forage, such as frogs, snakes, bugs, and berries. Though it looked horrible and smelled even worse, it maintained life, as it were. Jake preferred it to "Ham and Eggs", but Patrick ate his daily portion holding his nose to cut off the smell and the taste. Near the end of the week, the aggressors were less victorious. The patrols, both in daylight and in darkness, were much improved. Slowly, skills developed by repetition. The Pit became fun and First Sergeant Jackson a favorite instructor.

The confidence course proved to be one of the most valued experiences of Recondo for Jake. They ran the course on the last day, fatigued, and at a time he had little confidence in making his body perform for him. Every day, he had stared at the obstacles at OP Charlie, towering thirty feet or more above ground. The obstacles looked impossible. As the time to run the course neared, fear and dread lay heavy. A slip of the foot, the momentary loss of balance, or the failure to grasp a pole tight enough to hold all one's body weight meant a fall to the hard ground and rocks below.

With a fall, broken bones were assured, and death a possibility. Though no one talked about it, Jake was not alone in his fears. Every cadet in 5th Company had the same thoughts, the same fear, the same dread. The course loomed before them, the obstacles imagined more difficult and dangerous with each passing day, each man questioning his ability to muster the courage when the dreaded time arrived. When the time did arrive, the pent-up fear and anxiety in every man was converted into support and cheering as each passed through the obstacles. It was an individual event for each man to master his fear and to have confidence in himself, but it was done as a unit, a team. In its progress, Jake marveled at how important the support of the team was to one's ability to rise above one's own self-imposed limitations. He walked away from the confidence course, as did all his classmates, knowing that within the realm of reality, there are no limitations on the inward mastery of one's circumstances, and that fear is insidious, cuts off thinking, and makes men less than they have the potential to claim.

With completion of the confidence course behind them, 5th Company again strapped on the heavy loads and ran the five miles from OP Charlie to the banks of Lake Popelopen. In contrast to the start of Recondo, the cadets now ran with confidence and pride and enthusiasm for the week was finally behind them. The five mile run held more pain than the first run. More pain, for the cadets were exhausted from covering endless miles through the hills with no sleep, no food worth eating, muscles sore and tired, and feet that had not felt fresh air for seven full days. They ran with the pain, and they ran with more exuberance for life than they had ever known before.

On the banks of the lake, the cadets finished Recondo with the Slide for Life. Each cadet climbed the ladder of the tower, grasped the handle of the cable wheel, and jumped. The wheel sped down the cable for a hundred yards, high above the lake, gaining speed with every second, where just short of hitting the pole at the other end of the cable the cadet dropped from twenty feet into chest-deep water. Exiting the lake, Major Rock was paid homage with another fifty perfect pushups. Recondo was finished.

In the showers at Tent City, Jake and Patrick sat on the concrete floor naked, gingerly peeling the thick layers of dead and rotten skin from their feet. Their feet were swollen and had the appearance that the entire foot was rotten to the bone.

"Well," Patrick said, pausing as he stared at his feet. "I reckon taking our boots off and putting on a clean pair of socks at least once would've been smart, huh?"

"That for sure!" Jake replied. "We rotted our boots out in the swamps and The Pit. You'd think we would be smart enough to have suspected what was happening to our feet. Oh well. If I'd taken my boots off and seen this mess, I'd have thought I was crippled for life. Just goes to show, what you don't know, don't hurt. I wouldn't have missed Recondo for the world." Patrick smiled as he continued to peel the dead skin. "Hate to admit it, but I wouldn't trade this past week for anything either."

"Hey, Patrick," Jake said, grinning. "You can grab your pecker now without getting shot."

Patrick threw his soap with a near miss of Jake's head, and both started laughing. Tears mingled with the dirt.

CHAPTER ELEVEN

2100 Hours
12 November 1970
New York, New York

CHERYL TERRY casually walked around the large living room of the condominium looking at the displayed collection of beautiful crystal and expensive accent pieces that decorated the tables and shelves throughout the room. The apparent wealth and refinement on display in the elegant surroundings were intriguing. Perhaps someday she, too, would possess the extraordinary things in life. That is what she wanted. To be more than she had been. To be more than any of her family had ever been. And, as she strolled about the room admiring its possessions, she knew that she would reach her goals. The family farm in Indiana was far away, her undergraduate degree at Princeton would be finished in another semester, and her quest for law school at Harvard was merely a matter of a few months and checking into the residence hall.

"I hope you like your martini very dry," Sukarno stated loudly from the kitchen.

"I don't know whether I do or not," she called back. "I've never had one," she continued almost to herself. Cheryl sat on the sofa and continued her survey of the room while Sukarno mixed the drinks he claimed he could make so well. The room made her feel warm and expectant. She liked it. It seemed to be a preview of an apartment she might someday have for herself. And, if it were so, she had earned it. Cheryl Terry had strived against all the odds to be where she was and where she was going. No one from the small rural community outside Evanston, Indiana ever thought a poor black girl from the farm, even one as pretty as she was, would ever make it to Princeton University, much less excel with grades high enough to get her into the most prestigious law school in the country. But she had done it. She had done it with total commitment to the task, long hard hours studying to overcome the limitations imposed by an underprivileged rural school system, and full-time jobs to pay the exorbitant tuition demanded of her.

"Here we go," Sukarno said, entering the room with a crystal martini glass in each hand. "Thank you, Sukarno," Cheryl said politely. "I've never had a martini before. I don't drink at all."

"Well, one drink will not hurt you. Besides, this is the university. Liquor. Or drugs. It's a university pastime."

"Not for me," Cheryl quickly replied. "I don't have the time, nor the inclination to do either. It's all I can do to study and make enough money to stay in school. I should be studying right now. I don't know why I let you talk me into coming here with you. I hardly know you."

"Of course, you know me. We shared a class together. I don't remember what it was, but I do remember you."

Cheryl sipped her martini, pursed her lips at the taste, and giggled. "A class with about fifty others. Besides, we never even had a conversation until tonight. That's hardly enough to say we know each other."

"I know you."

"Oh? And what do you think you know about me?" Sukarno shifted in the deep leather chair, set his glass on the table next to it, and made a steeple with his hands as he stared at Cheryl. "I know you are magnificent."

Cheryl laughed without comment, uncomfortable with the remark and the coldness in Sukarno's eyes.

"Do you have a boyfriend?" he continued, maintaining his stare. "I mean, do you have one man that you make love to, or, do you sleep with many men."

Cheryl was stunned. She was angered by his question, and, she was frightened by the way he had asked it. With her hand shaking, she set her glass on the coffee table in front of her and rose to her feet. "I must go. Thanks for the drink, but I really shouldn't be here."

"Sit down!" Sukarno shouted, his face flushed with anger as he quickly sat forward in his chair.

Cheryl hesitated at the command, but then stepped briskly around the table toward the front door. Sukarno spun her around by the shoulder, smashed his fist into her stomach, then slapped her hard across the cheek. She crumpled to the floor in pain.

"You American bitch." Sukarno grabbed one arm and dragged her across the floor to the sofa. "Sit. Do not defy my orders again."

Cheryl sobbed from the pain she felt, but more so from the terror of being alone with Sukarno. She feared all the possibilities of what he might do to her before she could get away from him if she could get away from him at all.

She picked up her glass, trying to put on an appearance of calmness, though her heart raced near a panic level.

"You are foolish, Cheryl. My question angered you. That is so typically American. I know you sleep with men. Lots of men. What is it they call it? Free love," Sukarno said with a twist of sarcasm in his voice.

Cheryl was again shocked. "Sukarno, I sleep with no one. I don't have a boyfriend. I don't even date. I don't have time to have a relationship. All I want to do is graduate in May and go to law school. I…"

Sukarno sat forward suddenly, angered again "Liar. All American women are whores. I have been in America for a long time. I know what is going on around me."

"But..."

"You will sleep with me. You will sleep with me tonight." Cheryl was tempted to rise from the sofa but was frozen with fear. Calmly she said, "No. No, Sukarno, I am not going to sleep with you. I am going to leave."

Sukarno moved quicker than Cheryl could react. Again his open hand hit the side of her face, knocking her sideways into the sofa pillows. When she regained her balance, he was back in his chair, staring at her. "I've killed a man, you know? I may kill you."

Cheryl said nothing. Sukarno's eyes were cold, and his face appeared as hard as a stone. Not for one moment did she doubt that he had killed, or, that he was capable of killing her. In her mind's eye, she saw her life vanishing, and all that she had worked for, and all that she had dreamed.

Sukarno paused. He sipped his martini without a sign of stress as he watched Cheryl wring her hands and sob. "Cheryl. Stand up and take off your clothes. I wish to watch you undress. I want you to stand naked before we make love. Do what I tell you, and I will not harm you."

Cheryl stood, unable to control her sobs. The work, the study, the climbing over endless obstacles one by one, was not enough to reach her dreams. Here was yet another demand. A horrible demand stood in her way for mere survival. With trembling hands, she pulled her sweater over her head, exposing her bare breasts, then pushed her jeans and panties to the floor.

2200 Hours
12 November 1970
United States Military Academy
West Point, New York

THE ROOM WAS COLD. Someone of apparent high authority held the belief that having the cadets live in the barracks without heat in the early months of winter would acclimate them to the colder months ahead. Impatiently, and with daily bitching and moaning, the cadets awaited the day for hot steam in the radiators. Seeing one's breath while attempting to study was distracting, and taking a shower was downright irritating. Jake reclined on the upper bunk, attired in heavy sweats and a black wool cap pulled over his ears. Within reach were his physics text propped against his leg, his slide rule in one hand, and a new number-two yellow pencil clenched between his teeth. Patrick and Wayne sat at their desks studying with OD (Olive Drab) green comforters wrapped around them, head to toe. Jake looked at the two large green lumps hunched over the desks and smiled at the visible puffs of vapor rising from underneath. The only distinction between the lumps was that one had the bill of an orange baseball cap protruding from underneath.

Yearling year thus far was in stark contrast to the plebe year gone by. On the one hand, it was pleasant living without being harassed constantly about things that did not appear to have a bearing on life and eating like a human being, but on the other hand, the academic load more than canceled the good deal of being a yearling. With nothing else to do, the yearling was destined to stick his nose in a book and leave it there for a long nine months. His course load consisted of chemistry, physics, statistics, differential equations, statics, dynamics, psychology, history, literature, foreign language, and military science. To make it more unpleasant, every course had an uncanny way of being calculus-based, thus extending the misery of The Green Death's mind-numbing content. Without overcoming the misery of The Green Death as a plebe, the upper level courses for the yearling year would be impossible. Eight-plus hours of study outside class was typical six days a week, and the preferred activity for free time on weekends was to get horizontal on one's bunk. Though the academic requirements were onerous, the academy had a workable incentive plan. If a cadet makes a "D", he will be turned back a full year. Earn an "F" and catch a bus back to Podunk, U.S.A. Having to make a "C" or better in every class to survive has a compelling way of motivating the otherwise unmotivated. Somehow, the concept of making West Point a five year, or six year, experience, instead of the standard four, maintained turbulent stress levels throughout the Corps.

The two upper classes ignored the yearlings for the most part. The only expectation held for the yearling was that he handle the military protocols of cadet life, and that he successfully overcome the brutal second year academics. The plebes learned quickly. All they had to do to get along with yearlings was to stay out of their way, and recognize that they would remain in a perpetual bad mood all year. Occasionally, however, a plebe would forget that cardinal rule and thereby suffer the unleashed fury from one who truly appreciates the privilege of being on the other side of the fence. God grants no greater fury than a yearling operating on three hours sleep a night.

"Break!" Wayne said as he slid the comforter from his shoulders. "Who gives a hoot about thermodynamics and statistical mechanics. I hate this stuff. If one has a hard time going to sleep? No problem. Just read a physics book for five minutes."

Jake closed his book and swung his legs over the edge of the bunk. "Not me. I love this stuff. Think I'll stay here during Christmas leave, so I can really get into it. You know, and to get my Christmas jollies working a few extra problems."

"I'm tempted," Patrick said. "It'd be fun to stay here Christmas. I hate the idea of going home and getting warm. And, God forbid, getting to sleep again."

"Sara coming for Army-Navy?" Wayne asked.

"Nope. Got a letter from her today. She has some sorority project that weekend and can't make it."

Patrick snapped a glance at Jake and saw the disappointment on his face though the tone of his voice denied it. Jake had not talked about anything else for months except Sara coming for the game. Admiral and Mrs. Hollifield had invited them all down to Annapolis for the weekend, and they were anxious to bring Sara into their fold. Since last year's after-game dinner, the Hollifield's had become like a second family, and Sara was a part of it, though they had never met her. Patrick fell silent on the subject. Sara was not coming, and he knew Jake well enough to know that the last thing he wanted to do was to discuss it. The letters came less often now that she was at the university, but both he and Jake thought it not too unusual. After all, Sara was busy with her studies, and her sorority kept her free time occupied.

Nevertheless, Patrick felt bad for Jake. He knew how much he missed her and how important it was to him that she come for the game. As it stood, Jake would be the only one at the Hollifield's without a date. He, Cantrell, and Steve had arranged dates for the weekend.

"It don't mean nothin'," Jake said, as Steve was accustomed to saying. "It's only fifteen days from the game to Christmas leave. Fifteen days is no big deal.

CHAPTER TWELVE

1300 Hours
5 December 1970
J.F.K. Stadium
Philadelphia, Pennsylvania

THE STADIUM ROARED as the capacity crowd gathered for the annual battle between the Army and the Navy, and light snow fell as the teams took the field. The pregame antics had been typical. Army had marched on the field first and Navy second with the Brigade of Midshipmen slightly distracted by the whooping and jeering from the Corps of Cadets. And, of course, it did not take long for a war to break out once the midshipmen took the stands. Eight sailors rushed to the middle of the field to implant signs spelling B-E-A-T A-R-M-Y, but as to be expected, Navy's enthusiasm was immediately met by the surge of over a hundred screaming cadets pouring out of the stands onto the field to capture the bold sign bearers. The eight terrified middies turned tail and hustled to safety amongst their own four thousand while the cadets demolished the signs like a pack of wild dogs. For a moment, it looked as though a serious riot was about to occur on national television, but somehow the senior midshipmen were able to maintain control over the highly irritated Brigade.

The Corps knew that the Brigade was not in the best of moods already, and for good reason. During the past week, a recon mission was executed wherein a dozen Ranger-type mentalities covered the 260 miles to Annapolis, entered the enemy's territory with stealth, and exited the same way, with Billy, the Navy goat. For a week, Billy had enjoyed eating and visiting with Trotter, Hannibal, and Buckshot. The Army mules seemed to like their white-haired guest, and the Corps assured the enraged Brigade of Midshipmen that Billy would be treated with all the cordiality offered a prisoner of war under the terms of the Geneva Convention. Billy was scheduled to be formally released at midfield during halftime, and the recon team stood proudly in fatigues, combat patrol web gear and pack designed for a light load, and appropriately camouflaged faces to escort Billy back home.

The Navy's exchange tactical officer, Commander Jenkins , was ready for a transfer. He had experienced all the exchange tactical officer business he wanted. Nine months at sea in a rowboat would be easier. During Army-Navy week, he became severely depressed after entering his office Monday morning to find one-hundred live, giant crabs sharing his space. The crabs covered the floor, they were in the desk drawers, and they crawled through the file cabinets. They were everywhere. Commander Jenkins's commanding officer, an army colonel, standing nearby to witness the expression on his face, apologized with a smile for the brashness of the cadets who had flown to Boston to fetch the giant crabs. He assured the commander, again with a broad smile, that the guilty cadets would be severely punished if he could determine exactly who the guilty cadets were. And, as to be expected, the midshipmen retaliated by shoveling a yard of mule dung into the office of their exchange army officer.

All was going well for Army through the first quarter of the game. They had scored a field goal early, but Navy's passing game was beginning to set the Corps on edge.

Being sandwiched between Patrick and his date, Laura, and Cantrell with his fiancé, Jenny Sanders, Jake was made to participate in conversations on both sides of him. It was a party of five, and his friends were determined that he not feel alone. This was Jenny's fourth Army-Navy game with Cantrell, and she was due to make the flight from Amarillo only one more time. She would come for graduation in June and a military wedding in the chapel. Jake made a big "to-do" about the miniature West Point class ring she flaunted and would proudly wear the rest of her life as her engagement ring. But mostly, his admiration was directed to the thought of the miniature ring for the Class of '73 that Sara would wear.

By halftime, the Corps was much quieter, and the Brigade of Midshipmen much louder. Navy led 14 - 3. As the cannon shook the stadium signifying the end of the second quarter, Jake trotted to the north goal for the traditional halftime meeting with Steve. While he was standing under the goal post waiting, he watched Billy ceremoniously escorted to his proper owners. Jake was startled out of his amused revere when he was grabbed from behind in a bear hug. Instantly recognizing his friend's laugh, Jake laughed and called out, "Texas lowlife!" Steve released him, and the two old friends hugged again as brothers before shaking hands.

"You're gonna owe me a B-robe this year," Steve said, with a wide grin.

"There you go again, thinking this battle is won. I'll have my second Navy B-robe hanging in the closet before the day is done."

"Sure, Jake. Sure." Steve extended his hand to a petite little redhead with emerald green eyes who had accompanied him to the goal post meeting. "This is Julia. Julia, this is the scum of the earth, John Paul Jacobs, sometimes known as Jake, sometimes by names that can't be repeated in mixed company. Julia is he daughter of Admiral Dane. She probably knows more about aircraft carrier tactics than most of.the officers in the Navy."

"Julia. The pleasure is mine," Jake said, taking her hand. "You are far too lovely to be seen with a lowlife sailor. I'd be honored, and you'd be much better off if you'd spend the remainder of this game on the right side of the field in the capable hands of a proper gentleman. Being seen in the company of this skuzball is not fittin' for a lady as beautiful as you."

All three burst into laughter and Julia slipped her arm under Jake's as though she had just accepted the offer. "You're both charming, and I am tempted. But since my father is an admiral, it's probably best if I stay with the white hats. If I went with you, I might be shot for desertion when I get home. My father gets quite emotional about this game."

"Well," Jake said with a smile. "I understand how you must cover-up your true emotions in the name of family honor. It's a grand and noble sacrifice you make this day to stand by the men in blue in their hour of defeat."

"I've heard a lot about you from your greatest admirer," Julia said. "Steve talks about you all the time and the things you did together back in Texas. I'm glad to meet you in person."

"We have to run, creep!" Steve said, slapping Jake on the back as the Navy team entered the stadium, and the cheering from his side began. "Sorry, Sara couldn't make it. Admiral Hollifield will have a van meet us at the Sheraton after the game."

"Got it," Jake replied. He stood watching as Steve and Julia walked quickly, hand in hand, around the corner of the field and disappeared in the mass of midshipman. He paused a moment to survey the stadium and the excitement, then turned toward the West and walked slowly to the Long Gray Line.

0200 Hours
6 December 1970
United States Naval Academy
Annapolis, Maryland

THE GIRLS HELPED Mrs. Hollifield clear the table while Admiral Hollifield ushered his guests to the den. As they entered the masculine room, the young men were drawn to a wall that held several pictures the admiral had accumulated over his years of service. They were fascinated to see a thirty-year military career displayed as a pictorial history. Mounted proudly in the center was an old photograph of a Navy football team, and on the sofa table below it, a football from the Army-Navy game played in 1945. The admiral had been the team captain his first class year at Navy, and the team had autographed the ball as a memento. The fact that Army had won that year and had been declared national champions with an undefeated season had not detracted from the glory of the memory for the admiral.

The wall also displayed the admiral as a young man in Korea, standing by a fighter on the deck of an aircraft carrier, and another with him standing casually with a platoon of Marines. Beneath the pictures, in an oak frame, was the Navy Cross and its citation depicting heroism in aerial combat over the skies of North Korea. Another like picture frame cited heroism in combat when the admiral's aircraft was shot down, resulting in his capture by the North Koreans and his subsequent escape after three months as a prisoner of war, driving three other American servicemen across a hundred miles of frozen enemy-occupied territory without clothing for warmth, food, or weapons.

Vietnam had also seen the admiral. Twice he had served. Once he served with a command of a carrier and again on a joint service general staff in Saigon. He was in his second year as superintendent of the U.S. Naval Academy and would hold that post for another three years. Following his assignment at the academy, expectation was that his next assignment would be at the Pentagon as Chief of Naval Operations and the Joint Chiefs of Staff. The Naval Academy would be a stepping-stone to the highest rank in the Navy. The boys saw on the wall the history of the officer they already liked and respected merely as a man.

"Now, we aren't going to sit around and talk shop, are we?" Suzanne Hollifield said as she and the girls came into the den.

"For God, sakes, John. Turn on some music for these people. It's too quiet around here. They're going to think we are a couple of stuffed shirts." The Hollifield's were gracious and experienced hosts. Although they had no children of their own, they had no trouble with age differences. Those cadets and midshipmen thirty years their junior, and undeniably junior on the military's customary social ladder, felt very much at home. Nonetheless, no one dared call the admiral anything but Admiral, or sir, and Suzanne was quite pleased to be called Mrs. H. She knew the young people felt uncomfortable dropping the formalities. Mrs. H was just fine, knowing it was respectful but at the same time informally affectionate.

Best intentions of completely avoiding conversations of the military were abandoned when the admiral and Steve could not resist celebrating Navy's victory and gloating while Jake, Patrick, and Cantrell passed it off as merely a temporary aberration in nature. "Have your fun now, sir, you'll only get to brag about this for a year," Jake said, in a deferential manner. "I sure feel sorry for the plebes. Losing the Army-Navy game puts everyone in a foul mood, and they're the butt end of it for the rest of the year."

"Daughters, too!" Julia said. "When Navy loses, it's horrible around the house until the next game. Dad stays grumpy. Just the mention of the game makes him snap into a fit of depression. He played on the same team as Admiral Hollifield, only a year behind him. He always told me that the Army-Navy game isn't a matter of life and death. It's more important than that."

Laughter by all validated the truth in Julia's statement, and Jake said, "Sportsmanship, especially at the academies, is a double-edged sword. Just about impossible to say, "Hey, it doesn't matter whether you win or lose. What counts is how you play the game". Can you imagine what would happen if we went to war with the same attitude? I can hear it now. "Men, it doesn't matter whether you win this battle or not. It's only important that you get out there and fight the best you can. If you get killed, your family and your country will be proud that you did your best and got yourself killed in a sportsmanlike fashion. Winning isn't everything"."

"That's exactly right, son," Admiral Hollifield said in a serious tone. "We play our games, and there is such a thing as gentlemanly conduct, but don't you guys ever forget that winning is everything. I wouldn't give a hoot 'n hell for a commander who thought otherwise. In our business, if you don't win, the enemy does, and people die, or worse yet, a war gets lost. We're paid to win. It's our job."

"Exactly, sir," Jake replied, grinning. "That's why we sent a team down here to capture your goat. It was warfare. The objective was to defeat the enemy."

The admiral squirmed in his chair with the reminder that the Naval Academy's most prized possession had been pilfered by Army under his watch. "Well!" he said, returning to his three-star command voice. "If I had my way, son, I'd load the whole damn Corps of Cadets on the Enterprise, drive it to the center of the Atlantic, and walk all four thousand of you Army pukes off a short plank for that despicable act."

"Oops!" Jake said, still grinning. "So much for sportsmanship."

The room burst into laughter, including the admiral.

CHAPTER THIRTEEN

2100 Hours
20 December 1970
Comanche, Texas

JAKE HAD TAKEN a bus from West Point to New York, then a commercial flight from Kennedy Airport to Dallas. From there, a second classman accommodated him by driving fifty miles out of his way to drop him off in Comanche. Jake was glad to save his parents a long trip. Steve was already home. The Naval Academy had sent him home a day early to address the local Veterans of Foreign Wars Christmas banquet. Jake was disappointed that the academy had denied him permission to accept the invitation with Steve. It would have been fun to do it together, and even more importantly, it would have given him an extra day of leave.

Jake was disappointed, too, that he could not get Sara on the phone in Austin. It would have been nice for them to have had a few hours alone together between Dallas and Comanche. As the car carried him the last twenty miles, his thoughts and anxieties of the past three months became more intense. He was troubled about Sara. More specifically, he was troubled about Sara and himself. What was happening? He could not lay his finger on any one thing. The letters came less often, but that was understandable. The content of the letters was not even all that different. But something was happening. He could sense it. He could feel it. But, he couldn't quite figure out why the words seemed to be out of context. A thousand times, he had asked himself if she had changed her feelings toward him, but each time he reassured himself that he imagined things, gone crazy from the life he lived every day. As soon as he got home and held her, everything would be all right, and his fears would disintegrate. He had thought a lot about the fear he had of losing Sara and concluded that such a fear was legitimate. After all, in so many ways, Sara was his life, his future, his happiness. All that he was and all he hoped to be were inextricably tied to his relationship and love for Sara. Sara was so much a part of his identity, so much a part of his soul. Such a fear was akin to the fear of losing someone loved through death. The thought of such loss was painful and brought immediate thankfulness that the loss was only imagined and not real.

The streets of Comanche seldom held traffic in broad daylight and even less at ten o'clock on a cold winter night. Jake got out of the car on the west end of town, wrestled his B-4 bag from the trunk, thanked the upperclassman for the ride, then watched the car's taillights disappear into the darkness of the open road. He put on his long overcoat and pulled the brim of his hat down tight against the cold wind as he paused on the quiet street. Should he walk the four blocks to his house, or a bit further and two blocks over to Sara's? The decision was instantaneous. He wanted to see Sara now. The six-month wait to be with her was over. He gripped the handle of his bag and began the short walk to the Lowell's house.

The Texas night was cold, the light wind chilling to Jake's face and ears, but his uniform and caped overcoat were made for the icy winds driving down the Hudson River. He walked the few blocks briskly to Sara's, anticipation of seeing her growing with every step, the smile on his face broadening with every block. The closer he came, the better it felt to be home. Even in the darkness, the familiar houses and landmarks he had known all his life brought thoughts of his days as a boy and his years of going to school in the little town. They were pleasant memories. Comanche had been an excellent place to grow to manhood, and now, returning to it after living months in a different kind of world, years past seemed to embrace him and welcome him home. The brisk coolness of the night, the memories brought forth by familiar sights, and the excitement of seeing Sara made him acutely aware of how glad he was to be home.

Jake paused at the walkway in front of the Lowell's house. The beautiful old home was as familiar to him as his home a few blocks away. He had spent half his life in this house, being with Sara and raiding Valerie Lowell's refrigerator. And there, in the broad front window, stood a flashing Christmas tree, meticulously decorated just like it had been every Christmas since he could remember. Home.

Setting his B-4 bag on the top step, Jake crossed the wide wooden porch and knocked on the screen door. Anticipation growing, Jake could hear Bob Lowell from within yell that he would get it, and his footsteps coming to greet him. In a matter of seconds, Bob Lowell opened the door and stood behind the screen door with an astonished look on his face.

"Merry Christmas!" Jake said with excitement in his voice. "Got a warm fire for a soldier come home?"

Bob Lowell continued to stand behind the screen, making no move to open the door. For years he had been like a second father to Jake, and Bob loved him like a son. Yet, here he was with a screen door between them, an impenetrable wall of sadness, of defensiveness, and of undeserved betrayal. Those protracted seconds crushed Bob Lowell's soul. Still, the screen door remained closed, with no move made to open it.

Jake was confused. Only seconds had elapsed, but he recognized that something was wrong, terribly wrong. Something had drastically changed in the man that had always been jubilant to see him and counted the days until the marriage to Sara truly made him a son. The recognition emotionally flooded over Jake more quickly than thought could be processed.

Bob Lowell stared at Jake in silence for a moment through the screen, then at the floor beneath his feet as he spoke. "I figured you'd go straight home. I thought your folks would be the ones to tell you."

"Tell me what?" Jake asked, his body rigid as every muscle tightened and his eyes widened.

"Ahh. Jake. Jake, I don't know how to tell you this. Jake, Sara isn't here." Bob Lowell's eyes rose from the floor to meet Jake's. The eyes Jake saw were sad. They held pain. "Jake, Sara got married three days ago."

Jake stood frozen, a look of terror on his face. His fists tightly clenched the sides of his overcoat as though that act might keep his hands from involuntarily clawing into his face. He stood stunned and speechless, somehow detached, in a hideous sort of way, by the screen door between them as Bob Lowell again lowered his eyes.

"I'm sorry, Jake. The marriage came as a surprise to Valerie and me, too. "After a moment's pause, still not looking up from the floor, Bob Lowell stepped back and slowly closed the door without another word.

STEVE SAT on the sofa with his forearms resting on his knees, staring down at the white hat he twirled around and around in his hands. He was still in full uniform from his evening with the Veterans of Foreign Wars. Oliver Jacobs paced back and forth in front of the coffee table, covering each time the full length of the room, then unconsciously looked at the face of his wristwatch, disgusted that the minute hand had hardly moved. Laura Jacobs sat on the arm of the recliner, peering through the slight opening she made with her hand in the curtains. She kept a vigilant eye on the sidewalk in expectation of her youngest, and now the only son,

There was a strange mixture of wanting Jake to come walking through the door, and at the same time, a dread. The Jacobs had found out about Sara the day after the marriage, and Steve the moment he stepped off the plane in Dallas to greet his father. Oliver Jacobs had considered calling Jake while he was still at West Point, but Laura had convinced him that it would be much better if they broke the news themselves, in person. After all, it was only one more day. Laura could not stand the thought of Jake finding out over the phone, so far away and alone. Oliver had asked Steve that afternoon if he wanted to be present when Jake arrived. Oliver thought, having Steve there might somehow help. He was almost frantic about how he was going to tell Jake, knowing that there was no way to comfort him or make it hurt less. But, he sure wished he could keep this hurt away from his boy. He did not want his Jake to feel this horrible hurt.

There was already hurt. More hurt than could be explained because to do so would require understanding. The Lowells. The Jacobs. They were all hurt to the core. They were overwhelmed by Sara's decision. It was as though she had suddenly become someone they did not know.

Bob Lowell had gone to Oliver's office with the news, and he had been a wreck for having to do so. He did not agree with Sara's decision, but as her father, he would stand by her all the way. Oliver understood that. He would do the same for Jake if the circumstances were reversed. Bob was disappointed because Jake was like a son to him, and Oliver, a brother. Long ago it had been accepted that they were all family. Jake and Sara made it so. But with tears in his eyes, he delivered the news that hurt the people he loved. It would hurt that son, that brother, that family. Oliver knew how deeply Bob hurt and told him they were still brothers. They would all deal with this and always be a family. They agreed that Oliver should tell Jake first thing when he got home, and Bob openly admitted that facing Jake in the days to come was going to be one of the hardest things he would ever have to do.

"Where is he?" Oliver asked, gazing at his watch again. "He should have been here an hour ago."

Not moving her eyes from the sidewalk cast in light by the front porch light, Laura answered, "They might have stopped for something to eat along the way. I wish now we had insisted on picking him up in Dallas. I didn't have the heart to argue with him when he said he had a ride." Tears began to fill her eyes again. "He sounded so happy. So excited about coming home."

Steve glanced from his hat to Mrs. Jacobs, then back down again in silence as he heard her sniffle. Oliver Jacobs began his pacing.

The ringing of the phone shattered the silence. All three were startled, and they glanced at each other before Oliver walked briskly to the phone on the desk. "Hello," Oliver said, half expecting it to be Jake calling from a phone booth downtown.

"Oliver. This is Bob. Jake was just here. Is he home yet?" Bob Lowell sounded frantic.

"You mean he went to your house? What happened? Did you tell him? When did he leave?" The near panic in Oliver's voice was obvious. The fact that Jake had gone to the Lowell's first terrified him. Laura and Steve were on their feet, staring at Oliver.

"I should've called as soon as he left. I figured he'd go straight home. That was a half-hour ago. I'm sorry, Oliver. I was surprised to see him when I opened the door. Oliver, I didn't handle it well at all. I'm sorry. "

"Calm down, Bob. It's ok. You say he left a half-hour ago?"

"Yes. About that. I didn't expect him. I didn't know what to say to him," Bob said, still shaken.

"But, you did tell him about Sara?

After an audible sigh, Bob said, "Yes. I told him. He knows it."

"Which way did he go when he left your house? Did you see him leave?" Oliver tried to think where Jake might go this late at night. It was only four blocks to the Lowell's. A five-minute walk. Where could he have gone? "We'll find him, Bob. Thanks for calling to let us know. We'll find him." Oliver set the receiver in the cradle without another word to Bob.

"Steve. Call your house and see if he's there. He might have gone to see you."

Steve immediately walked to the phone and dialed the number as Oliver stood meeting Laura's worried stare, trying to think where else Jake might go at this hour under these circumstances.

"He's not there," Steve reported.

"Where would he go?" Laura asked, becoming more frantic.

"He wouldn't hurt himself, would he, Oliver?" Tears filled her eyes at the thought of having to bury her other son. Burying Charley had been all she could bear. She could not do that again.

Oliver read her thoughts and crossed the room to hug her. "Don't be silly, honey. You know Jake better than that. We need to find him and get him home."

Laura Jacobs shook her head and wiped away the tears. She knew Oliver was right. She felt a little embarrassed at letting her mothering instincts overreact. Sometimes it was hard not to still see Jake as that little freckled-faced boy with tears in his eyes and a fresh scrape on his knee. She missed those days, and how good it felt to make those little scrapes better, and those tears disappear so easily.

"I think I might know where he went," Steve said. "You mind if I go check it out?"

"You mean alone?" Oliver asked.

Steve thought for a second, then replied. "Yes, sir. If Jake is there, it's because he wants to be alone for a while. He and I used to spend a lot of time there."

"Oh. You mean you think he's at the bridge over Chandler's Creek where you two used to sit and drink hot stolen beer from my garage and smoke cigars, thinking no one the wiser?"

Steve grinned. "You knew about that?"

"I knew," Oliver said. "I saw you guys sneak out with the beer and had Charley follow you, to make sure you weren't going to get hurt. You guys didn't hide much, though. You left your bicycles on the side of the road. Charley said he heard lots of giggling and coughing."

Steve laughed. "We got sick, too. It's a wonder we could ride our bikes back to town."

"You think that's where he is?" Laura asked.

"Probably," Steve replied. "Spent a lot of time under that bridge just kicked back shooting the bull, all the way through high school. That's where we first talked about going to the academies. We spent hours under that bridge."

"You sure you don't want me to go with you?"

Steve understood the concern in Mr. Jacob's voice but firmly rejected the company. If Jake were at the bridge, it was because he was not ready to see anyone, including him. "Tell you what, sir, if I'm not back in ten minutes, you'll know that I found Jake and that he's all right. If he's there, we may be under that cold bridge awhile. We'll be here when he's ready. OK?"

The wind was cold against his face as he stepped away from the warm old Buick. Steve instinctively flipped the collar of his long wool coat around his ears and walked down the curving path that led to the belly of the bridge. It seemed so long ago that he and Jake had lounged so insouciantly in this place away from the eyes and ears of others. The pounding in his chest reminded him how much he hoped to find his friend here now. As he rounded the final turn in the path, now obscured by darkness and the overgrowth of brush from the lack of use, Steve was both startled and relieved to hear the voice so close to everything essential to him.

"You sailors are terrible at sneakin' up on people. Good thing I'm not dangerous."

"Hey, buddy," Steve said as he tracked the sound of the voice to a darkly shadowed rock. Jake was hardly visible in his gray overcoat and hat pulled low on his forehead. Had Jake not spoken, Steve was sure he would have returned shortly to the Jacobs's house empty-handed. Silently, he climbed the cold, sharp rocks toward Jake, still not knowing whether he was entirely welcome or not. Even as he sat next to Jake and bundled himself against the chill, Jake said nothing and continued his mindless stare into the dark water below him.

"If I could stand the taste of booze, I'd get drunk," Jake said.

"I'll hit you in the head with a hammer if you think that will help," Steve replied.

"Hatchet." Jake said, "Use a hatchet."

Steve rose from the rock and pulled Jake to his feet. Let's get you home. I'll come to get you for breakfast, and we'll talk about it some more if you want to, but right now let's get out of the cold."

As the old Buick fired to life and the heater struggled against the night air, Jake asked, "Why'd she do this, Steve?"

"You're a soldier, Jake," Steve said matter-of-factly. "This comes with the uniform. Let it go."

CHAPTER FOURTEEN

2200 Hours
31 December 1970
Dallas, Texas

THE GUESTS of the Mosher family milled around the Turtle Creek mansion with long stem crystal glasses filled with imported champagne while two dozen professional waiters offered an array of delicacies from silver platters. In small groups, the formally dressed guests held an assortment of conversations after having passed through the receiving line to congratulate the new Mr. and Mrs. Brent Mosher and to exchange the customary Happy New Year greeting. In the ballroom, a nine-piece band provided music to meet the occasion and to fill the mansion with the proper spirit, Dallas style, to celebrate a wedding and the final moments of the old year. John and Delia Mosher were determined to salvage, as much as possible, the social aspects of the marriage of their only son, Brent, to Sara Lowell.

They had nothing against Sara. On the contrary, John Mosher had been quite taken by her beauty and grace on the few visits she had made to Dallas in the past two months with Brent. The problem was the social expectation. As one of the city's most prominent and wealthiest businessmen, the marriage of an only son was expected to be an event, a spectacle of grand proportion. He knew that it was not the end of the world. His business associates and contacts could care less about yet another Dallas wedding to attend, but to Delia, it was a significant crisis. Brent and Sara's marriage by a justice of the peace in Austin with absolutely no fanfare whatsoever had deprived her of creating Dallas's social event of the year. Worse yet, within her circle of friends, gossip was abundant. Real or imagined, Delia feared that her friends thought less of the Mosher family because Brent and Sara had not had the good taste to marry properly. Delia cultivated the Mosher's social superiority with the same vigor and protectiveness that John used to cultivate the business. This marriage was just not acceptable. Not so much for her son, but for herself and all that she had strived for over the years. She had worked frantically over the past ten days, complaining to John at every phase of the organization, to deliver a combination wedding reception and New Year's ball. Many had canceled prior plans for the evening in deference to the Moshers, but for the most part, in the minds of many of Delia's friends, it was indeed the social event of the year to see how well Delia could salvage her social graces.

All but the fashionably late had already arrived and had passed through the receiving line when John Mosher demanded of Delia that they, too, join the party already an hour commenced. Sara was relieved to move from her post in the foyer. Never had she met so many people so quickly. At first, it had been amusing to meet the social elite of Dallas and believe the sincerity of their congratulations, but as the hour wore on, the words and smiles all seemed the same. The belief of earnest sincerity lost its credibility. It occurred to Sara that being married to Brent Mosher, of the Dallas Moshers, would change her life in more ways than she had anticipated. Those people, as insincere as they were, were a part of Brent's life, and she would have to adapt to an entirely different kind of social awareness. She was a Mosher now, and this was who the Moshers were.

"Sara, dear," Delia said as she pulled Sara's arm to follow her, "Come with me. I want you to get to know a few of the young girls you'll be playing tennis with at the club." Sara followed obediently, looking over her shoulder at Brent in smiling resignation as he held his glass of champagne in a salute of understanding. He understood his mother's motives, and he favored them. Now that he was out of school and had returned to Dallas to work with his father, it was important that his bride join the proper society. It was certain that his mother would see to it.

Brent wandered to the far side of the ballroom, having spied the gathering of his fraternity brothers enjoying yet another party for a fallen member of their clan to the institution of marriage. The sight was familiar. He would miss the university life. The past four years had been wonderful.

"Brent! Welcome, brother. How does it feel to join the ranks of the establishment? Job. Work. Wife." Brent took another glass of champagne from the tray as the waiter offered. Well, it feels grand, Jimmy, my boy. No classes, lots of money, and lots of good lovin'."

"Hell, Brent sounds like nothing's changed." Another brother smirked, causing the girls to laugh at the well-known truth. "You hardly ever went to a class in your whole four years at Texas, and that Porsche outside proves you haven't exactly been down to your last dime getting an education, and last but not least, we can all testify that you tried to bed every new class of freshmen girls. You are a married man now, Brent, but that's not likely to mean you won't be trying to have an affair with half the women in Dallas. Same old Brent, different city."

"True enough," Brent said, raising his glass as though returning a toast, taking pride in the admiration of his brothers and their recognition that he had indeed led a grand life for four years at the University of Texas. "True enough," he said again, as Sara made her way through the crowd toward Brent and his friends. "I had a great time at the university. You are my brothers, and I love you, but it's time for me to settle down."

"Settle down my ass," Jim Moore said with a laugh as Sara slid her arm under Brent's. "All you want is to stay in Texas and keep your ass out of Vietnam. The ole college deferment has expired, Brent." The group laughed.

"That's true enough, too," Brent said, laughing with the others. "You won't catch me in a soldier suit driving a tank in Vietnam when I can be in a camel hair coat driving my Porsche down Central Expressway. That army crap is for idiots. By God, if being married doesn't keep the draft board off my ass then we'll get us a baby. Ain't that right, honey?"

Sara stared into Brent's eyes, disbelieving what she had just heard him say. He had never before said such things. He had never expressed his concerns about being drafted previously, or how happy he was that their marriage was going to extend his military deferment.

"Ain't that right, honey?" Brent asked again.

"Yeah. Sure, Brent. You're right, of course," Sara replied, stunned by the conversation.

"Damn right I'm right!" Brent was boastful. Sara softly removed her arm from Brent's and walked swiftly toward the stairway with her head down, and Brent's words reverberating in her ears with every step. He said he would do whatever he had to do to keep out of the military, which would include getting married, having a baby.

Alone in the downstairs bathroom designated ladies only for the evening, Sara leaned forward on stiffened arms against the sink, staring at herself in the mirror. Her breathing was heavy and quick. She was astonished at the reality that consumed her expression, acknowledging fully that she had succumbed to half-witted advice from her sorority sisters. As the moments ticked away, her expression remained frozen. Sara wanted so badly to cry. But for now, she could only stare into the mirror. Her face a reflection of horror at the reality of what she had done, of what Brent had done. She had committed her life to a man who wanted her only to avoid military service. In recognition of the reality, she also recognized the price she had paid for a love she no longer understood. She had broken the heart of the man who had loved her from deep within his soul. "Oh Jake," Sara whispered to herself, staring into the mirror as the tears began to flow and the sobs choked her words, "What have I done?

1800 Hours
4 January 1971
United States Military Academy
West Point, New York

PATRICK AMBLED through the door with a broad grin on his face, glad to see Jake after two weeks, and pitched his B-4 bag on his bunk before playfully messing up Jake's black hair. "Hey, buddy. The Tennessee man has returned. Good to see you. How was Texas?"

Jake did not raise his eyes to meet Patrick's, nor did he alter his reclined position, clad only in a pair of athletic shorts, his chair tilted back on two legs, and his bare feet crossed on top of the desk. "Texas was the pits," Jake said without much emotion in his voice. "I've been right here the past five days. Glad you're back. This place is eerie when you're the only one here."

"What do you mean you've been here the past five days?" Patrick asked, totally astonished.

"Came back early. Like I said, Texas was a lousy place to be."

Patrick could hardly believe his ears. No one, absolutely no one, cuts leave short by five minutes, much less five days to get back to West Point early. Patrick was speechless. All he could do was stare at Jake in disbelief.

After an uncomfortably long pause, Jake turned his head to Patrick's. "Sara got married three days before I got home. Self-pity is a lot easier here than in Comanche, so I came back here. Not so bad. I ate at the Officer's Club and down at the Thayer Hotel. "

Patrick was twice as stunned now. He felt behind him without looking for the touch of his chair and finally managed to drop himself into it with a disbelieving stare on his face. " You have to be kidding me. She got married, to some other guy?"

"That's about the size of it," Jake said with false calm in his voice. "You know what I know, which is nothing." Jake slowly lowered the front legs of the chair to the floor, swung his feet off the desk, and rose to move to his upper bunk. "Don't know who. Don't know why. Don't know anything."

"You're kidding," Patrick said again in awe.

"Guess it's just as well I don't know. Wouldn't make any difference even if I did."

"Well, what are you gonna do about it?" Patrick asked as though Jake could somehow fix this problem with the same ease he had fixed the apple pie in the mess hall.

"I'm gonna rest," Jake replied confidently as he swung himself to the top bunk. "Wake me up for dinner formation, will you?"

"You mean you're going to sleep?" Patrick asked, his eyes wide and his jaw hanging open.

"That, too." Jake rolled over on his side to face the wall and covered himself with his comforter. "That, too, my friend. That, too."

CHAPTER FIFTEEN

0930 Hours
16 February 1971
Princeton University
Princeton, New Jersey

Dr. Samuel Wellburn Shaw, president of the university, sat stiffly behind his oversized, walnut desk trying to control his disgust with the two visitors sitting in front of him. He was not pleased with the circumstances surrounding the need for this meeting, nor was he comfortable having the State Department involved in the affairs of the university. And, he despised himself for the obvious moral compromise he was about to make.

"There is absolutely no proof of the young lady's accusations," Bob Lacey said, his words coordinated with the flip of his hand in the air. "Dr. Shaw, there is no substance to this at all."

Sukaro sat calmly, almost detached from the conversation altogether, as the mid-level U.S. State Department official defended him. Though regretful that there was a noticeable incident at all, he found it humorous that the American government was defending him and applying all the pressure it could bring to bear to preserve his attendance at the university, and his freedom from criminal prosecution.

Shaw shook his head slightly. "The young lady, Miss Terry, says that Mr. Bangjar raped her. That is a serious allegation. I've reviewed her university file, and I see nothing that would indicate that she would lie. She has not been involved in any radical activities, nor anything else that would hint that she might have a hidden agenda. Miss Terry has been a model student. She is extremely bright, is conscientious about her education, and as far as our investigators can determine, she has had no social activity to speak of in the three years she's been at Princeton."

"That's no proof," Lacey stated coldly.

"My God, Mr. Lacey, the girl left the university on the verge of a nervous breakdown. She has thrown away law school at Harvard in the fall. That may not be proof sufficient for a court of law, but that is damn strong circumstantial evidence. Cheryl Terry didn't throw away everything she has worked for without reason, emotional or otherwise.

Lacey smiled. "Well, Dr. Shaw, if circumstantial evidence is to be a factor on who is believable in this matter, then what do you have to say about Sukaro Banjar's records? I mean, hasn't he been an exemplary student at Princeton? Do you have any documentation to support a claim that he is a radical of any sort, or that he is the type of person that would rape Cheryl Terry? I think not, Dr. Shaw. We both know that Sukaro is a very bright student, and he has given this administration no reason to persecute him or suspect him of any wrongdoing. The fact is, Dr. Shaw, Cheryl Terry made all this up, for whatever her bizarre reasons. Maybe she just cracked under the academic pressure. Maybe she wanted a reason to quit and go home."

Shaw sighed in resignation. It was true. Sukaro's file was every bit as clean as Cheryl Terry's. It was her word against his with no hard evidence. And, Cheryl Terry had lost any hope of making the charge stick by not reporting the incident immediately. Three months was a long time to wait before telling anyone that she had been raped. The wait did not weaken her credibility in his mind, but it would for the district attorney that would have to take the case before a jury.

"Mr. Banjar." Shaw said, "Miss Terry claims that you told her that you had killed a man before. She said that you would kill her." Sukaro said nothing. He continued to sit calmly with his legs crossed and his arms relaxed, forcing Shaw to ask his question directly.

"Well. Have you killed a man? Did you physically threaten her?

"This is ridiculous," Lacey said in an irritated tone. "Of course, he didn't."

Sukaro shifted his eyes from Shaw to his fingernails, as though he thought the condition of his manicure more important than a question about murder. "Cheryl Terry has made all of these accusations falsely, Dr. Shaw," he said without looking up from his hand.

Shaw was disappointed. He wanted badly to see Sukaro's eyes while he lied.

"I have killed no one. I did not threaten Cheryl Terry, and I certainly did not rape her. Other than seeing her in one class we shared last year, I do not even know Cheryl Terry. I have never spoken to her."

"See," Lacey said condescendingly. "This entire situation is nothing more than a figment of Cheryl Terry's imagination. And, Dr. Shaw, I think the university owes Mr. Bandjar, his family, and his country an apology. Need I remind you that Sukaro's father has made substantial contributions to the university foundation in the past, and I have reason to believe that there will be future contributions as well. You should be thankful that the Bandjar family and the Indonesian government are not more offended than they are."

Shaw leaned back in his chair and paused, forcing himself to control the anger he knew was visible on his face. None of this was right, but he had no choice. "Very well, Mr. Bandjar. This investigation will terminate. I'll document your university file accurately. That is that all the facts are circumstantial and there are no reasonable grounds for legal prosecution on the matter."

Sukaro smirked slightly as Dr. Shaw leaned forward. "

Yet, I think you are lying. I think you did rape Cheryl Terry. There is nothing I would like better than to see you tried and convicted, expelled from Princeton, and deported. Your arrogance disgusts me. And, as for you, Mr. Lacey, I can't tell you how much I resent the State Department interfering in the affairs of this university and the justice system of this country based on political expediency. I don't give a damn if Indonesia is politically and economically vital to U.S. interests, no one should be exempt from the laws of this nation and rescued by the State Department. I am appalled. You, sir, have raped Cheryl Terry just as surely as Sukaro Bandjar raped her."

"Are we finished here, Dr. Shaw?" Sukaro asked coldly. Shaw quickly rose from behind his desk, further expressing his anger and indicating that the end of the meeting was more than welcome to him. Sukaro also rose, continuing his stare at Shaw, then quickly turned for the door while Bob Lacey followed without a word.

CHAPTER SIXTEEN

1930 Hours
6 March 1971
United States Military Academy
West Point, New York

LIEUTENANT COLONEL WILLIAM BLEVINS again shuffled through the two files on his desk. He had one more selection to fill the ten openings for airborne training and Ranger School. All graduates are granted sixty days of leave following graduation. Following leave, they report to Ft. Benning, Georgia for mandatory Ranger School. However, for the highly motivated and those evaluated as having an exceptional aptitude, ten cadets were selected each year for early training.

Though it was an honor to be selected from the numerous volunteer candidates, the program called for relinquishment of one's summer leave, the endurance of an extremely difficult summer, and rearrangement of the cadet's typical training and command schedule. Those selected proudly wore their jump wings and Ranger tabs for the following two years, and it is an enviable distinction in a radically competitive environment.

Colonel Blevins's problem was that he had two anxious cadets sitting in the foyer, both equally qualified, awaiting their acceptance or rejection. Blevins again scanned the file of Cadet Leonard W. Hancock. He was Top ten percent of his class in academics, a linebacker on the varsity football team, a member of the West Point debate team, and in his past life as a civilian in Patterson, New Jersey, he had earned the rank of Eagle Scout. No doubt Hancock would have an outstanding career ahead of him with a general's stars now in the making. Folding the file and setting it aside, he slowly opened the second file. Cadet John Paul Jacobs. He was Top third of his class academically, which was acceptable but not exemplary, on the varsity pistol team, from Comanche, Texas, and the Brigade Middleweight Boxing Champion. Colonel Blevins raised his eyes to the 1st Cavalry emblem on the wall and leaned back in his chair.

"You ought to see those two sweating out in the hall," Colonel O'Quinn, the deputy commandant, said as he entered Blevins' office. "They look like they're expecting a baby."

"Good evening, Colonel," Blevins said as he rose from his chair.

"Well, you've whittled it down to only one remaining slot. You've picked a fine bunch, Colonel. Who's the last one? I'll need to report to General Carter on this first thing tomorrow morning."

"Yes, Sir," Blevins said, still in deep thought as he rounded the corner of his desk and sat on the edge. "You've interviewed both cadets, sir. Perhaps you might advise me on my choice between Hancock and Jacobs."

"Shoot," Colonel O'Quinn said, crossing his arms over his chest.

"Hancock is an obvious, sir," Blevins said with that all familiar "but" hanging in the air. "The kid has everything going for him. He's star material for sure." "He's sharp, no doubt about it. Sharper than Jacobs."

"So, what's the problem, Bill?" Blevins stood slowly.

"The problem, Colonel, is that I saw the Brigade Boxing Tournament last year. In a combat situation, as you and I both know, there's a big difference between the sharp and a naturally great combat commander. I saw the way Jacobs strategically whipped a superior boxer by knocking Jonathan Scott into next week. That kid has heart. He has guts like you don't see very often. He had Scott beaten before the first bell because he went in that ring to win no matter what kind of beating he took himself. And Colonel, he's about to do it again next week. He's already in the finals. One at a time, all season long, he has beaten each of his opponents with persistence and guts. I tell you, sir, in a tight spot, when life or death is seriously in question, I'd take Jacobs by my side over Hancock any day."

With that said, Colonel O'Quinn grinned. "Well, Colonel. It's your task to choose. Which one of those men go to Ranger School?"

Blevins stiffened as though he were about to take a moral stand, he might be criticized for taking. "It's Jacobs, Sir."

O'Quinn reached for the door. "You've done a good job on this, Colonel." Pausing, he smiled. "I'd have stood by either choice you made, but I happen to agree with you picking Jacobs. He would have been my first choice. Ranger School is for warriors and leaders of men in combat. Jacobs will do well. As for Hancock, he'll find his niche in this army. He will go to Ranger after graduation. We need him, too."

The sigh of relief was visible on Blevins' face. "Thanks for the time, Colonel. Having a sounding board was helpful."

"Goodnight, Bill. Give those two puppies sitting in the hall the news, then you go home and get some rest. Job well done, Colonel."

JAKE WALKED to the barracks area from Colonel Blevins's office with the collar up on his short overcoat to block the cold wind blowing off the still-frozen Hudson River. Though spring was near, and the end of the Gloom Period was at hand, piles of snow bordered the slab and walkways at West Point. Jake walked slowly. The hundreds of lights in Washington Hall were in stark contrast to the darkness. Behind the lights, cadets went about the routine of study hall and preparation for tomorrow's recitations and exams.

As he walked, Colonel Blevins' words in choosing him rang in his ears, and for the first time since Christmas, he was again glad he was a part of the academy. Washington Hall, to his left, was overpowering in size and beauty, while to his right beyond Trophy Point, the moonlight glimmered on the magnificent frozen Hudson. For the moment, Jake was enjoying the coldness of the night, the beauty of West Point in snow-covered darkness, the freedom of having thoughts inside himself of the events of Christmas leave.

Jake entered the 50th Division and ascended the winding stairs to the third floor. The division was quiet with cadets at the books for the next several hours. As he climbed the stairs with slow deliberation, it occurred to him how little he was in the mood to join the others for concentrated study. The news from Blevins was worthy of a reward, like an evening of leisure, and Jake knew it was going to be harder than usual to settle into the books.

As he entered the room and pitched his hat to his bunk like a frisbee, Patrick and Wayne jumped from their chairs, stood side by side, and went into their three wise monkeys routine of "hear no evil, see no evil, speak no evil." As always, they looked like a couple of idiots standing there with one finger stuck in an ear, their eyes squeezed tight, and one hand over their mouths. To make the scene even more obscene, Wayne wore a Goofy hat he had bought at Disneyland that had two big eyes, a twelve-inch bill, and long black ears that drooped to his shoulders. As for Patrick, he was wearing what he wore every night at study hall. His study hall standard was a West Point B-robe decorated with a half dozen Army divisional patches, his University of Tennessee baseball cap, and his Mr. Bunny fuzzy slippers.

"Well, what's the poop?" Patrick asked with animated curiosity. "Surely they're gonna let you go. Aren't they?"

Jake said nothing. He knew Patrick was dying of anticipation, and it was so much fun to watch him squirm. He hung his over-coat on its hanger, unzipped his dress-gray coat, and went about the chore of changing into his study attire. He remained silent. After a moment of watching Jake undress in silence, Patrick jumped to his conclusion, which Jake knew he would, and dramatically played out all his emotions as he circled the room several times with arms flying, B- robe falling open, and bunny ears flopping frantically as he stomped his feet.

"Damn! How could those pencil-pushers reject you? Ain't fair! By God you're the best infantry warpo in this whole damn place! It ain't fair, I tell you! I won't have it. I'll write my congressman. No, I'll write the President. Hell no! I'll teach 'em. I'll write my mother. They'll be sorry. They've done made me mad now!"

Jake sat in his chair, now also dressed in B-robe, the Yankee baseball cap Charley had given him, and an identical pair of Mr. Bunny slippers that Patrick had given him for Christmas. Jake leaned his chair back on two legs, crossed his bunnies on top of the desk, and smiled at Patrick. Patrick raged around the room while Wayne sat on his desk, looking sad underneath his Goofy hat. Jake continued to smile while Patrick ran wild with his presumption. Finally, Patrick became vaguely aware that Jake was having no reaction to this horrible news. He knew how much going to Ranger School meant to him. He knew that Jake needed very badly to have something worthwhile happen in his life to take his mind off of Sara and get him back to a functioning level at West Point. He had not been himself since Christmas leave, and Patrick was hopeful that an opportunity to go to Ranger School would snap him out of his feeling that his life no longer had direction or purpose.

"What are you sitting there grinning at?" Patrick snapped from across the room. "How come you ain't mad? Like me."

"Because I like to watch you get yourself all worked up.", Jake replied nonchalantly, still smiling.

Patrick's eyes widened, and his jaw dropped slowly. "You

scumbag! You didn't get turned down at all. Did you? You got accepted. Didn't you?"

"Matter-a-fact, I did," Jake said as his grin widened. Patrick let out a loud rebel yell that roared throughout the barracks and threw his baseball cap across the room ceremoniously. Wayne sprang from his desk, grabbed Jake's arm, and lifted him out of his chair. The tiny room was jubilant in earnest congratulations with all the appropriate handshaking and back-slapping that comes so natural with heartfelt good news.

"Colonel Blevins came out of his office, walked over to me and Hancock, and said, 'Congratulations, Cadet Jacobs.' That was it. No explanation. No nothing."

"Was Hancock upset about it?" Wayne asked.

"I'm sure he was," Jake said. "Just like I would've been in his shoes. But he took it right. You'd never have known he was as disappointed as I know he was."

"Hancock's a great guy," Patrick said seriously. "But Blevins chose the right man. You'll do great at Ranger School. Nobody deserves this more than you, little buddy."

"Thanks, Patrick. You, too, Wayne."

"What about next week, Jake?" Wayne asked. His tone was serious. "You've made it to the brigade boxing finals this year simply because you've been mad at the whole world. It's not like last year. You were motivated to win last year. What about next week, Jake?"

Jake leaned forward in his chair and lowered his head as though ashamed. He knew how he had behaved the past two months. He knew he deserved whatever reprimand he might receive from his friends.

"You've been a real pain in the ass, Jake," Patrick said deliberately, and honestly. "You don't talk unless you have something sarcastic or derogatory to say. Mostly, you sit in silence and mope. It's wearing me and Wayne plum out trying to cheer you up. You are not eating right, you don't sleep worth a hoot, and you sure haven't been training for that fight next week." Patrick paused.

Jake still had his head held low, his eyes on the floor. "She's gone, Jake," Patrick said firmly. You know West Point as well as I do. If you don't snap out of it, and quick, they'll throw you out of here." Spoken firmly, Patrick said, "You have to accept it and get on with being John Paul Jacobs."

CHAPTER SEVENTEEN

0700 Hours
7 March 1971
Dallas, Texas

THE ALARM SHATTERED THE SILENCE, and Sara fumbled for the clock radio on the nightstand without opening her eyes. Finally, her fingers blindly felt the familiar snooze button for another seven minutes of half-sleep before the buzzer would again blare its obnoxious tone. Brent made it their routine during the week to sleep through the first and grumpily crawl from the warm bed on the second. Sara did not mind. Seven minutes of half-sleep gave her some warning that another day had arrived and to consciously prepare herself internally, or perhaps half-consciously to do so. This morning was different. The absolute silence of the early morning after that first blast of the alarm was absent. There were voices. The voices were faint. Sara struggled to identify the voices in her groggy state of mind. After a few moments of trying to focus on the conversation, it occurred to her. The television was on. Confused, Sara opened her eyes, propped herself on one elbow, and stared at a morning talk show with the volume turned down low, just as she had left it when she had fallen asleep. Brent had worked late again at the office. When he did so and came home late, he turned off the television.

Sara glanced at Brent's side of the bed. He was not there. She swung her legs to the floor and swiftly walked to the bathroom, expecting to see Brent shaving or in the shower. She was confused, still half asleep. She walked back into the bedroom, trying to figure out why this morning was so abnormal, so disorienting. As she approached the bed, Sara stopped in the middle of the room and stared at it. The realization that Brent's side of the bed was not rumpled shook her to full awareness. Brent did not turn off the television because Brent did not come home last night. Again, the alarm blasted for the second time, and Sara scurried around to the other side of the bed to terminate the awful sound. It was even more obnoxious than usual. Sara slid her robe over her long night-gown, passed through the door of the bedroom, and walked briskly toward the kitchen, hoping that there was an explanation for Brent not being in their bed all night, and that he was in the living room or the den asleep on the sofa. The walk to the kitchen confirmed that he was not. He was not in the house. Sara turned on the light and prepared the morning coffee, just like she did every morning. It was routine, and her motions did not interfere with her thoughts about Brent's whereabouts for the night. Her greatest fear, and the most likely possibility was that he was with another woman. But afraid to jump to that conclusion, her mind wandered to the other possibilities. Had he been in an accident or was he hurt?

As the coffee brewed, Sara became more awake and was focused on the reality that Brent really was missing, or at least missing from where he was supposed to be. Sara sat at the kitchen table with her cup of steaming coffee, and then the thought struck her that he might be in the house. His car might be in the garage. Sara dashed through the kitchen, struggled with the locked door to the garage, and finally managed to swing it open. The Porsche was not there. Brent was gone. There was no mistake about that now. Sara went back to the table and sat alone with her thoughts and her coffee. The clock on the wall read seven o'clock. As the minutes ticked away, Sara sat in a silent state of worry and fear and anger. Then she heard the Porsche coming up the driveway and stop in front of the garage. Sara sat silent. Moments later, sounds of the front door opening and closing preceded footsteps on the oak flooring as they moved toward the bedroom, then after a silent pause, toward the kitchen. Sara said nothing as Brent walked tentatively into the kitchen.

"Hi, honey," Brent said as though nothing was abnormal about the morning. He was still dressed as he had been when he left the house the previous morning, including a buttoned collar and cinched tie. Sara remained silent and watched Brent's face as he went to the coffee pot to slowly pour himself a cup.

Finally, Brent turned sharply, leaned against the kitchen counter, and said, "You're not going to believe what happened."

Sara's upper lip tightened as she silently acknowledged that Brent's last statement was likely to be the only truth she would hear. She could feel the back of her neck stiffen as anger began to well up inside her.

"I fell asleep on the sofa in my office," Brent spit out rapidly. "It was late, and I was going to rest for a minute or two, and before I knew it, it was morning. I would've called, but it was so late. I was afraid I would wake you."

Sara still sat silent. The anger in her was almost overpowering. A ten-year-old could tell that Brent was lying. Not only was his excuse flimsy, but it was also the way he said it. The look on his face and his eyes testified against him as an eyewitness to the truth. Sara was not surprised. Though against hope, she knew this was going to happen sooner or later. The night of their wedding reception told her to expect the worst from Brent. And here it was, after less than three months of marriage.

"You believe me, don't you, baby?" Brent asked, peering over the top of his cup as he took a sip of his coffee.

Sara paused, then stared into her cup. "No. No, I don't believe you, Brent."

"Well, screw you. Bitch!" Brent yelled as he slammed his cup down on the counter, spilling half its contents. "I was up there at that office working my ass off, so you can live in this big fancy house, and drive that big fancy car. Some thanks I get. I was working my ass off, and all I get from you is no appreciation whatsoever."

"You bought the house, Brent," Sara said softly without looking up from her cup. "You bought the car, too. I didn't ask you for either."

"Screw you! You don't appreciate a damn thing I've done for you! You wouldn't have squat if it weren't for me. And don't you forget it!" Brent stomped out of the kitchen.

Sara sat silent, staring out the window. Tears filled her eyes, as they had on New Year's Eve, for times lost and for a future that promised more pain than she could have ever imagined.

1400 Hours
12 March 1971
United States Military Academy
West Point, New York

JAKE EXITED the dressing room with Patrick and Wayne at his side. As they entered the main gymnasium, he recalled the sensations of last year's brigade tournament and how he felt inside as he was about to face impossible odds against Cadet Captain Jonathan Scott. None of those feelings were present today. The crowd roared as Jake entered the ring, just like they had last year when Scott climbed through the ropes to meet his opponent. The crowd, as a whole, expected him to win simply because he was the titled champion, and because they had witnessed a miracle a year ago. He was expected to repeat the miracle in the same dramatic fashion. Though not the last fight of the day, this was the bout everyone had come to see. Again, the gymnasium was filled with cheering spectators. The oval track structure above the gym floor, used primarily by cadets doing circuit training by running and lifting weights, held standing fans leaning against the railing with a bird's eye view of the ring. Cadets with their lady guests, officers with their wives, and dateless cadets by the hundreds in designated company areas cheered as Jake crawled between the ropes to face his opponent already in the ring. Company C-4 held a large banner with his name emblazoned across the top, a comical caricature of a combat-ready infantryman, and the company slogan which read 'Yea, though I walk through the valley of the shadow of death, I will fear no evil. For I am the meanest SOB in the whole damn valley'.

"Talk about pressure," Jake commented to Patrick and Wayne from his corner. "Wish I was in my rack this afternoon. Sounds crazy, but I'd even prefer to study this afternoon than be here."

"You'll do all right," Wayne said calmly. "Don't pay any attention to the crowd."

Jake turned toward the center of the ring and, for the first time, focused on his opponent. He had not met Ben Cruikshank in the ring during the intramural season, and though a classmate, he had little reason to know him since he was in another regiment. But, of course, he had caught a couple of his fights when he could catch them. Bottom line was that Cruikshank was mean. He was mean in the ring. He was mean outside the ring. Overall, he was just plain mean. Rumor had it that he took great pleasure in ridiculing plebes and had been reprimanded on several occasions for incidents that bordered on physical hazing. In the boxing ring, he was worse. Cruikshank was a good boxer, and he enjoyed walking on the edge of fighting a dirty, even illegal, fight. He was not opposed to beating an opponent without honor—as long as he beat him. Like Jake, he too was undefeated for the season. It was unfortunate that Cruikshank's opponents did not simply have a few aches and pains after a fight with him. Most opponents required a visit to the infirmary for a broken nose or cuts on the face that needed sutures. In some circles Cruikshank might be considered a good boxer, but his means of winning a fight demonstrated a lack of compassion. And that was likely to be Cruikshank's downfall at West Point. Compassion is a requirement to be a good officer.

"Don't let that creep psyche you out, Jake," Patrick said as he wiped the sweat from Jake's forehead with a towel.

"Right." Jake mindlessly stepped to the center of the ring toward Cruikshank and the referee.

Jake and Cruikshank stared into each other's eyes as the referee gave his instructions, but neither boxer paid much attention to the words since they had heard them a hundred times before. Cruikshank pounded Jake's extended glove downward as Jake offered the customary pre-fight handshake, then turned away muttering through his mouthpiece how he was going to beat Jake to a bloody pulp.

Jake walked deliberately back to his corner without a word as the crowd roared its approval that the fight was about to begin. Patrick leaned over the ropes close to Jake's ear to whisper his final thoughts before the opening bell, "I know your heart isn't in this fight, Jake. And that's ok. Just go out there and fight the best fight you can fight. If you win, you win. If you don't, you don't."

Most spectators expected this fight to be determined by points rather than by knockout, which favored Jake. On the other hand, it could be that the winner of this fight might significantly be determined by Cruikshank's success or failure at injuring his opponent.

The bell rang. Jake looked at Patrick, nodded his head, and stepped lively to the center of the ring to meet Cruikshank.

Likewise, Cruikshank enthusiastically came to the center of the ring, but with rage in his eyes. Cruikshank took the offensive by moving forward with a roundhouse right swing. Jake quickly stepped to the right, ducked under the swinging fist, and simultaneously delivered a hard, left jab to Cruikshank's mouth. Further enraged by Jake's jab, Cruikshank quickly spun his body three hundred-sixty degrees and caught Jake across the bridge of the nose with the full force of his elbow.

Jake rocked backward in pain as the blood began to pour from his nose. No doubt about it, this nose was broken. The referee rushed to reprimand Cruikshank for his foul play. "Don't you pull that Recondo, hand-to-hand crap in my ring, mister! I'll throw you out of this fight so fast it'll make your head spin!" the referee yelled. The ref then pointed to the scorning table and indicated one penalty point was to be deducted from Cruikshank's score for the infraction. Cruikshank was more than willing to sacrifice the penalty point for the enhanced probability of a technical knockout.

But the damage was done. Cruikshank had literally gone for a kill, and Jake had a broken nose to show for it. A few inches lower and the elbow would have crushed Jake's larynx, making it impossible to breathe short of an emergency tracheotomy. The crowd roared its disapproval. A riot and a lynching were not out of the realm of possibility for all those who had witnessed the atrocity just committed in the ring.

Jake stumbled to his corner when the referee ordered the clock stopped. After he had flopped down on the stool, Patrick grabbed Jake's head for a closer look at the twisted nose. Following a quick survey of Jake's nose and watery eyes, Colonel Edwards, an orthopedic surgeon from the infirmary, took control of the situation.

"It's broken, son," Edwards said.

Jake said nothing. He stared at the doctor through watery eyes.

"We need to call this fight. You…"

"I'll fight, sir," Jake interrupted. "Just get the bleeding to stop. I'm ok."

The referee came to Jake's corner after physically taking Cruikshank to his corner with threatening instructions to stay there.

"What's the verdict, Colonel?" he asked the doctor, genuinely concerned as he looked at Jake. "Do we need to call this fight?"

"I'm ok," Jake said, half choking on the blood gushing down his throat.

"Well, this gauze should temporarily control the bleeding, but he shouldn't fight," the doctor said. "We need to get him to the infirmary and run some x-rays. No way to tell how much damage is done till then."

"No offense, Colonel, sir, but I'm ok. I can still fight."

"His eyes are clear, sir," the referee stated on Jake's behalf."

"Whatever you say, Colonel. If it's ok with you, I'd let him have another go at it. If not, I'll call it right here and now. If he doesn't go back in the ring, I'll call it a technical. Jacobs will win and still hold the title. If Jacobs fights, and if Cruikshank fights clean, that nose might just cost this kid the fight. It isn't fair, but that's the way it is."

"I'm ok," Jake stated again firmly.

The colonel and the referee both looked deep into Jake's eyes for any flicker of a reason to indicate that the broken nose might be more serious than it appeared. As if to cinch their decision, the roar of disapproval from the crowd at Cruikshank's cheap shot further encouraged them to let Jake have another try.

After a long pause, the colonel stated dogmatically, "All right, Jacobs. You can have your fight. But one little sign of trouble and this fight will be over. I mean it. That nose starts bleeding, or you start acting like you aren't one hundred percent, I will throw in the towel. You got that, Mister?"

"Yes, sir," Jake said as he pushed the towel away from his face, rose from the stool, and walked sharply toward the center of the ring with the referee following.

The crowd immediately went into a frenzy. Jacobs! Jacobs! Jacobs! the crowd began chanting as the two opponents met in the center of the ring again. Cruikshank seemed not the least regretful at either the sight of Jake's blood-soaked C-4 T-shirt or his illegal blow that caused it. As Jake extended his glove a second time for the customary handshake, Cruikshank again hammered it and muttered viciously through his mouthpiece.

The referee signaled, and the bell rang. Cruikshank charged forward swinging wildly with both fists. Jake stepped back one step to miss any contact from the wild man, planted both feet solidly on the canvas, and hammered his right glove into Cruik-shank's mouth with such a force he couldn't believe he had in him. The force of the devastating blow might have KO'ed another opponent, but not Cruikshank. He was stunned, but only for a second. But it was less than a second before Jake summoned everything he had in him and unleashed an earth-pounding left-right combination that rocked Cruikshank backward and dropped him stunned to the canvas. With a resounding thud, Cruikshank fell and landed ignobly onto the seat of his black silk shorts.

Jake went to his corner with the referee's instructions to do so, and the crowd roared its approval that justice was indeed being served. Cruikshank came to his feet as the referee began the count and did his best to convince the spectators that he had not been knocked down, but rather had lost his balance and tripped.

After checking Cruikshank for physical damage, the referee motioned for the fight to continue. Jake moved quickly to the center, breathing heavily through his mouth. His nose was crammed with gauze. Angry, Cruikshank charged with rage, his fists swinging wildly. Jake rose to his toes and shuffled quickly to his right, to avoid Cruikshank's right fist and forcing him to follow. After a full wide circle with Cruikshank still unable to strike, Jake saw an opening, stepped inside the momentary open stance, and rammed his left into Cruikshank's ribs, stepped one step back, then delivered a crushing hard right to his opponent's cheekbone. Cruikshank was dazed. He pulled his glove to his face and backed away from Jake. Jake pursued. With a flurry of combinations, Jake dominated the remainder of the round. As the bell rang ending the first round, Cruikshank found himself in serious trouble and surrounded by a crowd screaming for his defeat.

"Great job, little buddy!" Patrick said excitedly as Jake slumped down on the stool Wayne slid under him. "I've never seen you box so well. You're doing great!"

Colonel Edwards climbed through the ropes and squatted in front of Jake to examine the broken nose and the clearness of his eyes. "Well, I guess my patch is holding. I'm surprised. But so far, so good. Good fight, son. Keep it up if you can, but don't you be afraid to drop out of this fight if you need to."

"Thanks, Colonel," Jake said as he gasped, trying to catch his breath. "I'm still ok."

The bell rang for the second round, and the fans increased the feverish pitch of their enthusiasm. This round, Cruikshank did not charge as he had before. He was deliberate in his movement, almost as though he were stalking a prey, waiting to spring a predetermined trap. Jake circled to the right and followed Cruikshank, attempting to initiate the imminent exchange of blows that were inevitable. Harmless jabs were thrown by both combatants, each seeking the proper opening in the other's defenses. Cruikshank repeated a flurry of left jabs to Jake's head but simultaneously dropped his right-hand several inches as he focused on working his left hand. Focusing on offense with his left hand and defense with his right demands thinking under pressure, and Cruikshank momentarily failed in that mental process. Instinctively, at the moment the last jab moved in his direction, Jake dipped to the right, stepped forward, and planted a left jab of his own to Cruikshank's jaw, then followed it with a power-right to the nose, and yet another powerful left to the jaw. It was a full left-right-left combination that was delivered with power and precision. Cruikshank staggered backward, bounced lightly off the ropes, came back, then stepped momentarily on Jake's left foot and shoved him off balance with his body. As Jake dropped his arms to maintain his balance, Cruikshank hammered a solid right to his broken nose.

The crowd, already on their feet, roared its disapproval in an instant. The referee had been out of position, behind Jake, and saw nothing out of the ordinary. The damage was done. Jake caught his balance, but spun to his left in agony, raising his gloves to cover his face. He staggered to the far side of the ring, dropped to his knees, and coughed blood onto the canvas. The gauze was thoroughly soaked, and fresh blood streamed freely from his nostrils. He was in trouble. The bleeding was so profuse that blood was flooding his throat and blocking his airway. His exerted lungs screamed for oxygen. With every gasping breath, he coughed. He coughed blood mixed with air and spittle.

The crowd was in pandemonium. They were angry, shocked, and horrified at the sight of Jake on his knees, holding onto the bottom rope, bleeding and choking. Colonel Edwards scrambled through the ropes and reached him just as Patrick cradled Jake's head like a parent with a hurt child. With the professional and technical expertise that had earned him his eagle, the colonel took charge to give Jake his needed medical aid.

Cruikshank danced arrogantly at his corner with his arms defiantly and victoriously waving above his head, proclaiming himself the winner.

The referee assured that Jake was receiving the medical attention he needed, walked briskly to Cruikshank's corner and declared him the winner of the bout by a TKO, or technical knockout. The referee sensed from the reaction of the crowd that there was more to that last punch than he had seen, but as the referee, he had no other choice but to call the fight as he had seen it. What he had seen was Cadet Jacobs's nose hemorrhage from a Cruikshank right, which led to Jacobs's inability to realistically or safely continue the fight. He'd done his job to the best of his ability, whether the crowd agreed with the outcome or not.

With the spectators still in an uproar, two enlisted medics from the infirmary entered the ring with a stretcher, carefully strapped Jake to it, and exited with Colonel Edwards, Patrick, and Wayne at his side. Shortly, the canvas was wiped of blood and two more cadets stood ready at their respective corners, each ready for the next fight of the Brigade Boxing Championship.

1900 Hours
14 March 1971
United States Military Academy
West Point, New York

JAKE WAS RECLINED in a semi-sitting position on his infirmary bed trying to make sense of his physics assignment when he saw Patrick and Wayne enter the ward and sheepishly glance from bed to bed trying to find him. He knew they would come tonight after dinner and before study hall. They were a welcome sight, but he was somewhat embarrassed at the way he looked. The emergency surgery had left his nose swollen three times its size, or at least it felt that way, and dark blue circles under nearly swollen shut eyes.

"Good grief! You look just like the last guy that made a pass at my baby sister after I done put a world a hurt on him." Patrick said jokingly, as he stepped close to Jake's bed.

"You don't have a sister, hick," Jake said.

"Oh yeah. I forgot." Patrick put his hand on Jake's shoulder and looked concerned as he surveyed the broken face. "How you doing? I mean, you look downright poorly."

Jake grinned. "No problem, buddy. The doc said I'd have these black eyes a week or so, but other than that, I'll be up and running in a few days. I'm not sure what all he did to my nose except rearrange a little bone and cartilage. He says I'll be fine, and if I want to, I can box again next year."

"Well, I'm glad to hear that!" Wayne said relieved. "Come next year, you have to give Cruikshank the thumping of his life. They ought to kick that creep out of the academy for the way he cheated."

Jake grinned again. "I been thinking about that all day. And I think you're right. I'm not mad at losing the fight. You guys know as well as I do that I didn't deserve to win. I wasn't prepared, and that's my fault. But I don't like Cruikshank being the champion either."

"Nobody wants anything to do with him," Patrick said. "Technically, what he did isn't an honor violation, but it's so close, it's hard to say it isn't. I think the Corps would like to throw him out for cheating, but it can't be done."

"I don't want him thrown out," Jake said seriously. "I want to give him a boxing lesson next March. With your help, as we did together last year against Captain Scott, we'll make him wish he'd been kicked out for an honor violation."

"You got it," Wayne said enthusiastically.

"Damn straight!" Patrick quickly added. "I can hardly wait. Cruikshank is dog meat!"

"You guys better hustle." Jake glanced at his watch through squinted eyes. "Study hall in ten minutes."

Patrick and Wayne both simultaneously checked their watches and started to leave at the recognition of the time. At the end of the bed, Patrick paused and turned to face Jake again. "You know, buddy, you were already ugly. But you are some really ugly now."

"Get out of here, creep," Jake said affectionately, as he reached behind him, grabbed a pillow, and threw it in Patrick's direction. "You're double ugly."

CHAPTER EIGHTEEN

1800 Hours
25 May 1971
Dallas, Texas

THE PHONE RANG TWICE before Sara could rinse her hands at the kitchen sink and lift the receiver from its cradle. She was irritated, and the telephone ringing only added to her agitation. Brent was late getting home again, which had become the norm. She was home late herself with dinner hardly started, and the afternoon, overall, had brought her mixed emotions and uncertainty.

"Hello. You have reached the Brent Mosher residence," Sara said, just as Delia Mosher had instructed her on how to answer the phone correctly.

"Sara! I'm so glad to hear your voice. I've been trying to get you all afternoon."

"Mother." Sara feigned gladness in her voice though her mother was one of the last persons she wanted to talk to at the moment. In fact, of all the possibilities, her mother was the second on the list, right after Brent. This evening, Brent was number one on her Last-Person-I-Want-To-Talk-To list.

Valerie Lowell immediately began the usual barrage of chit-chat without giving Sara much opportunity to answer any of her questions or to respond in any fashion. Sara leaned against the wall, extended the phone an arm's length away momentarily, and mumbled something inaudible while rolling her eyes skyward, then returned the phone to her ear.

"Well?" Valerie Lowell asked.

"Well, what, Mother?" Sara tried to hide her irritation. "Weren't you listening to me, dear?" her mother asked as though her feelings had been hurt. "I asked you how you would feel if your father and I moved to Omaha."

"Omaha!" Sara was stunned. "Omaha, Nebraska."

"That's what I've been trying to tell you, dear. Your father has an offering for a wonderful job in Omaha. It would be foolish for us to turn down the offer. It's almost twice the money he makes here in Comanche. He's so excited."

Sara did not know what to say. As her mother talked, the only thought that ran through her mind was that the last remnant of her life, before Brent, was about to be loaded on a big truck and moved several hundred miles north. She would never see Comanche again. Worse yet, with mixed feelings about whether she would want to, she would never see Jake again either. Somehow, she had assumed, or perhaps daydreamed, that someday she would run into Jake in Comanche. Perhaps there would be a coincidental meeting at Christmas, or a serendipitous meeting on the street in front of the drugstore where they had met so many times before. The possibility of such a meeting frightened her because she did not have the slightest idea what she would say, or how Jake might react. But with the worst possible scenario, she wanted to see Jake more than anything in the world.

"Well? What do you think?" Valerie Lowell pressed.

Sara replied slowly after her thoughts of seeing Jake faded. "I hate to see you leave Comanche. But if moving to Omaha is what you and daddy want, then I think that's just fine."

"We'll come back to Comanche, to visit our friends," Valerie said as though she almost sensed what Sara was feeling. "Oliver and Laura Jacobs are excited for us, and they've promised they'll come to Omaha for a visit sometime."

Tears almost rose to the surface at the mention of the Jacobs family. "How are the Jacobs?" Sara asked nonchalantly.

"They're fine, dear," her mother said softly. "And they get a letter from Jake fairly often. He's doing fine, too. They said he lost that boxing thing he does. You know, that contest he won last year. He got a broken nose and was in the hospital for a while, but he's fine now."

"When is he taking his summer leave?" Sara asked, trying to act casual with the question.

"Laura says he isn't taking leave this summer. He's going to Ranger School or something like that, then he has to report to West Point as soon as he's finished. I guess he won't be home until next Christmas."

"That's a long time without going home," Sara aimlessly stated, lost in her thoughts about Jake staying away from Comanche.

"Are you all right, dear? You seem kind of down today. Is something wrong?

"No, Mother. I'm fine."

"Now, Sara," her mother said sternly, "you have something bothering you, and I want you to tell me what it is. I'm not getting off this phone till you tell me what's bothering you. You don't sound like yourself today at all."

Sara paused and considered whether she should confide the results of the day with her mother. "Ok, Mother. I went to the doctor today."

"Are you sick?" Valerie quickly interrupted. "Have you been feeling bad? Have you been taking your vitamin C? I told you to take that vitamin C. If you'd take your vitamin C, you wouldn't get sick. I give your father vitamin C every morning, and he hasn't had a cold in three years."

"I don't have a cold, Mother!" Sara said in an irritated tone

"Well, if you're not sick, then what is it?

Sara paused. "I'm pregnant, Mother. I'm going to have a baby."

"A baby?" Her mother squeal with excitement. A moment's silence passed between them as both tried to think of what to say next. "How did Brent react to the news?"

"He doesn't know yet," Sara responded with concern and uncertainty in her voice.

Valerie reflected momentarily on the mixed signals she was getting from the news. Ordinarily, the announcement of a baby was cause for celebration. What was it in Sara's voice that made her feel that Sara was not happy about the news, and worried about Brent's reaction? "Well. He'll be happy about this. Won't he?"

"Oh, I don't know, Mother," Sara replied dejectedly. "Probably not the way you would expect."

"Sara," Valerie Lowell said in a genuinely surprised manner. "I thought everything was fine. I thought you and Brent were happy. I thought you were happy. What's happening? What's wrong?"

Sara broke into tears. The sobs almost choked off her ability to continue the conversation. After a moment of struggling to regain her composure, she continued, "Oh, Mother. I've made such a horrible mistake."

"Mistake? What mistake?" Valerie Lowell asked in a tone somewhere between genuine concern and anger. Sara's determined and unannounced decision to marry Brent Mosher five months ago had not been an easy adjustment for Bob and her. Sara had had her way. She had married Brent. But the price for them had not been pleasant. Their expectations for their daughter had evaporated overnight. They had envisioned a college education for her. And, a marriage to a young man who was already like a son to them. Her husband, Bob, was heartbroken for Jake and haunted by the look on Jake's face when he had told him the news that cold December night. Sara's choice to marry Brent had changed their lives, and now, she was hearing her daughter sob and say what a mistake it all was. In part, what Sara said made her want to hug her and comfort her, and in part, what she heard made her want to scold her.

"Mother. I made a mistake when I married Brent," Sara said, the sobs coming under control. "He doesn't love me. Brent just needed a wife so he could be married. I think he just wanted to dodge the draft. Mother, he's seeing other women. He's...."

Valerie interrupted. "Listen, Sara. You listen to me. You're upset. Being pregnant sometimes causes a woman to be overly emotional. I'm sure that Brent loves you. And, I'm sure he isn't seeing another woman. You've got to get yourself together."

"But, Mother," Sara said, "you aren't listening to me."

"Yes, I am. You may think your marriage isn't what you thought it was going to be, but you have to give it some time. Marriage isn't all that easy, you know? It's hard work. Besides, you are the one that made the decision here. You wanted to marry Brent Mosher so badly, and that's what you got." Sara sat on the floor, leaned against the kitchen wall, and listened to her mother as she accepted that her feelings and the truth of her marriage were falling on deaf ears. Her mother's beliefs about marriage and its permanence, despite the circumstances, were never more apparent. She did not believe her about Brent, or at least she did not want to consider it. Her statement about Brent seeing other women had not brought the emotional support she wanted. It had only brought her mother's denial. As the lecture continued, all Sara could do was to listen silently and reflect on how alone, how scared, and how trapped she felt.

"Well, dear, I know you're busy trying to get dinner ready for Brent. I just wanted to tell you about Omaha."

"Omaha is ok with me, Mother," Sara said without much thought or enthusiasm. "Whatever you and dad want to do is fine with me."

"All right. Now you take care of yourself and write to us about the baby. I want to know everything. Try not to worry, honey. Everything will work out fine. Brent will be so excited about the baby, and you two will work out your little problems. Just give it time."

Sara surrendered to a total agreement with her mother, which was all she could do, said her goodbyes, and slowly set the receiver on its cradle. Water boiled on the stove. Foam from the large pot bubbled over the top and onto the red, hot metal, hissing and crackling as if it were screaming for attention. Sara sat against the wall with her knees cradled in her arms, staring past the boiling pot to no place specific. "I'm in trouble," Sara said aloud in her trance.

2200 Hours
28 May 1971
United States Military Academy
West Point, New York

WITH HIS LEGS crossed on his desktop, Jake wiggled his right foot from side-to-side and smiled. Watching his slipper's bunny ears flop from one side to the other was much more interesting than the differential equations text. After a full minute of staring at the bouncing ears, Jake leaned over, removed the shoe, and threw it with deadly accuracy at Patrick's head. The flying bunny hit him on the nose and dropped to the pages he was studying. Without comment, Patrick slammed the text shut with both hands, leaving one bent ear protruding from the pages.

"Thanks, Jake said. "He was a communist, you know?"

Patrick leaned back in his chair and frowned. "I've thought so for a long time now. How did you know?"

"It was the way he wiggled his ears," Jake said. "It was un-American. They had that Commie kind of a wiggle. You can spot them every time."

"You know what I think, Jake?

"What?" Jake asked in a disinterested tone.

Patrick smiled. "I think you've gone completely nuts. That's what I think."

"You giving up, already?" Wayne asked.

Jake was quick to respond. "I'm not surrendering. I'm announcing a victory. I know that stuff. Another two or ten hours of study won't make a twit of difference on the final tomorrow. I'm done. Yearling year at the books is a done deal."

"Me, too," Patrick said as he casually pitched his chemistry book in the same general direction that Jake's book had landed, and the dead commie. "How 'bout it, Wayne. You gonna be a tenth boner and study until dawn?"

Wayne stared uneasily at Patrick, then back to his book for a moment. "What the hell." He slammed the text shut and lobbed it like a grenade to crash with the others.

"Well, what shall we do now, gentlemen?" Jake asked sarcastically. "Shall we wander down to the lounge for a whiskey, or shall we wander around campus searching for voluptuous sorority girls?"

"Listen to this guy, Wayne. He's gone plum crazy. The boy has forgotten where he is. This is John Wayne University, Jake, my boy. There ain't no whiskey, and there ain't no sorority girls. Besides, you aren't the least interested in either."

"No, I'm not. But I can pretend I am," Jake replied. "Two more days and I'll be out of this hole for three months."

"You'll think hole," Patrick smirked. "Where you're going is a bigger hole for sure. Jeez! Anyone that would volunteer to spend his leave jumping out of airplanes, and crawling around the woods eating snakes isn't all there. You know what I mean?"

Jake did not answer. The comment was rational enough, but he managed a smile at the knowledge that neither Patrick nor Wayne understood that the rigors of Airborne School and Ranger School were precisely what he needed for leave. Whatever hardship he had to endure would somehow feel right. Jake hoped the ordeal would purge him, or cleanse him, or even harden him against what he felt on the inside.

Patrick and Wayne would not be taking their leave until the first of August. They had both been assigned to the first detail, four weeks in July, of Beast Barracks. Their duty assignment for the summer was to indoctrinate and train the new incoming plebes. Their June would be spent at West Point learning every detail on how to carry out that assignment with as much precision as they had received themselves two years earlier. Mainly, June was class-work on how to teach new cadets. On the first day of July, the new cadets would arrive, and the skills the old cadets learned would be applied. For plebes, Beast Barracks is hard and exhausting. For old cadets, the cadre, it is even harder and more exhausting. Each day is spent step-by-step with the plebes, and at lights out, the plebes go to sleep while the old cadets begin hours of paperwork and planning for the next day. As with everything else at West Point, they would be continuously monitored for leadership skills and graded daily.

"I'm not going to be crawling in the mud on my leave," Patrick said as he daydreamed about his status quo on summer leave. "I'm gonna eat my momma's cookin' till I drop, sleep 'til noon, and dance all night. Thirty days of the good life. And I'm not gonna think about you, or worry about your scrawny butt one single second. No, sir. I'll eat my steak rare, hot off the grill, and drink cold beer. I'll not be the least bit concerned that you have bugs and snakes for dinner. I'll return to this wonderful land of the perpetual good deal with a golden tan, a potbelly, and a gal on each arm leading me through the post gates. And you, my friend, will come back with skin that looks like leather, scrawnier than you are now, with bags drooping under your eyes so bad you'll step on them, and blisters so bad the skin peels off by the pound. No, sir. I'm gonna have a good time. I ain't gonna worry about you at all. Not one little bit!"

Jake looked over his shoulder at his raving friend. "I love you, too, Patrick."

Embarrassed that his concern was not so well hidden, Patrick waved his hand in the air as though it all meant nothing to him.

There would be two more months for Wayne and him at the Point, but Jake would be flying to Georgia in two days. He had heard many tales of Ranger School, and of course, he had vivid memories of its minor introduction, Recondo. He was afraid that the summer would prove to be a bit more grueling than Jake anticipated. Not everyone made the grade. Many good men failed Ranger School for one reason or the other. Jake, with nine other classmates, were going to be going through the program with older and more experienced soldiers. Jake would finish jump school in three weeks and Ranger School in nine. If all went well, he would have just enough time to grab a plane back to New York for the first day of classes in the fall. Best guess was that for the entire summer, Jake might get two or three short weekend passes, hardly a leave, and certainly no break from the military routine they had known for the past eleven months.

Jake laughed. "I can see you two commanding a squad in Beast Barracks. Two years ago, we were all scrambling around with Cantrell yelling at us all day long. Who'd of thought it'd ever be our turn to break in a new bunch of plebes? Patrick, no offense, but I'm having a hard time imagining you playing the super-straight cadet."

Patrick did not reply. The vision seemed queer to him, as well. Somehow, a change was about to occur in all of them. He could feel it. The first year, as a plebe, had been horrible, but simple. All one had to do was to remain in a panic mode for eleven months and jump sky-high whenever an upperclassman spoke. Yearling year had been almost as simple, though made horrible by the academic load. The third year, or cow year, had arrived. It was time to learn and apply command skills. It was their turn to ensure that West Point continued the generations of the Long Gray Line. For the next two years, it was they who would make the corps function by doing their share to lead the plebes and yearlings so that when their turn came, they could do likewise. Graduation, the gold bars of a second lieutenant, and Vietnam still seemed far away, but for the first time, awareness of getting prepared for those things seemed pressingly more important. If the next two years went as quickly as the last two, then Vietnam and responsibility for a platoon of living, breathing flesh was right around the corner.

"Super-straight cadet?" Patrick asked more to himself than to Jake or Wayne. "You're rubbing off on me, Jake. I reckon I'll manage to do my duty this summer. Fact is, I'm looking forward to doing my duty."

CHAPTER NINETEEN

1030 Hours
1 June 1971
Atlanta, Georgia

DELTA FLIGHT 788 made its final approach for landing. The stewardess walked the aisle reminding the passengers to put their seat backs in the upright position and secure their seat belts.

Jake had enjoyed the flight from Kennedy Airport. He could have easily hitched a ride from Stewart Air Base to some location in the vicinity of Ft. Benning. But Jake thought it worth the extra expense to fly commercial. Actual leave time for the summer was practically nonexistent, and the luxury of flying commercial and mingling for a few hours with real civilians seemed the thing to do. It had been fun watching the people in the airport, going to who knows where. It had been so long, five months to be exact, since he had been around people dressed in civilian clothes going about their day-to-day lives. He was fascinated by how different the world seemed outside the gates of West Point. Of course, the world's reaction to him was a mixed bag because in uniform, some responded kindly and respectfully, while others either stared at him with piercing, angry eyes or more vocally expressed their anger with some derogatory comment. Though he knew better, it was apparent that some wished him to feel ashamed to wear the uniform of an American soldier.

The tires on the airliner screeched as they touched the concrete runway and the stewardess's voice immediately came over the loudspeaker to remind the passengers to remain in their seats, with seat belts securely fastened, until the plane came to a complete stop at the terminal. Before she had finished, the well-traveled unfastened their seatbelts and began shuffling their carry-on luggage in preparation for what they hoped would be a rapid exit at the terminal. Jake sat, amused at the scene. He had not flown much, but it seemed comical that the passengers in the rear of the plane somehow thought they could get off the plane faster than those in the front. As the plane rolled to a stop, the aisles filled with passengers cramped together for the long, uncomfortable process of deplaning.

The Atlanta Airport was a beehive of travelers and a haven for one who had an hour to waste. His ride to Benning was not due for an hour. The sign overhead indicated the exit and a coffee shop somewhere down the long ramp, so Jake walked in mass with the others in the designated direction. Something to eat and a table with a view of the innards of the airport would be the perfect way to spend his free hour and to enjoy his tiny bit of freedom.

Finding the coffee shop, Jake located a table next to the ramp and set his duffel bag in an empty chair. Within moments, a portly waitress approached the table. Warming, idle chit-chat was not in her job description. She was all business with not so much as a "hello," her demeanor demanding Jake to rattle off his order. Before he had finished the last syllable, she was turned about and walking toward the kitchen. Jake turned his attention to the crowded gateway. Businessmen passed by in their pressed suits and briefcases, mothers did their best to herd their children to the desired gate, young lovers held hands, a military uniform occa-sionally passed by, and a myriad of people unidentifiable by their dress as to occupation or purpose in the airport drew Jake's attention. It was exciting for Jake to see people moving around doing whatever their lives dictated they do, oblivious to the eyes of someone who thought their lives were excitingly unique.

Jake was focused on the crowd when the waitress returned with his cheeseburger. He thanked her as she set his order on the table, though she acted like she was disgusted with the task and turned her back to him as quickly as she could. As she turned, she bumped roughly into a young man who was about to sit at the table adjacent to his. A young man of apparent Southeast Asian, or perhaps, Polynesian descent extended his apology stoically, and she stormed off toward the kitchen without a word. Jake smiled at the young man in acknowledgment that their shared waitress was not the most cordial to be found. In return, the young man, dressed in a black suit, smiled at Jake as he took his seat. Jake started to initiate a conversation, but the young man averted his eyes just at the proper moment to indicate that he was not interested in talking to a stranger. Jake could not help wonder if it was again the uniform, or if it was merely that the man wanted his privacy.

The waitress approached the table, just as she had Jake's without a word, and with pen, and pad in hand. Sukarno gave the woman a menacing look with his dark eyes and ordered without removing his stare from her eyes. Unnerved, she quickly wrote down his order, then scurried away from the table.

It was here, in Atlanta, that Sukarno had come to complete the second step of his instructions from his father. He was no longer Sukarno Bangjar. He was Sayed Dijani, a Jordanian businessman, and the fabricated passport in his left breast pocket proved it. Should anyone seek to track his movement out of the Princeton or New York areas, the trail would end at the Atlanta airport. Within an hour, he would be on a Pan Am flight to London as Sayed Dijani. Once in London, his instructions were to register at the Hotel Intercontinental and await contact for directions to his next destination.

Inwardly, the change in identity had heightened his zeal for the mission. After months of contemplating the future, this exchange was the first tangible action taken toward his destiny. Another member of his cell had not elaborated on the training he was to receive, but he was confident that his father would arrange for the best training available through his connections in the Muslim community at large. Though not looking forward to physical discomforts, a training camp for the tradecraft necessary for jihad was a requirement.

Sukarno sipped his hot tea and glanced at the young man in the gray dress coat and white starched trousers. West Point cadets were often seen in New York City. He had not expected to see one in Atlanta, but then, the cadets come to West Point from all the states of America. A smirk crossed Sukarno's lips as he watched the cadet enjoying the mass of strangers in the busy airport with no awareness that a significant threat to his country was at the next table.

As Sukarno was served his meal, the cadet rose from his chair, swung the duffel bag to his shoulder, and walked to the cashier. Sukarno watched the cadet intently and noticed the confidence and bearing that the young soldier seemed to possess. Sukarno had heard of West Point and was aware of the influence it had on American military history, but it occurred to him that he lacked real knowledge of why West Point had such an impact. As the cadet positioned his hat on his head correctly and walked out of the coffee shop, Sukarno made a mental note to himself to study the American military academies. But, for now, there was no time for such trivia. It was time to board Pan Am Flight 302 for London. Sukarno pulled the passport from his pocket, glanced at the picture of himself with the name Sayed Dijani typed beneath it, and placed a twenty-dollar bill under the empty cup of tea before walking away from the table into the crowded gateway.

1030 Hours
15 July 1971
Fort Benning, Georgia

MAJOR ROBERT ROGERS, the father of the American Rangers, wrote his nineteen standing orders in 1759 during the French and Indian War. Number fifteen was an irritation for all generations of Rangers, which is "Don't sleep beyond dawn. Dawn's when the French and the Indians attack."

Jake sat upright in the makeshift hole he had hastily dug for himself a mere two hours ago, rubbed his sleep-filled eyes with a hand that was charcoal black, and rummaged through his gear with his other hand for a small box of cold C-rations. The candidates were allowed to eat one cold meal each twenty-four-hour period.

Five days in the woods around Benning was a practical exercise for the skills the candidates had learned in the past three weeks, but primarily, it was intended to semi-acclimate the uninitiated to the conditions they would face in the remaining six weeks of the program. Ranger School was 818 hours of instruction, known more technically in the Pentagon as course 7-D-F4. The nine-week course was in three phases. The first being the Benning phase. The second, the Dahlonega phase, was in mountainous terrain in north Georgia. And the last phase was the jungle warfare training in the Panhandle of Florida. The first three weeks consisted of brutal physical conditioning, and classroom instruction on skills the candidates would need for the remainder of the course. To succeed they would need to know compass and map reading, demolitions, ambushes, insertions, extractions, rappelling, artillery support, kill zones, hand-to-hand combat, small-unit tactics, and reconnaissance. The mountain phase forced the candidates to apply the skills that they learn in the classroom, and their physical fitness and endurance were pushed to the limit. By the time the candidates arrived in Florida, they were half-starved, exhausted, and exhausted. From this condition of despair, the candidates were pushed toward a mental breaking point. Long before the Florida phase, the candidates were well aware that the course description and reality were vastly different. Officially, the stated mission of the Ranger program was "To develop a superb infantry soldier, with exceptional endurance, skilled in the techniques of fieldcraft, survival, and mountain, jungle, air-land, and amphibious operations." To Jake, and the other two hundred in his class, neither the official stated objective, or what was ahead of them for the next six weeks was particularly meaningful. The only reality was the present darkness, the present exhaustion, and the present hunger. If the worst was yet to come, Jake and his companions would just as soon not know about it.

Captain Harriman walked slowly through the dark, getting the candidates mentally ready for the new day. "Fifteen minutes, gentlemen. If you have rats, you better eat them now. We've got twelve miles to cover this morning. At zero-seven-thirty, our first little stroll for the day will be done. Fifteen minutes."

Jake put a stale cracker to his lips and quietly made a quick mental calculation, "Zero-seven-thirty roughly two and one-half hours, twelve miles. A little stroll, my ass. That's a twelve-mile run." Within ten minutes, he had finished his meal and stood to load his forty-pound pack and rifle, securing the straps tightly to prevent them from beating him too severely for the next few hours.

Ranger School was not necessarily a delight, but Jake had no real quarrel with the rigors of the program. So far, it met his expectations. He knew it would be both mentally and physically tough, and it was. Airborne School in June had been less of a strain. He had played the game for three weeks and had made his five jumps. As he pinned on his hard-earned wings, he felt a certain amount of pride at having overcome the natural fear of jumping voluntarily out of a perfectly good airplane. There was a bit of insanity in the act, but the madness fit well with his chosen path for the summer of '71. The only real trouble he had at jump school was breaking the desire to look down when he stood in the door of the airplane. Looking downward on his first jump had sent him tumbling to the short end of the static line and a temporarily twisted chute as he fell through the air. The instructor on the ground reprimanded him that he had to look to the horizon when he jumped. Otherwise he was likely to go into a forward roll that would eventually tangle the lines of the parachute, and he would have a swift trip down to Mother Earth, with no opportunity for a repeat performance. "And, son, I'd have to flunk you for that," the instructor had said only half-jokingly.

The past three weeks had been mentally and physically grueling, and every bit as fast-paced and competitive as the academic year at West Point. Between classes, field exercises, and the most hostile physical training he had ever experienced, there was no time to think about anything external to the training and survival. If the historical numbers of attrition at Ranger School remained the same for his class, at least twenty-five percent would not be wearing the little Ranger tab in late August. Sprains, fractures, and snake bites would take some out of the course, but most of the attrition would come simply from poor performance, by the school's standards, or poor attitudes. As the weeks rolled by, attitude was to become increasingly more important. Without the right attitude, it would be near impossible to persevere the physical and psychological stress.

Each candidate was given 1050 points to his credit the day he walked through the gates at Ft. Benning. It took 683 of those points to graduate. At each phase of the course, instructors or lane graders, composed of both officers and noncommissioned officers, would be stripping those points away from the candidates. Each candidate had to lead a half-dozen patrols and pass at least half. Get the patrol lost, and one would flunk. Lose a member of the patrol, and one would flunk. There would be a hundred ways to fail, but only one way to pass. A soldier had to lead the patrol successfully on its mission and keep everyone theoretically alive. Unless one fails miserably and it is determined that the soldier is untrainable, to flunk meant that the Ranger candidate could recycle through that phase at a later date.

Jake had thought that some of those that recently graduated from The Point might be in the class, but he had no one to commiserate with since they were all on their sixty-day leave and would not start entering Ranger School until the late summer and autumn cycles. He was glad to be fighting the heat of midsummer rather than having to cross icy rivers and withstand freezing weather like those in the later cycles would have to endure. And, the other nine cadets from West Point were not available for encouragement either because they were spread throughout the company, leaving each to stand on his own,

The arrangement of not having contact with other West Pointers suited Jake. It did not remove him from West Point entirely, because after two years, his psyche was an embodiment of all that West Point is. Still, at least he could talk to and get to know others who had a frame of reference of army life that was not one hundred percent encapsulated on the banks of the Hudson River.

Jake was very much impressed with his enlisted companions. They were tough, and they were highly motivated. Every man had specialized training behind him, and most had experience either in a command position or in combat. The men teased him for the first week about being a hot-shot West Pointer, and how he, the future officer, was going to teach them how to do this Ranger business. But they eased off when they realized that he thought of himself as ignorant at the business at hand. With this realization, the men then became eager to teach him what they knew about the army from an enlisted man's perspective, and he was equally eager to learn. Reciprocally, and unexpectedly, the enlisted men responded readily to Jake's confident leadership style. He cared about his fellow candidates and inspired an exceptional level of trust in his decisions, while he remained aware of his own strengths and weaknesses. The enlisted men found Jake to be persuasive, in a positive way, and capable of bringing the men in the patrols he led together for the accomplishment of the mission. The thought crossed Jake's mind by the end of the second week that if he should flunk the course, he would still gain invaluable experience by living and working with these men for nine weeks. The enlisted men assured him that it was they who ran the army, not the officers, and Jake readily agreed. When it comes to the tactical side of the business of warfare, the enlisted man is where the rubber meets the road.

1300 Hours
15 July 1971
United States Military Academy
West Point, New York

"O-DEN! O-DEN! O-DEN!" the eight New Cadet Companies chanted in unison as they stood on the slab, under arms, awaiting the order from the King of Beast to form by companies on the parade ground. The sound of twelve hundred men chanting in a deep, loud voice was a thunderous resonance across The Plain, an auspicious prelude to the pageantry of the pass in review. Oden, the ancient Viking god of weather was traditionally beckoned at parade formation in the hope of inclement weather. If it started to rain, then the parade would be canceled. The chant was never known to have worked, but the Long Gray Line of one hundred sixty-nine years kept trying. It is said that tradition dies hard. But at West Point, tradition does not die at all, even when the results are dismal.

"Get your eyes to the front, smack!" Patrick barked as he walked down the rank of his squad to check their appearance one more time before the parade. "Lane, if I catch you gazing around one more time, I'll have you reciting poop till you're old and gray. You keep your head and eyes to the front. You got that, Mister?"

"Yes, sir!" New Cadet Lane popped-off.

Patrick slowly walked the line with a scowl on his face. Only last night he had sat at his desk, feet propped on the desk like Jake was in the habit of doing, and laughed aloud at the transformation, or more precisely, the appearance of a transformation that had taken place in him. To the new plebes, Patrick appeared to be the ideal Mr. West Point. His uniform was always immaculate, back straight, shoulders back, shoes as reflective as a mirror, and possibly the meanest man on the planet. Patrick laughed at the thought that a mere sixty days ago, the tactical officer had to threaten to put him on the area before he would go to the barbershop and get his weekly haircut. Mr. Gung Ho was nowhere around, then. But now, he was a model upperclassman, doing his duty.

One surprising thing to Patrick was how dumb and scared the new plebes were. "When we were new plebes, we were cool. We were sharp.", he said to a classmate. Seeing the plebes and training them made him realize how much he and Jake had grown in two years. In many ways, it had been a speedy two years. It seemed like yesterday that they were standing ready for parade with Cantrell walking the line, yelling, and screaming just like he was doing now.

As the orders were given, the squad stepped-off for the pass in review. There was nothing more to do with the plebes until the parade was over. If one of them screwed up, an upperclassman at the back of the formation would let him know about it, and he would then put on his hard-core look and throw a tantrum in military fashion. Tradition. Plebes get away with absolutely nothing.

"Peterson! Mister Swanson tells me that you were out of step for the entire parade. Martin! You dumb smack! What's this about you not keeping your elbow tucked in and letting your rifle cant to the left? That's not a hobo sack on the end of a pole, you know! It's a mighty M-14 with a full-dress bayonet on the end of it. You better get it together, Martin, or I'll run you out of my beloved corps in a heartbeat! Mr. Stith!" Patrick roared as he faced the new cadet, an inch from his face. "You sloppy beanhead! The next time you don't keep your chin in and chest out, you're gonna sweat dimes on my wall! You got that, Mister?"

"Yes, sir!" Stith popped-off as sweat poured down the sides of his face from underneath his hat.

"You know how to sweat dimes, scumbag?" Patrick snapped.

"No, sir!"

"You'll brace, or stand at attention, so hard that the back of your neck will hold dimes flat against my wall. You'll brace so hard, Mister, I bet I could count maybe twenty or thirty wrinkles in your chin. Would you like to sweat dimes for me, Mister Stith?"

"No, sir!" Stith barked in horror.

"It's up to you, Mister Stith. You either learn how to keep your chin in and look like a cadet on your own, or you'll brace at my wall for hours. One way or the other, you are going to get this mess in front of me straightened out." Patrick turned sharply, marched to the front of the squad to give them all another menacing stare, then snapped his next order in an angry tone. "Ten minutes! You have ten minutes to stand tall against my wall. Uniform is as for bayonet training. Fatigues under arms. Don't you girls dare forget your field bayonet. Dis-Missed!"

The band of ten new cadets immediately did an about-face, shouted "Beat Navy" at the top of their lungs, and ran for the stairway leading to the fourth floor of their barracks. Ten minutes quickly vanished when one had to change into a different uniform and be immaculately groomed for special inspection against Mister McSwain's wall. Cadet Patrick McSwain tolerated nothing short of perfection and was especially obsessed about tardiness. It had taken the new cadets only two formations to learn that it was better to come improperly dressed than to arrive late. McSwain was the meanest man they had ever met.

"I don't know about all this, Swanson," Patrick said casually to his classmate as they entered the stairway for a slow climb of the stairs. "I'm just not cut out for this upperclassman stuff. I'm not very good at training these plebes. You think I'm doing all right with them?"

Before Swanson could answer Patrick's question, a new cadet with apparent panic in his eyes dashed past them trying to get to an upper floor as though someone had announced a bomb was about to blow the first floor to smithereens. He brushed Patrick's shoulder and was around the next landing, taking two steps at a time.

"Hold it right there, smack!" Patrick shouted. Though out of sight, the solid thud of the plebe slamming his back to the wall was heard. Patrick turned his head and smiled at Swanson. The sound of a plebe hitting the wall was like no other sound in the world, and they had both heard it thousands of times. Patrick and Swanson continued their slow ascent around the landing to face the fear-frozen plebe whose eyes were firmly fixed on some imagined spot on the wall.

"What's the rush, young man?" Patrick said in a gentle voice. "Are you in a hurry?"

"Yes, sir!"

"Well, why are you in such a hurry, Mister?" Patrick asked in the same soft tone.

"Sir, I got lost. Sir, I went into the wrong barracks, and I only have ten minutes to get to the next formation. Sir, I..."

"Are you suggesting that my classmate and I are detaining you. That we're keeping you from going to your next formation, Mister?"

"No, sir. I..."

Patrick moved his nose to within a fraction of an inch from the plebe's, took a deep breath, and exhaled his wrath. "You, beanhead! You, crot! You, hairless dumbass, don't you ever let me catch you running past an old cadet in the stairway or the hallway without slamming your back against the wall and asking for permission to pass! You got that, Mister?"

"Yes, sir!" the plebe popped off, sweat rolling down his cheek.

"And, Mister, when you're asked a question, you have four answers and only four. You may answer "Yes, sir," "No, sir," "No excuse, sir," and "Sir, I do not know." You understand that, Mister?"

"Yes, sir!"

"I'm not interested in your flimsy excuses about getting lost, or about your ass gettin' chewed out for being late to the next forma-tion. You don't give excuses, Mister! You got that?"

"Yes, sir!" the plebe shouted.

"Post outa here, smack. That means move it like your pants are on fire. The next time you are in the hallway and pass me, I better hear ribs crack when you get your scrawny ass up against the wall. I want to hear glass break when you ask permission to pass, you got that, crot?

"Yes, sir!"

"Post. Get out of my sight. You make me sick," Patrick said disgustedly.

The plebe popped-off another "Yes, sir" and continued his scramble up the stairs. Patrick stared after him, and Swanson broke into a gut-splitting laugh.

"What are you laughing at?" Patrick asked.

"You. You're what's so funny. Two minutes ago, you were all worried that you weren't doing a good job being tough on these plebes and teaching them the ropes. Patrick, you're doing fine. You're doing just fine."

CHAPTER TWENTY

1300 Hours
22 July 1971
Southeast of Qom, Iran

SUKARNO SAT in the shade of the headquarters building, which consisted of a one room, plywood structure, with his back resting against the wall. As Rahid Abudiun gave yet another emotional lecture on the evil features of the Western imperialists, Sukarno's concentration focused on the ramblings of a large scorpion approaching his leg. The political lectures of the Hezbollah, the Party of God, had been the same for the past ten weeks. Sukaro was bored with the illiterate attempt to politically indoctrinate, or brainwash, the trainees in the desert. After ten weeks, all but he was influenced. His fellow trainees in the camp were now highly emotional and enraged at the West and ready to sacrifice their lives by striking a deadly blow to the enemy in the name of Allah. Sukaro had a different purpose. A different destiny. At the emotional climax of the lecture, Sukarno raised his AK-47 slowly, then crashed its butt down on the scorpion. The lecture ended with Sukarno still grinding the dead insect into the dirt.

The weeks at Qom had not been a waste, merely an excruciatingly long period to learn basic tactics and the subtle recognition that the people of the Hezbollah, and the other PLO organizations like it, were usable by individuals like himself. Without a firm plan of action, he did know that his fellow jihadist was a resource. For the most part, the jihadists were fanatical and emotional. Sukarno knew that when the time came, he could use these soldiers for his cause. If the surface of his cause were draped in the same fanaticism, then these soldiers and others like them would be quick to join his side. They are open to manipulation, and that manipulation would make him a powerful man.

Sukarno had become one of them, at least in appearance. He wore olive drab pants, a khaki shirt, and a surplus cap from the U.S. Army, and he grew a full beard on his sun-darkened faced to blend well with the others. As far as anyone in the camp knew, he was Sayed Dijani, a poor Jordanian who had joined their cause out of hatred for westerners. No one questioned in depth who he was, where exactly he was from, or what his beliefs were. And, he remained aloof from the others. They knew him no better after ten weeks than they did the day he arrived.

The tactical training at the camp had been elementary, but effective. The camp taught nothing of military tactics. The only legitimate military skill learned was that of marksmanship, and even that was without much success. Most of the trainees were better at firing their automatic rifles into the air during one of Rahid Abudiun's lectures than actually hitting a target with any accuracy. Where the camp did excel, however, was in demolitions. Sukarno learned how to make letter bombs, booby traps, car bombs, and bombs intended for airplanes, buses, and railways. He was now confident that if he so chose, he could kill many people very brutally and very dramatically. He did not expect to do anything like that himself, personally, but there was value in knowing what was possible so he could send others to do it.

Training with the Hezbollah was near its end. In a week, he would take a bath, be driven to Teheran as Sayed Dijani, and fly to Paris to meet with his father. As far as he could tell, his father had intended that he learn precisely what he had learned. Kuwat Bangjar was a very deliberate man. He had not sent him to the desert for eleven weeks of nonsense training. There was a purpose. Surely his father did not think that he would become a raving zealot and personally drive a car rigged with plastic explosives through the gates of an American embassy. No. It was more likely that his father wanted him to understand fully and commit himself to their Indonesian based Darul Islam. The Indonesian government Kuwat served would not hesitate to imprison or execute him if they discovered his loyalty to Darul Islam. That clandestine loyalty reflected his firm belief in the Doctrine of Taubid, the oneness of God. While Kuwat worked daily in the functioning of the government, and a participant in the creation of laws and regulations, his real beliefs were that only Allah held the right to govern and formulate laws. Any individual or institution or government that infringed on Allah's rights was an outright unbeliever and should be a target for jihad. Sukarno knew that, at some point, he would have to defy his father openly. Darul Islam and its fanaticism had no place in his destiny unless it served him personally.

2300 Hours
3 August 1971
Paris

KUWAT BANGJAR ENTERED the library from the south wing of his Paris residence to find Sukarno browsing intently through the rows of books that lined the ceiling-high bookcases. Kuwat smiled. It was heartwarming that his son had inherited his appreciation for books, art, and music. He believed that those cultured in the world were born to it. Others merely acquired quasi culture employing study or environment. Sukarno truly appreciated these things. It was in his blood.

"Someday the collection will be yours," Kuwat said as he closed the large doors to the library. The setting for the conversation he was about to have with his son was important, its context demanded surroundings such as these, including absolute privacy. No one would ever know of this conversation, and yet, with respect to Kuwat Bangjar's point of view, it was to have a significant impact on the entire Muslim world. It would because he, as the Minister of Natural Resources for the Indonesian government, had the opportunity and position to make it happen, and he had absolute trust in Sukarno to execute his plan in every detail.

"It's a fine collection, Father. How many books do you have, fifteen hundred? Two thousand?"

"A good guess," Kuwat said proudly. "The collection is just under two thousand. Some of the finest and rarest in the world are on those shelves. It's taken years of collecting, and a couple of million U.S. dollars, but worth all the effort. There are still so many fine volumes I hope to purchase."

"Well, the room is magnificent. A perfect setting for a perfect collection," Sukarno smiled admiringly, then turned from the bookcases toward a large leather armchair near the fireplace.

"As I said," Kuwat repeated, "someday the collection will be yours. This house and this library as well, I might add. That's what I want to talk to you about." Kuwat Bandjar poured glasses of wine and joined his son in the adjacent leather chair.

"I see your taste in wine has remained impeccable, Father. Sukarno could care less about the wine or the precious volumes in his father's library. He had learned long ago that these things pleased his father and that it was easier to encourage goodwill than to show his real indifference. Besides, his father had summoned him to Paris from the desert of Iran for a purpose. As much as he resented his father's involvement in his future, it was required. After all, it was his father's wealth and power that would carve out his destiny.

"You've trained well, Sukarno," Kuwat plainly stated after he had sipped the wine. "My sources from Qom tell me you performed with true dedication."

"Thank you, Father."

Kuwat tilted his head slightly backward in a hearty laugh. "Dedicated. Sukarno, I am greatly pleased that you have matured in our faith. Praise, Allah."

Sukarno said nothing, while his smile confirmed to his father the truth in his words. In reality, Sukarno's smile was a false message. He was a Muslim, but contrary to his father's belief of him, he was a moderate Muslim. Almost ninety percent of Indonesia's population was of moderate Islamic faith, and only a small number were considered radical. Among the small number of Islamic radicals was his father, who hid his beliefs and agenda from everyone but him. Darul Islam's goal, based on Taubid, was the reality of an Islamic State in place of the current Indonesian government. Sukarno did not quarrel with such a thing, but the truth seemed a weak fantasy in light of the moderate parliament and Indonesian demographics. Besides, Sukarno did not think it had anything to do with his goals, one way or the other.

"It was an interesting experience, Father. It will serve its purpose someday." Sukarno said, to encourage his father's belief that they were partners in ideology.

"Exactly!" Kuwat said excitedly. "I knew you would see the truth and reap the real benefits of your months in the desert." Without confirming what Sukarno had learned in the desert, Kuwat continued to tell him, by assumption, what he had learned. The knot in Sukarno's stomach tightened while his smile broadened to encourage his father that he was correct in all his assumptions. "Now you have the practical tools to entrench yourself in the future politics of our country, and you know first hand that our brothers are available for the jihad that must come."

"Just what do you have in mind, Father?"

"What I have in mind, my son, is that you will someday soon be positioned to have power in a new Indonesia. You know of the unrest in our country. A new order in Indonesia will emerge that will reverse our country's adaptation to Western Culture. We will return to Islamic fundamentalism."

Sukarno sat slightly forward in his chair, awaiting more detail. His father was a brilliant man. Educated in England and comfortable in all the European cultures, Kuwat Bangjar had achieved significant power over the years, and he had survived political upheaval and treachery at every turn. He despised his father for being the kind of man he was, but at the same time, he respected his craftiness at survival and deception. Either way, Sukarno had gained an appetite for his power, his craftiness, his destiny, and like it or not, for the time being, he was inextricably dependent on his father.

"There is to be great turmoil in the Muslim world for the next decade," Kuwat coldly stated as he leaned back in his chair and sipped his wine. "The British and the Dutch abandoned Indonesia, for their problems at home, and that created a vacancy for your namesake, Sukarno, and his corrupt New Order to take control. It is a shame that the parliament and President Sukarno did not return our country to Allah. And, there was another chance to do that in 1966 when Suharto overthrew Sukarno and established yet another New Order. The government today consists of infidels, and the only solution is jihad. You and I will have a significant impact on that jihad. Now is the time for Allah, and you.

Sukarno could see the sadness in his father's eyes. His concern over the death of the Muslim world as he had known it was genuine, but he knew that Western culture had greatly benefited the Indonesian people. He knew that a return to the old culture of strict Islamic law was destructive to the welfare of the people. Of the sadness, Sukarno was not particularly concerned. His concern was his father's intentions for him.

"Yes, Father, I have seen these things, too." Sukarno lied.

Kuwat Bangjar paused to light a Cuban cigar before continuing. "My son, there are as many political factions in the Muslim world as there are branches on the tree. What makes the difference is loyalty to Allah. Those that do not follow the law are unbelievers and deserve jihad. They deserve death."

"Yes, Father, I understand. But why are you so confident that I will be of any importance in the new government?" Sukarno said, leaning forward, expecting to learn something never said before from his father.

"Because you'll have the financial resources to become powerful. You'll have the resources to be influential with the new government. Money corrupts that way. If you have money, and a lot of it, then you automatically have corruptible influence."

Sukarno placed his glass on the table. "That is all well and good, but it is you that is the wealthy man. I am not. And, if I pursue this goal, I forfeit my chances of achieving wealth in my own right. That is, of course, if your plan for me does not materialize."

"I understand your hesitation," Kuwat said seriously. "I ask much of you. I realize that. I am asking you to trust me." Kuwat took another sip of his wine and thought carefully of his words before continuing. "And I must trust you. This is an ambitious, but attainable venture upon which you and I embark. It is the only way for you and your sisters to be safe. If I do not take action now, Suharto's New Order government will execute or imprison all the high officials loyal to Durul Islam and the Taubid. We must trust each other implicitly." Again Kuwat paused while Sukarno remained silently sitting forward in his chair.

Kuwat smiled. "I have five hundred million dollars. U.S. Dollars, I might add. And I want you to deliver these funds to the cause of Durul Islam over a period of time."

"You're not serious," Sukarno said, genuinely surprised.

"But I am serious. I have five hundred million dollars. And, delivered to Dural Islam prudently and wisely, Indonesia can be made to serve Allah."

Sukarno was stunned. He knew that his father was wealthy, a millionaire many times over, but he never dreamed that his father had accumulated wealth to that extent. "Father, I had no idea. From where did such money come? What have you done with that much money?"

"There lies a part of the problem that you must help me solve, for our mutual benefit, our mutual cause," Kuwat said with a frown on his face. He rose from his chair, walked to the table, and picked up the cut crystal decanter and poured a perfect measure of wine into his glass. Momentarily concentrating on the wine, Kuwat swirled the glass in the palm of his hand, smelled the wine's bouquet, and watched its vintage legs form and flow down the sides of the glass. With this long pause, while Sukarno sat in shock, Kuwat took a moment to scan the library that was so meaningful to him and strolled to the fireplace.

"What do you mean, Father? What problem?" Sukarno finally asked.

"I'll not be able to stay in Indonesia much longer. Confiscating my assets both at home and abroad is a given. Not only will I likely be brought back to Indonesia and executed, but you and our family will be penniless. I can't allow that. I have the funds, which we'll talk about specifically in a moment, but by acquiring them, I'll be in exile from our country. It's only a short time now. I stole the money. I have been shifting money from military aid and oil production for the past six months. I control the purse strings of Indonesian resources without oversight. It has not been difficult. I did the right thing, but it won't take long, maybe another six months before the red flags pop up and the loss is discovered. I must now take action to avoid that kind of investigation."

Sukarno sat silently. He was stunned that his father had the daring to steal millions of dollars from the treasury of their country. He was undoubtedly positioned to have done that. As Minister of Natural Resources, millions of dollars pass through a chest to which he was the only one with a key. Electronically transferring funds was easy for his father, and that is precisely what he had done.

"Our meeting here tonight is important, Sukarno. It is critical, to you, to me, to your mother and your sisters. I, if you wish to view it as such, stole a great deal of money from our country. I have no regrets, mind you. I believe I've done the right thing. And I believe that bringing you to power in an emerging new government will keep you safe and is the right thing as well. I believe in what we are doing. I believe in you. So, I took the money to make sure we are successful."

Sukarno did not know what to say. His destiny seemed even more real than it had in the preceding months. The euphoria he had felt in the cold-blooded killing of the man in New York was minor compared to the feeling he had at the moment. Power seemed imminent. Power seemed real. It was five hundred million dollars worth of real.

"I've arranged for you to be a signatory on the accounts. It's all in cash. You must have emergency access to the money, my son. Your mother, sisters, and I will disappear from Indonesia, and Paris, in another month. We'll be going to Sao Paulo, Brazil, under the name of Pasha. It's Pakistani, but it will suffice in helping us to disappear. As you might imagine, I'll not be popular when what I've done is discovered. In our meetings tomorrow with a banker I trust, you'll receive a new identity as well, to use in an emergency. The necessary documents will be signed for you to have access to the funds immediately." Kuwat walked to Sukaro's chair and knelt by its side, placing his hand on his son's. "You have to make me a promise. A promise you would die for."

"Anything, Father," Sukarno said sincerely, visibly returning his father's warmth and trust.

"Should I be caught. I mean, should I fail to survive, you must promise me that you will carry our plan forward, and you must promise to take good care of your mother and sisters. You must protect our family."

"I promise, Father. You can rely on me. I promise you I will protect and provide for our family, no matter what. You can rely on me, Father."

CHAPTER TWENTY-ONE

0200 Hours
3 August 1971
Mountains of North Georgia

JAKE STEPPED SILENTLY through the darkness, third in the line of yet another reconnaissance patrol deep in the Georgia forests. In their third week of mountain training, the patrol members thought they were near exhaustion and even closer to starvation. There was no real danger of either according the Army higher-ups, but apparently, some pencil pusher in the Pentagon decided that two hours of sleep per day and a cold meal was sufficient.

Mostly, hunger was a mental hurdle. It was discouraging to see your buddy's uniform hanging as though they belonged to a much larger man, or that his cheekbones look like knobs on the side of his face. With the absence of mirrors hanging in the forests of Georgia, one could only assume that the same hollow-eyed, emaciated type body was what they, too, had become. Food. Food became a subject of hallucination, of humor, and humility. The staff told a story from years earlier that has become a favorite among the Ranger family. Perhaps true. But, if not, it certainly could be. As the story goes, a healthy twenty-two-year-old from the 101st caused worry amongst the patrol early one morning when he awakened his fellow Ranger candidates by kicking the base of a nearby tree. The fact that he was kicking a tree was a little bizarre, but the thing that caused concern was that he kept yelling, "this damn candy machine ate my quarter! I want my money back! This damn candy machine ate my quarter!" And, when it happened, some Sergeant, a Vietnam veteran from the 24th Infantry, looked over at another candidate sadly and said, "Poor bastard, I know how he feels. I lost my damn quarter in that machine, too."

For the most part, the lane graders were agreeable to letting the Ranger candidates forage for food provided it did not interfere with the intensity of the training. After all, a part of the exercise was to teach the candidates to survive off the land. Several days before, the patrol had come upon a good-sized rattlesnake. Quickly, the patrol killed it. When the lane grader asked if the patrol could eat it, the captain said, "Sure, you can eat it. But no fires on this patrol. You want it. You eat it cold." At the first rest break, the patrol stripped the skin away, cut a chunk for everyone and washed down the gummy white meat with warm canteen water. "I like copperhead better," Jake announced. "Me, too," Toller agreed. "But you wait till we get to the swamps in Florida. Ain't nothing tastes better than water moccasin. Tastes like chicken."

The patrol was moving slowly in what Jake knew to be a north-westerly direction. Every hundred meters, he stooped to grab a handful of soil and rock. Jake could not see, but he could feel. Houlihan, a sergeant he had gone through jump school with, was the patrol leader for the evening, and Jake was glad the pressure was not on his shoulders. He had been the patrol leader four times already in the past three weeks and had flunked two patrols. The lane grader had failed him on the spot when he discovered that Jake could not tell him exactly where they were on the map. Since then, he had become obsessed about always trying to determine where they were. It did not matter where he was in the line of the patrol. He did not want to have to go back to West Point and tell

Patrick he had flunked Ranger School because he could not keep from getting lost. Patrick would never let him live that one down.

The patrol crossed a shallow ravine and then made a long, steep climb. To see the man three feet ahead of him required a focus on the slight glow of a fluorescent strip on the back of his hat. Though more tired than he had ever been in his life, Jake fixated on the hat. Every foot of ground brought awareness of how tired and weak his legs were becoming. Even the light patrol butt pack rig seemed to weigh more than it actually did. The patrol rig consisted of a web belt with suspenders and a butt pack measuring roughly eight inches in height, a width of nine inches, and five inches in depth. The advantages to the soldier are that it allows him to carry less weight than a full-sized pack, and its capability to add equipment to the belt and suspenders. Jake carried a flashlight and his compass on the suspenders, and two ammunition pouches, a first aid kit, and a folding entrenching tool on the web belt. As he topped the crest of the climb, Houlihan signaled with his red lensed flashlight for a rest stop. Jake moved forward another three feet, found a tree with his hand, and leaned his back and head against it for needed rest.

Jake could hear the muffled whispering of Houlihan and the lane grader and knew what was happening. Houlihan, the patrol leader, was being quizzed as to their location relative to the mission objective. A poncho covered them to prevent the enemy from seeing any light, which would expose their position. Based on the amount of conversation, it was evident that Houlihan did not have the slightest idea where they were. "Jacobs," the lane grader said in a normal tone of voice as he came out from underneath the poncho, "you're now the patrol leader for the remainder of the mission. Houlihan, you flunked this one. You'll never get us to that bridge before sunrise 'cause you don't know where we are. If I leave you in command, we're likely to find ourselves in a whorehouse in Atlanta by sunup."

Jake pulled himself from the tree without a word and covered the six feet to the captain. He did not want this patrol, but there was nothing he could do but comply with the captain's order. He unbuckled the belt of his load bearing patrol butt pack and slid his arms out of the suspender straps, then crawled under the poncho with his M-16 rifle.

"You know where we are?" the captain asked as the light spread over the map.

Jake concentrated on the map for a solid minute as the captain waited. "Yes, sir. We are right here, above this creek bed, and about a hundred meters west of this hilltop. That puts us three miles from the objective. If we shift our direction to due north from here, we'll arrive at the objective in two hours, give or take a bit."

The captain looked at Jake with skepticism. "How do you know this is where we are, Jacobs?"

"Sir. I know because I've been counting steps and checking my compass once every one hundred meters. We are at this creek because we just crossed it."

"There wasn't any creek back there. We haven't been wet for a week," the captain said, trying to make Jake doubt his judgment. "It was a creek all right, Captain. Dry, but still a creek. I've been picking up dirt, too. When we crossed that ravine, I grabbed a handful. Round rocks, sir. Sandy, too. Probably doesn't run in the summer. It probably only runs in the spring and late fall with the rains. It's a creek, sir, and this is where we are," Jake said, pointing at the map again.

"Outstanding, Jacobs. Guess you learned your lesson about getting lost. You understand the mission?"

"Yes, sir. We forge the Chestatee River, set demolition charges on the bridge by zero-five-thirty hours, and set up an ambush north of the bridge before sunrise. If the terrain matches the map, I'll use a linear formation along this stretch of road. Any suggestions or orders before we move out, sir?"

The captain had neither suggestions or orders. He smiled at Jake under the poncho and turned command of the patrol over to him. Jake gathered the men, gave them an updated mission order, and instructed them to recheck their gear for silence. In short, Jake took command and issued, in his words, Rogers' Rangers second standing order. "Have your musket clean as a whistle, hatchet scoured, sixty rounds powder and ball, and be ready to march at a minute's warning."

0900 Hours
29 August 1971
Florida Swamp

"ANOTHER TEN MILES and you men can tend to your blisters, feed your gut, and sleep for a week," Sergeant Brousard said in a loud voice, encouraging the exhausted men. "Ten more miles and you'll be a Ranger for life."

Jake was at the rear of the patrol struggling with his gear, and Sergeant Toller. Toller had severely sprained his ankle on the midnight amphibious assault of a platoon strength aggressor team. The mission, the final mission, was a surprise night attack on an acre-sized island in the Choctawhatchee Bay. The patrol had marched forty-eight hours through snake-infested swamps, paddled their light rafts two miles offshore, then immediately attacked a force three times their number. The mission was a success. The surprise was complete, and the aggressors surrendered helplessly within minutes. The candidates cheered the victory and even more so that it was the last exercise of Ranger School. They had made it, or so they thought.

At sunrise, helicopters touched down for their extraction, and the patrol boarded thinking that a short ride back to base and a shower was due. Discouragement and exhaustion doubled when the airlift took them back to the swamp, and Captain Graves announced that they had only a short twenty-two-mile walk through the beautiful wastelands of Florida to complete this, their last day. Max Brimmer, a kid no older than Jake, carried Toller's gear while Jake, for the most part, carried Toller. The ankle was bad. Jake had cut his boot away to give room for the swelling and Toller cursed every step of the way.

"I ain't gonna make it," the man in front of Jake said. "I can't believe they're making us hump this twenty after what we been through."

"We'll make it, Jim," Jake said between gasps for air. "The captain would love to see us drop out so he could flunk us just a few hours before graduation. No way I'll stop. He'll not walk me into the ground."

"Me neither," Toller said. "I got me a ride."

"Screw you, Toller!" Jake snapped.

"Sorry, Jake. I was only kidding. I do appreciate the hand. Graves would've loved for me to accept that airlift back to base. I'd have gotten there a lot more comfortable, but then he'd have the satisfaction of washing me out at the finish line."

"Well, you're not going to washout. We may have to go to graduation this afternoon like we are, me carrying you, but we'll be there. Ten more and it's a done deal."

The nine weeks were over. Ranger School was a done deal. Jake, and the others, less twenty-five percent or so, had earned their patch.

The beginning of the jungle phase had found them already weak and half-starved, and they were considerably more so now. They were hollow-eyed, blister infested, sick, partially eaten and drained by insects and leeches, and exhausted. Though unappreciated at the moment, the cadre had made the experience as real as possible. The past nine weeks had been as close to the physical and psychological stresses of war as they could make it. More importantly, each candidate who survived the course had discovered his inner-self. For a lifetime, each man would know the depths of his reserves, the strengths, and abilities that are still available even when the senses tell him that all is hopeless and defeated.

Jake would never forget the simulated Vietnamese villages that had been built for their benefit. They had been complete with booby traps and even civilians. The cadre prepared the candidates for their future, which was most likely an authentic experience in South Vietnam. The harder the training, the harder the cadre, the better chance those of this class had of survival. Jake could not help but think of Charley. He had lost his life in the jungle. It was all very humbling. Charley had been through Ranger School, and he had these same lessons. But he was dead.

The aggressor's role in the training was to represent the enemy. Most of the aggressors were a mixture of Vietnam veterans from various units, and they were as dedicated to making the training as realistic as were the instructor cadre. They were fierce. They were good. They were professional. Staff Sergeant Saul Apodaca learned to respect them the hard way and taught everyone in the course a valuable lesson in the process. He was taken prisoner on a moonless night from the rear of a normal patrol mission. They tied his hands, gagged him, and lead him to their camp in the Panhandle of Florida swamps. After a short discussion, the aggressors stripped him of his clothes, hoisted his tied hands behind him from a tree so that he was perched on the tip of his toes, then tied a noose around his neck. They repeatedly asked him who the members of his patrol were and the objective of their mission. As the hours wore on, Saul tired, his body ached to touch the ground and as his heels slipped downward, the noose around his neck tightened. He was near hanging himself when the aggressors cut him loose. He had not talked. But they were not finished. As the sun rose, they threatened to stake him to the ground naked and douse his body with syrup. The idea of ants chewing bits of his flesh away and crawling in his ears and nose was enough for Apodaca to tell the aggressors what they wanted to know. The aggressors wrote the names of each member of the patrol and the details of the mission. Twelve hours later, Jake and his patrol walked into an ambushed, and in theory, killed down to the last man. The aggressors made it real. Just like Vietnam, or any other war for that matter. Saul Apodaca did not flunk the patrol for breaking, but the patrol leader did. He should have known that Apodaca, or any man, could be broken. He should have anticipated that possibility and altered the execution of the mission to protect his men. He failed. He flunked.

1600 Hours
30 August 1971
Flight 616 to New York

THE STEWARDESS REACHED into the overhead bin for a blanket. The handsome cadet was fast asleep though the plane had barely left the runway and was still in its steep ascent. It had only been minutes before takeoff that she had brought him forward from coach to a vacant first-class seat. She stared for a full minute at the young man who seemed so strange. Although his gray uniform jacket and white starched trousers were immaculate, he had the look of one who had been through a horrible ordeal. His deeply tanned face and hands were drawn taut, like old weathered leather, and his eyes were sunken as though he had been off to a concentration camp—like those remembered from an earlier war. The scratches. His forehead and cheeks and knuckles had deep scratches, some old with dark scabs and some more recent, red and fresh. As the stewardess unfolded the blanket, her eyes fell to his chest. She did not understand the significance of what the grizzled cadet wore on his uniform, but she knew that the ordeal he had been through was directly related to them. On his chest, he wore the jump wings he had earned in June and a small black patch bordered in gold with the word "RANGER" affixed with a straight pin. She gently covered Jake with the blanket, smiled, then turned down the aisle to perform her duties.

CHAPTER TWENTY-TWO

0900 Hours
31 August 1971
United States Military Academy
West Point, New York

THE BUS ROLLED down Thayer Road toward the barracks area. Jake felt excited about seeing familiar surroundings and anticipating the reunion with friends. Though the summer had passed quickly, it seemed in some ways to have been the most extended summer ever. The place looked good to him. The river was beautiful this time of year, as were the gray granite buildings that had become his home.

Everywhere, immaculately groomed cadets in gray trousers with black stripes, white, starched shirts, and gray hats scurried in every direction. The old cadets had arrived the previous day. The start of another academic year was imminent. At ease, the upperclassmen were comfortable with the surroundings and amongst friends. But it was not so for the plebes. As in every new year, the plebes were scared. Yesterday, there were three plebes for every upperclassman. Now it was reversed. The plebes could only react to their brutal, abusive environment and learn subtle skills like never giving excuses for failure, taking responsibility for all one's actions, and performance under tremendous stress. Seemingly without purpose to the plebes, those character traits must be present in a leader of men in combat. The more important lesson, the more subtle lesson, was learned by the upperclassman creating that abuse and stress. As the upperclassman matures, he often concludes that as a commander of troops, there will always be those at the bottom rank of the unit that can be easily abused, belittled, and denigrated. The lesson learned is that an officer of honor treats soldiers with respect and fairness. The upperclassman learns this lesson of compassion by having been a plebe himself, then given the responsibility to teach it to others.

As the bus came to a stop in front of Grant Hall, Jake looked through his window and smiled at the look of terror on the faces of the new plebes and wondered if they comprehended how very long the next nine months would be for them.

Following a short walk to the barracks and a sign-in with the Cadet in Charge of Quarters on the third floor, Jake kicked the door open to his room. Patrick jumped from his chair. He was startled from his concentration of stamping his name neatly in each new textbook.

"Dang. You're doing the same thing you were doing the last time I saw you, three months ago," Jake said with a broad smile across his face, "just sitting on your scrawny ass."

Though expected to come stomping through the door sometime during the day, the combination of Jake's actual entrance and his unexpected physical appearance left Patrick momentarily speechless. He had not prepared for Jake looking like he did. After a moment of staring into Jake's sunken eyes, he snapped back to the reality of being overwhelmingly happy to see him. A broad smile swept his face, and then he flew across the room to grab Jake in a bear hug.

"Damn, it's good to see you. I've been a nervous wreck the past two days waiting for you to come sliding through that door. I thought a bear might have eaten you. And a poor meal you would have been. Where you been, son? We expected you Thursday."

"Graduation was Thursday. Yesterday, I spent the day traveling."

"Glad you're back," Patrick said as he took the duffle bag and threw it on Jake's assigned bunk. "I gotta say though, you look like death itself! What did those guys do to you down there, anyhow?"

"Same as you'll be getting in two years," Jake replied with a chuckle. "It was bad but not as bad as you think. Guess I look a little pooped, huh?"

"Pooped? No, you don't look pooped, buddy. You look like you just returned from the Bataan Death March. Those starving, Ethiopian babies look healthier than you do."

Jake grinned at Patrick's endless exaggerations. He had missed them. "Well, a few good meals and a week of sleep will put me back on the road. How about you? By the looks of your hair, you must have decided to go hippie on me."

"Yeah, right. An inch and a quarter on top and a month's growth on the sides is hardly hippie hair. Besides, I think it looks pretty good. I'll keep it as long as I can. It will probably be a couple of days before Major Griffin gets around to writing people up for haircuts."

"Wanna bet?" Jake asked. "I'll bet old Griffin is at supper formation tonight, barking down your collar to be at the barbershop tomorrow morning."

"Right. I think I'll have it shaved down to the bone in protest of the academy's failure to assimilate itself into modern society."

"You'd probably look better bald," Jake said. "And we'd all be thankful for that."

"Jeez! You've been back five minutes, and you're slandering a saint already. Speaking of saints, I know you'll be disappointed in me, but I wasn't one while I was home on leave."

"Gee, Patrick, that surprises me," Jake mockingly said as he slumped in a chair and propped his feet on the desk like he always did. "Go ahead. I'm your father, confessor. Tell me all your juicy and wicked sins."

"It was wonderful," Patrick began, delighted in recounting his thirty days of revelry. For the next half-hour, Patrick went through every detail of the dozen or so girls he had dated. It was apparent when he had finished that Tennessee was a much more tranquil place since his departure for New York. "Yep. It was wonderful. I wish you had been there with me. You'll have to come to Chattanooga for Christmas leave. I told every gal I met about you. They anxiously await the mysterious Texan. Course you'll have a hard time living up to what I told 'em."

"Knowing how much bull you're capable of spreading, I'd best stay away from Tennessee. Besides, if I were there, you might not find a woman available for yourself."

"Well," Patrick said in mock indignation. "I reckon Ranger School took the Sara outta you, huh?"

"No," Jake said, smiling cockily. "But I did learn to accept things the way they are."

"Jeez. You're hopeless. Let's go over to Grant Hall for a burger and show off that Ranger tab you're wearing."

"You mean a real burger?" Jake said as he jumped to his feet. "You mean with meat from a cow? Real meat?"

"Nah. I called ahead. The cook is making a snakeburger for you.

1800 Hours
31 August 1971
Dallas, Texas"

Look, Sara," Brent said in a disgusted tone. "I have to work. I have to compile this report and prepare all the charts for the presentation in Ft. Worth on Monday. You know how important this contract is to the old man."

"I know it's important," Sara said flatly, "but you promised me you wouldn't miss another Lamaze class. You've only been to two meetings. How do you expect to be able to participate in natural childbirth if you don't know the first thing about it? It's not supposed to be this way, Brent."

"I'm sorry, honey. I promise I'll make it up to you next week. I promise." The line was silent. Brent sat forward in his leather executive chair and put his elbows on the desk. He had played this silence game before with Sara. If Brent said nothing, she would speak first to try to confirm that he was not mad. She felt horrible when he, or anyone else for that matter, was mad at her.

As he waited, he lightly drummed the eraser of a pencil on the leather desk pad and stared out the full windows of his corner office on the fifty-fifth floor, in downtown Dallas. His father had leased the top floor of Dallas's newest office tower and gave Brent, his new Executive Vice President, an enormous corner office that overlooked all the northern part of the city. It was lavish. The furnishings and art alone cost as much as their house in North Dallas, and that was in the middle six figures. Brent enjoyed sitting in the office and admiring the beautiful woods, leathers, and works of art. Slaving over spreadsheets and attending boring meetings with his father was worth it. The satisfaction he got from the admiring and envious eyes of clients or salesmen who came to the company headquarters was worth every mundane moment. It gave him a sense of power to know how others envied his wealth and success.

"Brent?" Sara finally said in a beaten tone.

"What?" Brent replied, sounding disgusted, rather than the sense of satisfaction he felt.

"I'm sorry if I sound like I don't understand about you working late. I know you work very hard at the company. It's just that I wish you had some time for me, for us. In a few more months we're going to have a baby. We're going to be a family. I need you right now."

Before replying, Brent cocked his head to one side and rolled his eyes toward the ceiling. "Look, Sara. You're all worried about nothing. I'm working so we can be the family we want to be. I want to be able to give you and the baby everything the world has to offer. Surely you understand that I'm just a low executive. I have to work hard so I can take care of those I love. I'm sorry I can't make it to the Lamaze class tonight, but I just can't. I promise I'll make it up to you."

"You're not a low executive, Brent. You're the son of the owner, not to mention that he's the grandfather of our baby. You can do whatever you please at the company."

"Well," Brent said indignantly, "no one is giving me a damn thing down here. I'm the Executive Vice President because I work hard for this company. I'm sitting in this chair because I earned it. No one has given me a damn thing. Sara, I'm disappointed that you aren't more supportive of me and my work. It's my work that pays the bills around there, you know? Sometimes I don't think you appreciate all that I do for you and the baby."

"I appreciate it," Sara said, disheartened. "I guess I just worry sometimes that you don't love me at all, and that you don't want this baby."

Brent leaned back in his chair again and propped one foot on top of an open drawer. "Of course, I love you, Sara. And I can hardly wait for the baby to arrive. You shouldn't worry, and I'm excited about being a daddy. And over the years, you and I are going to have even more babies waddling around the house. I promise, Sara, someday I won't have to work as hard as I do right now and we'll have lots of time together. I promise."

Sara was silent. She was so acclimated to Brent's lies that the truth was becoming harder and harder to recognize. He made her feel like she was going insane. The double messages and his words contradicted his actions. Brent swore that he had changed, had grown up, since his days at the University of Texas, and that his priority in life was his life with her, their marriage, and their family. She did not know what to believe from him anymore. A part of the trust that was supposed to be there was missing, maybe lost forever. But she had made a decision to give Brent Mosher the best she had to give.

Their baby was soon to be born, and maybe her mother was right about time solving the problems between them. She had to keep trying. She had a baby to think about now. "Ok, Brent. I'm sorry if I sound like an old nag. I'll go to the Lamaze class by myself."

"That a girl," Brent said with a smile. "I'll be late, probably around midnight. Those charts will take me awhile. I love you."

Brent hung up the phone and walked slowly to the private bathroom adjacent to his office, combed his hair, straightened his tie, then returned to the large desk. After pulling his chair forward, Brent picked up the pencil again and, with slow deliberation, dialed seven digits on the phone with the eraser end. The phone rang once. It rang twice before it was answered. "Lisa. We're on. Let's have dinner at Chayn's, then back to your place."

CHAPTER TWENTY-THREE

800 Hours
1 October 1971
Sao Paulo, Brazil

SUKARNO APPROACHED the iron gates of the secluded estate as the sun tilted deeply to the west. His baggy, khaki pants and loose-fitting, olive-colored shirt were clothes out of character for him. They were the inconspicuous clothes worn by native Brazilians of the lower class. A straw hat and leather sandals completed the disguise, making him appear to be just another local. An unfamiliar automobile or even a cab driver to the estate would have drawn attention for anyone looking for the slightest variation from the normal, so he walked the last several miles. Even to a trained eye, Sukarno appeared to be merely one of many common laborers that worked the gardens or lawns of the surrounding estates.

Leaving New York and secretly traveling to Brazil had been a challenge, and Sukarno congratulated himself on going so far without being followed. It was merely a matter of patience and intelligence, he had concluded. A series of cabs and subway rides had allowed him to change into the clothes of a merchant seaman in a restaurant across from the Port Authority, then a brief walk across the street and a twenty-five-dollar ticket bought a bus ride to Boston, leaving behind him several Indonesian military agents frustrated at his disappearance. From Boston, under a false passport and another change of clothes, Sukarno traveled to Panama. There he purchased a 9mm Beretta and silencer at three times its value from a small-time criminal who fancied himself a world-class arms dealer, then boarded a Danish cruise ship for Rio De Janeiro. Sukarno retained the week-old stubble that was beginning to take form as a legitimate beard and mustache as it furthered his disguise and plans for entering Sao Paulo undetected. Upon arrival in Rio de Janeiro, he was rested by the four-day cruise and immediately found a greedy captain of a fishing trawler that would take him south without any questions. The trip had been debilitating and uncomfortable, but at last, he arrived to visit his family undetected by frantic agents of the Indonesian government, and his appearance and smell would fool even his mother.

"Bom dia!" the guard at the gate said in Brazilian Portuguese.

"Yes, it is a good day," Sukarno replied with the few words of Portuguese he knew. "Dr. Pasha. Tell Dr. Pasha I wish to speak to him." The guard understood little English but understood well enough that the vagabond in front of him knew where he was and that Señor Pasha lived on the estate.

"What is your name, Señor? I will see if the doctor will see you. Do you have business here?" The guard was perceptive. Perceptive enough not to be fooled by the dirty clothes and vagrant appearance. Though dressed like a peasant, Sukarno's bearing and manner were transparent. He was not a peasant.

"Tell the doctor that the one he loves and trusts most has traveled far. He will understand."

The hired guard rang the main house and repeated in Portuguese what Sukarno had told him. The translation was not exact, but close enough. A few minutes passed, then the gate opened as another uniformed guard from the guardhouse at the residence approached in a jeep.

Sukarno removed his hat as the guard drove the jeep down the long drive then stopped in front of the house. He touched Sukarno's arm, indicating that he should remain in his seat until told otherwise. A long moment passed. Sukarno saw the curtains part from a room several yards forward and instinctively knew that it was his father straining to identify the visitor. It did not take long. Even in the plain clothes and a dark beard, Kuwat Bangjar recognized his son.

"My son, it is so good to see you." Kuwat was genuinely happy to see Sukarno and nodded to the guard, indicating that this visitor was most welcome. "I didn't expect you. I thought you were going to wait in New York until I sent word that it was safe for you to travel."

"Don't worry, Father. It was safe. Especially the way I traveled. No one followed me. I can assure you of that."

Kuwat smiled, then instinctively glanced toward the gate in the distance with apprehension. To be followed would be disastrous. Of late, he had begun to wonder if he would ever be able to surface from the confines of the secluded estate. More than once, he had had second thoughts about the wisdom of his embezzlement. Though vast and beautiful, the estate was still a prison of sorts. The months had passed slowly. He missed the power he had as an influential man in the world, the luxuries of travel, public recognition, and the intellectual interaction experienced by the privilege of high office. Wealth and power without appreciation were less rewarding than he had imagined.

Sukarno met his mother in the foyer, as well as his two sisters. Eka, at sixteen had grown into a beautiful woman, tall and dark and elegant in manner. Sita, at seven, was aglow at the sight of her older brother and raced to him with a squeal of excitement. "My son," his mother said, in a gentle tone of voice, as she ran the palm of her hand across his unshaven face. "We've missed you so. These months without word from you have been the longest ever."

Sukarno kissed his mother's cheek and affectionately patted her back. "I've missed you. I've missed you all," he said as he reached to lift Sita in his arms. "I could not stay away from you any longer.

It took me two weeks by every means of transport, but I am here, safe and happy, and I am glad that all of you are safe as well. I have been worried."

The family moved together to the formal living area and time passed quickly as each recounted the past months. Within an hour it was as though they were all back in Paris on holiday or at home in Jakarta. Maria, the only household help, had selected clean clothes from a past manservant's quarters, not unlike those he was wearing, and Sukarno retired to a guest room for a shower.

He had made it. He had traveled thousands of miles without detection. No one knew where he was, and more importantly, his family was still undiscovered. Time was on his side.

2000 Hours
4 October 1971
Sao Paulo, Brazil

THREE DAYS WANDERING the vast estate and spending time with each member of his family had been a time he would always remember. His father irritated him, as he consistently did, but his sisters pleased him. Eka was utterly bored with her confinement. She was anxious to meet others her age in Sao Paulo and to participate in all the exciting things she had read about Brazil. She was eager to live her life. Sukarno laughed and assured her that her confinement was necessary for the moment but that it would not last much longer. Sita was in just the opposite frame of mind. She loved the freedom of life on the estate grounds, and much to his mother's horror, Sita was determined to climb trees and dig holes on the grounds for the pure sake of digging. She was a seven-year-old, typical of her age. Sukarno enjoyed watching her innocence and teasing her.

Kuwat was nervous the first day following Sukarno's arrival. He feared for their safety. His concerns soon vanished, however, and he was pleased to have Sukarno for conversation. Forgotten was his boredom, and his commitment to their quest for revolutionizing the Muslim world renewed his enthusiasm. Kuwat strolled every foot of the estate with Sukarno and pointed out its features and its natural defenses. The sea with a private beach and steep cliffs secured one side of the estate, with mountains to the rear, and dense forest on either side forced any visitor to enter the estate through the main gate. He had been careful not to invite curiosity. Maria traveled to Sao Paulo twice each week for anything needed to run the household, and only two hired security guards protected entry to the grounds. Kuwat could afford an army to defend him, but more security would raise questions. So far, his family's safety remained uncompromised, and he intended to keep it that way.

Sukarno entered the kitchen area and snatched an hors d'oeuvre. Maria grinned at him as he sheepishly shrugged his shoulders at having been caught. "You should wait, Señor Pasha. Dinner will be ready in a few minutes."

"I'm sorry, Maria. I'll not do it again." Sukarno poured coffee into a disposable cup and slowly stirred in a spoonful of sugar. "I'll take Pablo a cup of coffee. I'm sure he would appreciate something to drink in the guardhouse while the rest of us eat this fabulous meal you have prepared." Maria giggled at the compliment. She liked the young Pasha because he was so relaxed and considerate of her feelings.

"Pablo. I have brought you coffee."

Pablo quickly folded his newspaper, surprised that Señor Pasha had been so thoughtful. He was embarrassed, but also grateful. It was not often that one of his station in life was treated kindly by those higher in society. So long as he did his job correctly, those of a higher status ignored him.

"Keep your seat, Pablo. I don't want to disturb you. I just thought you might enjoy a cup of coffee while the family has dinner. You must get bored sitting in this guardhouse all day." Sukarno slowly wandered around the walls of the room, looking intently at the different black and white photographs that had been left by the previous owner.

"Thank you, Señor Pasha. That was very considerate of you. "Pablo sipped his coffee, uncomfortable around Sukarno, or anyone of his social status. He didn't know what else to say, so he concentrated on his coffee and said nothing.

Studying one picture at a time, Sukarno moved around the walls. When directly behind Pablo, he glanced over his shoulder to see Pablo again reading his paper. Sukarno turned silently, drew the silenced Beretta from behind his jacket, placed it within an inch of the back of Pablo's head, and pulled the trigger. The Beretta bucked lightly in his hand and made one soft spitting noise. Sukarno pulled the shades on the two windows in the guardhouse, darkening the room, then glanced at Pablo slumped over the table. Blood pooled around his head with the cup of coffee undisturbed and still steaming. Sukarno locked the door and closed it behind him before strolling to the main house for dinner.

Dinner was being served when he entered the dining room from the kitchen. Maria set trays of food on the long table as the other members of the family took their customary place at the table. Familiar mealtime chatter was underway Sita described to her father a new hiding place she had found in the rocks on the beach that bordered one side of the estate, Eka interrupted and pleaded with her mother that Sita had taken a stool and small table from her room to the new secret hiding place, and both Kuwat and his wife were trying to deal with both girls at the same time. Sukarno sat on the side of the table to his father's right and smiled. His father could negotiate the toughest deals in the world of international finance, but when it came to his two daughters, he was at a hopeless loss. He could magnificently arbitrate between kings and presidents, but he could never settle a dispute between Eka and Sita. Sukarno's mother, on the other hand, had a way of remaining calm. She would say "Yes, dear" to both, and somehow, both would feel vindicated enough to allow the crisis to end.

"Sukarno," his father said, "Why don't you take Eka to bed

Paulo tomorrow and buy some clothes. Also, we need an automobile. I've given it a great deal of thought, and I want you to buy something that will blend appropriately with this neighborhood. But I do not want it to be an automobile that attracts too much attention in the city. A nice car, but nothing lavish. I know that you will find something appropriate."

"Yes, Father," Sukarno said. "I will take care of it. I take it by your desire for us to go into the city that you are not concerned about our identification."

Kuwat Bangjar hesitated. "There is a risk. There will be a risk for many years. However, we cannot live in total isolation. That, too, can become suspect. Perhaps some visibility and movement is an asset rather than a liability."

Eka was ecstatic about leaving the estate. Months of confinement had been hard for a sixteen-year-old. Sita immediately made her pleas to join them, but Kuwat said no without hesitation. Sita knew that "no." Appeal to the higher court, her mother, would not succeed.

"I agree, Father," Sukarno said. "If the family has the appearance of being in hiding, then it won't be long until people notice. Gossip and rumors travel fast. Sooner or later questions would be asked. It is better to appear normal with nothing to hide."

Sukarno sipped his wine. "Excuse me. I think I'll have a white wine rather than red. Would anyone else care to join me?" Both Kuwat and his wife shook their heads to indicate that the red was the correct choice. A white wine was inappropriate for the meal. Sukarno slid his chair back and walked calmly to the kitchen with a glass in his hand. Maria was preparing dessert. "Wonderful meal, Maria," Sukarno said as he stabbed the cork of the bottle with a corkscrew.

"Obrigado, Señor Pasha," Maria said, appreciative of the compliment.

Sukarno drew the Beretta from his belt and walked calmly toward Maria. She did not notice his approach as she sliced the fresh tart, and Sukarno brought the weapon within an inch of the base of her skull and pulled the trigger. As she fell forward against the sink, Sukarno caught her at the waist to prevent her from falling. For a moment, he was surprised at the spatter of blood and gore on the white cabinets and curtain. The bullet had exited the front of her face, taking a mass of blood and tissue with it. Sukarno laid Maria's limp body on the floor softly to avoid any undue noise.

"This wine is marvelous. You really should try some, "Sukarno said as he re-entered the dining room. Kuwat glanced at him and smiled, then resumed his conversation with his wife while Eka and Sita argued again embedded in conversation about the missing furniture. Sita was almost convinced to return the stool and table in exchange for an old cot that was stored in the gardener's shed collecting dust.

Sukarno walked directly to his place at the table, set his glass of wine in its proper place, then casually unbuttoned his coat to draw the Beretta. Kuwat saw the pistol immediately and stared at it, his fork midway to his mouth. Sukarno pointed the gun at Kuwat without expression and quickly fired two rounds into his father's chest. Kuwat slumped back in his chair, blood flowing freely through the two holes in his white shirt, eyes wild with pain and confusion. The other members of the family were stunned. They were speechless at the horror they had just witnessed. Sukarno met his father's eyes, then turned the Beretta and is silencer toward his mother. He fired immediately. The first round caught her in the throat, and the second in the forehead. She was dead. Eka screamed and scrambled as quickly as she could toward the study. With only a dozen full steps behind her, Sukarno fired three rounds in her direction. Two rounds missed the moving target, but one round hit her in the center of her back. She toppled forward to the floor, made a feeble attempt to crawl away, then died. Sita was gone when Sukarno turned toward her chair. He turned his head toward the foyer and saw his baby sister racing up the stairs to the second floor.

Sukarno was not concerned. Sita would be easy to find. He

ejected the magazine on the floor and replaced it with a fresh magazine containing nine shiny 9mm rounds. Sukarno sighed, then faced his father. Kuwat was still alive. His chest drained life's blood and sucked air through the hole in his lung. "Well, Father," Sukarno said condescendingly after sipping the white wine. "Sorry, it had to end this way. I am sorry. Especially for my mother and my dear sisters."

Kuwat tried to speak, but his struggle was in vain as blood poured from his mouth, not words. His eyes followed Sukarno, consumed in sadness. There was no fear for the death that would soon take him. There was only the pain and sadness brought forth by deadly betrayal, and the sight of his wife massacred before him. A lifetime of lust for power and wealth evaporated in a flash of time. With death's grip, they were meaningless. Life, in its last moments, was simplified to its essence for him. His thoughts were of his wife, his daughters, and his love for them.

"All this wouldn't have been necessary, Father. But you were a fool," Sukarno laughed. "You thought you could steal half-a-billion dollars and get away with it. What a fool you are." Sukarno sipped again at the wine. "Don't worry. Your dreams will be partially fulfilled. I will be a powerful man. I don't yet know how or what, but I will be. That's what you wanted, isn't it?"

Kuwat closed his eyes for a moment, and a tear rolled down his cheek. He did not try to speak again. It was hopeless.

"You have to die, Father. They would take the money, and then we would all die. At least this way I shall survive. You wanted me to think of a way to make in-roads with a new Darul Islam government. Well, I don't know about that, but I can make in-roads with the current government. What could be better than to punish the great traitor of our country and to return the fortune stolen from the people? Well, not all of the money, you understand."

Sukarno raised the pistol and aimed it at Kuwat's face. Kuwat closed his eyes a mere second before the Beretta again bucked in Sukarno's hand. With slow deliberation, he poured his glass from the bottle and listened intently for any sounds coming from upstairs. There were none.

Sita had taken the steps on the staircase two at a time to the upstairs area only to find herself trapped. There was no one to turn to, and nowhere to hide. She was panicked and sobbing uncontrollably as she ran from room to room, searching for some reason to believe that this was only a bad dream and not real. Sita's mind did not want to accept that her brother had just killed her mother and father and Eka. Finally, after racing to every room, she found herself sitting on the floor in the corner of her parent's bathroom with her knees pulled tightly to her chin, immovable from the horror.

Sukarno climbed the stairs calmly, a glass of white wine in one hand and the Beretta in the other. He paused at the top of the stairs to listen for sounds that would tell him where Sita was hiding. Still, he heard nothing in the mansion. Eka's room was on the right, Sita's on the left. He quickly searched both. She was not there. Back in the hallway, he paused again for sounds of a terrified little girl. With no clues of her presence except an ever-tightening trap, he opened the door to his parent's room. Immediately he heard sobs behind the bathroom door. He tried the doorknob. It was locked.

"Sita. Open the door. Let me in."

Sita cringed tighter into the corner and hugged her knees with all her might. "Go away!" she screamed through the tears.

"Let me in Sita," Sukarno said calmly. "I won't hurt you. I promise."

"Go away! You hurt my mother! You killed my daddy. You killed Eka!" Merely saying it made it real. Sita started screaming and crying out of control.

Sukarno stood back from the door and fired three quick rounds at the doorknob, then stepped forward and kicked the door. It opened. Directly in front of him in the corner was his hysterically distraught sister. He walked into the room several paces and immediately fired the pistol at her. Again and again and again, he fired. Four 9mm slugs ripped through her legs and chest and face. The sobs stopped.

Sukarno stood for a full minute staring at her bullet-riddled body. The others had not bothered him, but the sight of Sita did. He leaned over the sink and vomited.

Within the hour, Sukarno started the jeep and drove down the long dark driveway to the gate. The telephone call to the banker in New York before he left would have dozens of Indonesian agents and Brazilian police at the estate before daylight. It was time to go.

"Good evening, Señor Pasha," the guard at the entrance gate said.

"Open the gate. I have business to transact for my father in the city."

The guard shrugged his shoulders. Since when was he one to question the coming and going of his employers? He reached inside the guardhouse and pushed the red button on the control box. The moment the gate started to open, Sukarno raised the Beretta and fired two rounds into the guard's chest.

Business in Sao Paulo was finished.

CHAPTER TWENTY-FOUR

1600 Hours
25 November 1971
United States Naval Academy
Annapolis, Maryland

Jake browsed through a journal from the Naval Institute and chuckled to himself as he paused on an article concerning the latest technology on sonar devices. The chuckle came from the recognition that Steve's world was as technical as his, only in different areas. He had about as much knowledge of sonar as Steve had of armored vehicles with air defense capability.

The Army-Navy game was only a week away, and it was his turn for an exchange visit. When given a choice between Annapolis or Colorado Springs at the Air Force Academy, the decision was easy. A week following his old friend Steve around would be fantastic. He had not seen Steve since last Christmas, and his rescue from the belly of the bridge over Chandler Creek, following the news of Sara's marriage. He was anxious to talk about old times.

Having arrived an hour early, the wait for Steve at Brigade Headquarters seemed an eternity. Every swabbie that passed said,

"Beat Army!", with a colorfully descriptive noun or two attached. The first two or three times he was greeted in such a manner, he was undecided as to how he should reply. Was he to say the first thing that came to mind? Would that be proper? After some thought, Jake decided that such answers were admittedly a bit too direct, especially since he was outnumbered by a mere four thousand to one. It did not seem the best of times to let his mouth lead him to the end of some sailor's gangplank. But, when the next midshipman passed with a smirking, "Beat Army!", Jake smiled back, violated his own counsel, and said, "Up yours," and returned his eyes to the outrageously boring article on sonar.

Though the time passed slowly, Steve finally burst through the door with a load of books under his arm. He had just finished his last class for the day and had run from the academic building to get Jake. Admiral Hollifield had made a suggestion to his deputy commander, who in turn, made a pointed suggestion to a squadron commander, and so on, that Midshipman Second Class Steve Ross has the honor of hosting their visitor, Cadet John Paul Jacobs for the week. Steve's official job was to take Jake with him to every class, every activity, and to have Jake bunk in with him. Steve's unofficial job, per the loaded suggestion of the superintendent, was to have a good time with his life-long friend.

Exchange visits between the three academies were traditional. The supposed purpose was to bring the branches of service closer together by learning the other's environment, but primarily the purpose it served was for a cadet or midshipman to get out of his hole for a few days by going to someone else's hole. For all concerned, it was fun. By this time of the year, the plebe system had grown monotonous. It was great fun having someone out of the ordinary in the barracks to pick on.

"You look fantastic!" Steve said excitedly as the two affectionately slapped each other on the back. "I've been pacing the floor since Admiral Hollifield called the barracks and told me you would be my roommate for a week. I didn't think I'd see you till next week at the game."

"Yeah. The Admiral must be pretty excited about setting this up for us. His office called me just a couple of days ago."

"Let's get out of here," Steve said as he held the door open for Jake and his gear. "Being around these brigade bigwigs gives me the willies."

"Don't worry about them. I swept those sailors off their feet with my charming conversation and civility while I was waiting."

"Missed you in Comanche last summer," Steve said with a smile across his face. "Didn't seem like the same place around there without you. I saw your parents. How was Ranger School?"

"Piece of cake."

"That bad, huh?" Steve asked.

"Bad enough," Jake said with a smirk.

Steve understood the unspoken language. There are some experiences in life, like one's plebe year, for instance, that is simply beyond description. One would have to be there to understand what 'bad enough' meant.

"I think it's great you did it," Steve said, smiling back at Jake. "You'll get a lot of ribbing in the barracks this week, but I'll tell you, all the guys have respect for that tab you're wearing. There are guys here that would likely kill for the chance to go to Ranger School, but only the Marine Corps warpos can enjoy that little exercise, of course. One of my roommates, Jerry Stiles, plans to go Marine. He's as gung-ho as you are. You two will have a lot in common, that is, deliriously stupid."

"Marine, huh?" Jake asked as his thoughts flashed back to two enlisted Marines in his Ranger company. "Had two of them at the course. Good soldiers."

"I'm sure they were sharp," Steve replied. "Not many of those jar-heads get the opportunity to do Ranger School. If they were there, they were hand-picked."

Steve held the door open to the barracks as they entered and ascended the stairs toward the company area. The decor was different, but the activity was the same. Plebes slapping their backs against the wall, yelling, "Sir, may I pubbl".

"Holy Crap!" a midshipman screamed as Steve and Jake rounded the corner. "Hide your wallets! We got us a gen-u-ine - Airborne-Ranger-West Point-Kadet on deck!"

Steve chuckled. Jake frowned. Jake reserved his opinion as to the exchange being fun. He expected a week of teasing but was hoping for brother in arms razzing rather than ridicule from some warped hatred for Army. Within moments his fears were put to rest.

"Ron Jarret. Welcome aboard, Army," the midshipman said as he offered his hand and a genuine smile. "Most of us here in the company feel like we already know you. If Steve likes you, in spite of your choice of service, then we will, too."

"Thanks, Ron," Jake said, relieved. As they shook hands, dozens of other midshipmen came out of their rooms to greet their visitor. "Beat Army! Beat Army! Beat Army" A chant began as they each, in turn, came to Jake for a friendly handshake. Jake was pleased.

The week at Annapolis could not have been more fun. One might have thought that Jake and Steve would have grown somewhat apart over the past two and one-half years. After all, they were miles away from each other, in different branches of service, and the life they had known together back in Comanche was nothing but a fading memory. So much had changed. They had changed. They had grown. But, as they learned during this one short week, real friendship does not change with time and distance. It only grows in tandem with the individuals offering the friendship.

1300 Hours
3 December 1971
John Fitzgerald Kennedy Memorial Stadium
Philadelphia, Pennsylvania

The game opened as usual with the traditional march-on by the Corps of Cadets and the Brigade of Midshipmen. Jake felt totally out of place in his Dress-Grays amongst the sea of white hats. Spending a week in enemy territory was one thing, but having to march on the field with them at the Army-Navy game was almost more than one should be expected to bear. As they marched to the beat of the band, Jake thought of how the cadets must have felt back in 1943. Due to the war and the restrictions on transportation, the Brigade of Midshipman could not make the trip from Annapolis to New York City, where the game was then played. Apparently, some desk jockey in Washington had a brilliant idea. That is, to split the Corps of Cadets in half and make one- half cheer for Navy. Unbelievable. They sang the Navy songs and cheered the Navy cheers as though they were midshipmen. Navy won the game.

The first volley of water balloons filled the air and crashed amongst the sea of midshipmen. The Army catapults, well-engi-neered with enough velocity and altitude to spare, were able to hit their mark with ease. A sign held by two plebes read for all to see. "Remember '69", referring to the same shameful stunt pulled off by Navy two years prior, but with less accuracy. The midshipmen were helpless. Four thousand white hats and a few gray visitors were tightly packed shoulder to shoulder, and all they could do was watch with indignation as the multicolored balloons fell while the stadium roared with cheers from the enemy. As the volleys continued in rapid succession, five Navy A-6 Intruders buzzed the stadium in close formation, and the midshipmen's cheer rose in volume as the roar from the jets diminished to the north. Army fired its howitzer. Ka-Boom! As if to intimidate the aircraft. Ka-Boom! The Navy cannon replied. Again, within minutes, the

Intruders strafed the stadium, north to south, at a fearfully low level and with such speed that the crowd of one hundred thousand shuttered at the power above them. "On, brave old Army team! On to the fray..." the cadets sang the Army fight song loudly with vigor. The Navy band had had enough. The melodious roar of "Anchors Aweigh" blended with the song of the West and all those present knew that the Army-Navy game was again underway.

The first half of the game had its usual ups and downs for both teams, with Navy leaving the field seven points in the lead. As always, game tickets were sold out in advance, and the television networks sold advertising time at a premium. Even with the unpopularity of the Vietnam War at home, millions of ex-military people and their families gathered around a television or radio to cheer for their favorite team, as did thousands around the world still in uniform whose pride for another twelve months was dependent on the outcome of the game. It did not seem to matter that the athletes themselves were perhaps much smaller or less proficient than might be found at some larger universities known for their football dominance. Army-Navy football was recognized and appreciated around the world not for its premium execution of the game, but for the sheer guts displayed on the field, the spirit of the services involved, and the enthusiasm exhibited in a good old fashion tradition of mutually respectful competition. Like all the games that had proceeded it, this game held adrenaline levels high on both sides of the stadium.

At the halftime goal post meeting, Jake spilled popcorn on Patrick and his date when he was physically spun around to face his attacker. "Last year you invited me to sit amongst the gray hats, then you ignore me for an entire year. What kind of gentlemanly conduct is that, Mister?" Julia Dane scolded Jake as she shook her finger in his face. "If you're not nice, I'll sic my daddy on you."

Jake stood shocked as Julia, Admiral Dane's daughter, joined the goalpost reunion and scolded him like a plebe. Steve interrupted by leaning over to plant an affectionate kiss on her cheek. "Jake. You remember the lovely Julia Dane, don't you?"

"Of course," Jake said, regaining his composure and recognizing that Julia was not some lunatic attacking him in the bowels of Memorial Stadium. "I'd almost forgotten how beautiful your green eyes are. I am a fool, aren't I?"

"Good God, you sure are, buddy!" Patrick popped off. "Miss Julia," Patrick continued, "if my idiot roommate has offended you in any way, I'd be happy to give you my phone number and address so we could get together so that I could comfort you in your obvious anguish." Patrick's date slapped his arm in mock offense as though to remind him that he already had a date and that a change in plans was not acceptable. "I mean, I'm... I'm ashamed of Jake. It's all I can do to keep this boy on the right track. You have no idea how hard it is on me, having to watch him every minute. I promise, Miss Julia, when we get back to West Point, I'll straighten him out."

"You won't have to straighten him out. I'll take care of that myself," Julia said as she slipped her arm under Jake's. "Come with me, Army. Buy me a coke."

Though Steve and Julia were semi-engaged to be married two-years hence, Jake and Julia started toward the concession stand away from the group. Patrick smiled from ear to ear. "Now, don't you be too hard on him, Julia," Patrick yelled. "He ain't much of a roommate, but he's all I've got."

CHAPTER TWENTY-FIVE

2000 Hours
3 December 1971
Sheraton Hotel

"MISTER JACOBS," Admiral Hollifield said cheerfully as he and the Green Beret colonel advanced on Jake. "You've met Colonel Strong?"

"No, sir." Jake nodded his recognition of the colonel and extended his hand. "Sir, I'd like to introduce you to Miss Julia Dane. Julia, this is Colonel Strong."

"The pleasure is mine, Julia," the colonel replied. "I know your father. I had the pleasure of working with him in the Pentagon a few years back. And how is your mother, Margaret?"

"She is fine, Colonel. She's still working on her doctorate. She has more time for it now that my brother and I are away at school. I remember father mentioning your name. If I remember correctly, you and father worked together right after you were awarded the Medal of Honor in Vietnam. He thinks the world of you, you know?"

"Well, I'm honored that he spoke well of me and that you remembered."

"Julia," Admiral Hollifield interrupted, "would you mind terribly if Colonel Strong and I steal Mister Jacobs from you for a few minutes? I know it's rude, but I promise we won't keep him long."

"Of course, Admiral. I need to find my date, Midshipman Steve Ross. He is a social butterfly and hard to keep up with when there are people to meet and hands to shake." All three of the men watched Julia cross the room to talk to Mrs. H.

"Julia is like a daughter to me. Her dad and I were only a class apart at the academy. A fine young woman," Admiral Hollifield said.

"Indeed, sir," Jake said, "and a whole lot better looking than her father. I mean, yes, sir, she's a fine young woman."

"Yes. Well, I'll pass on your sentiments to Admiral Dane the next time I see him," Admiral Hollifield said with a chuckle. "Truth is, Julia did get her mother's looks. If she looked like Bill Dane, she'd be as homely as an English bulldog."

All three laughed. Admiral Bill Dane was indeed homely look-ing, notwithstanding the fact that he was the best carrier fleet skipper in the Navy. "I'm glad we have a few minutes to visit, Jake," the admiral said seriously. "I had the opportunity to mention your name to Colonel Strong a year ago, and he asked to meet you. He could have gone to the academy, but he said he'd prefer to meet you informally. And, here we are."

Jake was puzzled as to why a full-bird colonel would want to meet a second classman at the academy? Graduation was a full year and a half away, and besides, colonels do not even talk to fresh young lieutenants, much less some cadet.

The colonel gave Jake a stern look. "You've got a smart mouth. Don't you, Jacobs?"

Jake thought a moment and quickly recovered mentally from the colonel's verbal attack. He had not been a plebe once in vain. "Yes, sir. I've been known to have a smart mouth."

Colonel Strong pulled a cigar from the inside pocket of his

dress blue coat, lit it, and blew smoke into the air as Jake, and the admiral watched, and waited, in silence.

"I pulled your file in the Pentagon," he said without looking at Jake. "And, I called Colonel Weber, your regimental commander at The Point. He told me everything I wanted to know about you, right down to which direction you wipe your butt."

He paused again. The admiral seemed unaffected by Colonel Strong's statement, but Jake was beginning to wonder what this colonel wanted with him.

"You know what your CO thinks of you?"

"No, sir," Jake replied.

"He thinks you have what it takes to be one of my very own snake eaters."

"Sir?" Jake asked, totally confused.

"The Army is changing, son. Warfare is changing. Oh, we are always going to have our big battle groups, customary divisional forces, but the world is changing, Jake. Special Operations is a small concept right now, but it's growing out of necessity. Small units will do a good bit of the fighting in the future. Highly trained limited forces in limited warfare. We've just seen the tip of the iceberg where terrorism is concerned."

"He's right, Jake," Admiral Hollifield pitched in. "When you think about it, the future is likely to hold actions similar to the mess we're in now. The Soviet Union sucked us into this war, but they aren't the ones fighting it. They supply the material, but the fighting is done by others, on soil far away from theirs. They're delighted to see us deplete our resources and spill our blood in indirect conflict with them. It's pretty clear that what we'll see in the future is a continued expansion of their strategy in other parts of the world."

"That's right," the colonel added. "We'll still have wars in the future that call for the big operational divisions, but Special Operations will have an important role there as well."

Jake was listening intently. If it had been just the colonel building a case for elite special troops, he might have been a little skeptical, but Admiral Hollifield was convinced of the concept as well. That made a difference. The admiral would not be selling this idea if he didn't believe in it, and in Jake's mind that made it essential. He trusted him.

"So why are you talking to me about all this, Colonel? I'm just a third-year man at the academy. It's a long time before I select a branch, and even when I do, I'm not so sure I have much to say about what assignments I get."

The colonel grinned and took a long pull on his cigar. "Oh, you have more to say about your career than you think you do. And don't bullshit me, son, you're infantry. You're Airborne Ranger Infantry if I ever saw one. Your Ranger commander says you are a natural, and that you love it. Your CO at West Point went so far as to say you're gifted."

"I've read your files, too, Jake," the admiral said seriously. "You've got a lot to contribute to the military if you put your aptitude to the best use. I've got a young man at Annapolis that has about the same potential as you. A natural-born SEAL. Sure, he's sharp enough to do anything in the Navy he wants, fly, command a ship, do anything. But I sure hope he flows where his talents take him. He may never make admiral by taking that route, but he'd be happier in the long run and serve his country better to boot."

"Which brings up a good point, Jake," the colonel interrupted. "I reckon you've figured out by now that the admiral and I would like for you to consider coming into Special Operations when you graduate, but you need to know all the facts before you make that decision. If you do, there are sacrifices to make. There's no question that you could go straight Infantry and have a brilliant career. Or Armor, or any other branch for that matter. Use your talents wisely and keep your nose clean, I can see you with stars on your shoulder someday. But if you go with Special Operations, you'll probably never get a star. Special Operations is not popular. Many in the service are so entrenched in the disciplines of conventional forces that a barrier of resentment exists. They're against what they call elite troops. They resent the whole concept of maintaining highly trained troops to perform covert operations."

"Yes, sir," Jake said. "I'm aware of the general opinion. I've experienced some of that since Ranger School. Some of my classmates resent or mock my being a Ranger. Kinda silly since they will all be Rangers eventually."

"It's a bit of envy, Jake," the admiral said seriously. "And in part, that's why Special Operations is generally disliked. Envy. There is an aura of superiority about those troops that breeds resentment."

Colonel Strong nodded his head in agreement. "Well, Jake. I just wanted the opportunity to visit with you. I'm the commander of the Special Forces School at Fort Bragg. Think about it. We could use men like you. We need good young officers that will carry this program into the future. I'll retire soon, and I worry about having enough tough officers on board to keep dragging this army into the twenty-first century."

"I'll give it serious consideration, sir," Jake said sincerely.

The admiral waved across the room and motioned for his wife to join them. He was pleased with Jake's response and his interest in what Colonel Strong had said. It would be a hard decision. The colonel's offer meant taking an enormous career risk. By choosing Special Forces, Jake would most likely sacrifice the opportunity to achieve flag rank, the benchmark of career success in the military.

"May I call you if I have questions, sir?" Jake asked as Mrs. H crossed the room.

Colonel Strong handed Jake his card. "Certainly. Any time. If you'd like to visit the school, just let me know. I'll do everything I can to help you make your decision, and, Cadet Jacobs, I'll respect whatever route you decide to go."

"Are you three finished gabbing?" Suzanne Hollifield asked teasingly.

"Of course, dear," the admiral replied. "The course of military history is now set for the next one hundred years. We have it all worked out."

ADMIRAL HOLLIFIELD and Mrs. H. sat at the head of the table with Admiral Dane and his wife, Julia's mother and father, while the other guests sat on either side. The after-game dinner that had started three years ago had grown in number. It had blossomed into a formal affair with over thirty guests. Cadets and midshipmen with their dates, other Navy and Army officers, and a few titled civilians such as the Secretary of the Navy and Secretary of the Army were in attendance, all by selective invitation. Though more formal, the cadets and midshipmen present were made to feel at ease. Admiral Hollifield's objective was for this dinner to feel like a family gathering, and it did.

Admiral Dane tapped his wine glass with a spoon as he rose from his chair. The room fell silent. "Ladies and gentlemen. I want to propose a toast."

Jake smiled across the table at Steve and Julia, then filled their glasses.

"About two weeks ago, and I believe it was late on a Saturday evening, I heard a timid tapping noise at my front door. It's not often that I allow a midshipman or junior officer to see me in my pajamas and bathrobe, but in this case, I could sense the urgency in the young man's voice. So, I let him come into the house. It was Midshipman Second Class, Steven Ross. Mister Ross looked as though he had seen a ghost."

Everyone at the table chuckled in anticipation of the story as Steve sat blushing in his chair. "Just like a sailor," Wayne said.

"Mister Ross sat on the sofa in my den and was having a hard time spitting out whatever it was he had on his mind. He was turning and twisting his hat. I thought he was going to wear a hole in it. To make a long story short, Mister Ross finally asked me for my beautiful daughter's hand in marriage."

"Just like a sailor," Wayne said again.

"I told Mister Ross that perhaps they should wait a few years," the admiral said with a chuckle. "You know what Mister Ross said to that?"

"We'd believe anything from a sailor, Admiral," Patrick said. Everyone laughed, including the admiral.

Admiral Dane continued. "He said that he didn't think waiting was a good idea because there was this guy up at West Point, named Jake, that Julia thought was a pretty swell guy. Then he asked me how I would like an army son-in-law."

Again, everyone laughed. Steve and Julia held hands, smiling at each other. "That's really like a sailor," Wayne said. "Blame it on the Army."

"I have to tell you people, the thought of my Julia in the hands of a West Point man sent shivers down my spine. After considering the situation for a minute, perhaps less, I suggested that he wed my daughter in the academy chapel immediately following graduation next June." The admiral paused while all the guests clapped at the good news. "I propose a toast to the engagement of my daughter to Midshipman Second Class Steven Ross. Mister Ross is a fine young man and will make a fine husband and officer in the United States Navy. Julia's mother and I are happy for both of you and wish you many years of love and happiness."

"To Steve and Julia," Admiral Hollifield said as the cadets, midshipmen, and officers rose in the presentation of the toast. Steve and Julia kissed, then fielded the congratulatory comments and handshakes from everyone present.

Following dinner, Admiral Hollifield tapped his glass with a spoon, and the room again fell silent. "Ladies and gentlemen, I hope you all enjoyed your dinner."

"A toast to the admiral and his lady," an Army captain said. All rose and lifted their glass in honor of their host and hostess.

"Thank you," the admiral continued. "Suzanne and I appreciate all of you joining us this evening. Needless to say, you were invited to this dinner tonight because I can call you brother. What I am about to say is confidential, for your ears only. For the past two years, this dinner has been a special event. I've been disappointed in the outcome of the game... two of those years. But even in defeat we have very much enjoyed this traditional dinner. You've probably noticed that a band will play for us shortly. And yes, Mister McSwain, they will be playing elevator music."

The admiral sipped his wine while everyone had the opportunity to laugh at his joke. "However, the band will not be allowed to join us until I've had a chance to make my little speech. This annual event started three years ago when Suzanne and I met Midshipman Ross, Cadet Jacobs, and Cadet McSwain in a restaurant after the Army-Navy game. I'm happy to say, that event changed our lives. For Suzanne, it gave her three sons to love and be the beneficiary of her concern. As for me, I've grown to feel the same about them. But, more importantly, knowing them and watching their careers develop has renewed my faith in the future of this country. I feel rededicated to my years of service, and I sense a new vigor in my stride to carry me forward in the service of my country."

The admiral paused to sip his wine. The small group focused on every word. Admiral Hollifield was one of the most respected men in all the branches of service, and any speech he might make deserved complete respect. His words were likely to hang in the halls of history, whether spoken to a small group such as this, or from the podium in the U.S. Senate.

"Vietnam has broken my heart. The war—if you want to call it that—is all but finished. The truth of the matter is, America has lost this war. The enemy didn't defeat us. We have been beaten by ourselves. Our diplomats discuss our withdrawal with our enemy, yet continue to send men to die after capitulation. Shameful." Admiral Hollifield paused to compose the emotions raging within him. "It brings tears to my eyes when I think of one soldier, or sailor, or airman dying on the fields of battle. Gentlemen, over fifty-thousand beloved brothers have fallen. I've asked myself, "Why, a thousand times fifty?""

The room was deathly silent, but for the admiral's words. Each in the room, and especially those in uniform, felt Admiral Hollifield's anguish.

"We wear our country's uniform to serve her. Our forefathers drafted a mighty Constitution which called for generations of dedicated men and women to defend it, and our leaders rightfully demand that we serve and protect without question. I'm proud to say that during this Vietnam Era, we have been faithful to our charge. However, I am sad to say, that the custodians of our Constitution, and the people that we have so ardently sought to defend, have abandoned us to die singularly and en masse in the horrors of warfare. Those custodians—the president, Congress, and the courts—use loose construction of the Constitution to engineer politics to a deadly degree for the achievement of their own self-interests. Our government abandoned us. They abandoned us by committing us to war without a declaration, then gave us orders not to fight for victory. In this way, our government has committed the most despicable of deeds. Our people abandoned us. They've forgotten that we are but their servants of those great and noble causes of freedom and liberty that we have dedicated our lives and service to. Those in the military today are often spat upon and ridiculed for their service to the country. Perhaps, these very people either don't realize or don't want to admit that they are the very ones who voted into power those who engaged us in war, and who have lengthened it by their lack of integrity."

Jake stole a glance across the table at Steve, then to the major sitting next to him. The major smiled through his emotional pain as he stared at the hand that was no longer there. Visions of Charley as a young man in Comanche flashed through Jake's mind, and he fought to control the swelling tears.

"Yes. The three young men at this table renewed me. A shiny new midshipman and two cadets showed me the future and gave me hope. While their peers ridiculed them, they took a stand. And, ladies and gentlemen, it wasn't just these three. There are thousands of young men and women who are standing with them. You know... Cadet McSwain shocked me three years ago. He said, "Sir, when I signed on at the academy, I didn't think I would live to see the age of thirty. I'll graduate. I'll go to Vietnam. I'll die"."

Patrick shuffled uneasily in his chair. To his way of thinking, it was dangerous for any officer of flag rank to remember what you say or do.

"Suzanne will attest to my bewilderment and frustration. How could these young people choose of their free will and volition to swim against the tides of criticism and abandonment? How could they stand for people and principles that they thought would steal their very lives? I'll tell you how, and why!" the admiral said with a raised voice. "It's simple. It's because there will always be young men and women who are willing to lay down their lives for the freedom of others and this wonderful nation of ours. Vietnam hasn't turned out to be about democracy in that country. Perhaps it could have been, but it isn't. Vietnam is about democracy and freedom in this country."

Suzanne rose from her chair and nestled close to her husband's side. Of those present, only she knew of the turmoil he lived night after night for ordering men into combat and death. The admiral put his arm around her waist, appreciative of the support she had given him over the years.

"Cadet Jacobs summed it up three years ago when he was still a runny-nosed plebe. Jake told me that he was at West Point to preserve America and that when he finished his military service, there would be another plebe training to do the same, and another following him. Cadet Jacobs, in his innocence and his idealism, was right. The perseverance of freedom in this country is paramount, despite the mistakes our voters and politicians make over the years. The freedom to live and love and pray is supreme. Not many today have the courage to stand for the perseverance of freedom, nor do many have the courage to stand by those who do."

Admiral Hollifield stood taller as a tear rolled down his cheek. Suzanne tightened her grip around his waist and looked up to him.

"Ladies and gentlemen, I'll not retire until they force me into a rocking chair. These last few remaining years of service are more meaningful to me than all my years preceding. Like you, I've never felt more needed by my country than I do today. It's a time of sadness. It's a time when those of courage stand all alone. I salute all of you here tonight. I love each one of you for loving my country as I love it.

Though indoors and uncovered, the admiral took one step back from his chair and executed a perfect salute. The military personnel at the table immediately rose from their chairs and returned the admiral's salute in unison.

EPILOGUE

WEST POINT of the trilogy *A Full Measure* ends following Admiral Hollifield's after-game dinner, and Jake and Patrick return to West Point for their remaining one and a half years to graduation. It could be said that cadets quickly embody the character and essence of West Point. Conversely, West Point is more than bricks and mortar in that it, as an institution, is a reflection of the character and essence of its graduates, and that reflection is The Long Gray Line. The process, down to the smallest detail, has placed Jake and Patrick in a transition from being in a position of teachability and enforced humility to the development of the capacity to lead, and more specifically, to lead men in battle.

Jake, Patrick, and Steve have established a bond that is likely understood fully only by those that have lived in a particular environment together and have shared hardships. The reader may, or may not, know this bond from personal experience, like military service or combat, but can sense its depth. And, if not a personal experience, the reader may find that such a bond would have been desirable in their life experience. Certainly, such a bond is inexplicable between members of military service components when no other commonality exists, like when they served or where they served. The bond exists only on that thin thread of shared sacrifice of military service. And while inexplicable, the actions and dialogue in the A Full Measure trilogy give the reader a notion of its authenticity.

Book I Jake and Sara's young, idyllic love for each other. Were readers surprised by this calamity? Some say, "yes," and they are saddened by Jake's heartbreak, and perhaps angered by Sara's actions. Others may have celebrated the circumstances, if for no other reason than to see the characters moved out of quixotism to normalcy, that is, to circumstances that are a bit messy. Book I ends with both Jake and Sara struggling with issues of personal loss. Jake seeks to accept the reality that who he thought to be his soulmate has rejected him for another and feels a deep sense of hopelessness from the absence of choice. Sara, on the other hand, suffers from the consequences of a bad decision. With thought preceding action, Sara is becoming aware that her delusional thinking has led her to consequences, not in the realm of delusion, but in the realm of objective reality, and that the reality is a place she never intended to go. Is there such a thing as soulmates, or a right love? If so, and if Jake and Sara are soulmates, are they foredoomed to fail in another love relationship? Will they find another love greater than the one they have lost? Or, will Jake and Sara find their way back to each other?

Sukarno Banjar, an Indonesian with a life of privilege and an American education from Princeton, has demonstrated a Mephistophelian lust for power without bounds. In *West Point*, the birthing of Sukarno's inordinate ambitions to destroy Western culture, and particularly that of America's, parallels Jake's development as a combat leader committed to protecting America from enemies both foreign and domestic.

Book II of A Full Measure will take the reader into the dynamics of that shifting sand, called life, for the characters, including Sukarno's steep climb to power by becoming the foremost source of financial resources for the purpose of radical Islamic terrorism. His American education and family influence position him to not only manage various legal investments, but also to fund terrorism through illegal means such as money laundering, trafficking conflict diamonds, organized kidnappings for ransom, slavery, fraud, and narcotics.

With a backdrop of the final days of the Vietnam War, Book II, The War Tocsin, is a compelling read where each of the characters is on a collision course with intense difficulty. As in life, the intersection of these lives is perhaps providential, but unknown, where seemingly insignificant decisions and choices weave the tapestry of *A Full Measure*.

ACKNOWLEDGMENTS

I would like to sincerely thank those who helped in the narrative of this book, including my wife, Debbie, for her support of this project through many hours of writing. I am grateful for Frank Eastland, Raeghan Rebstock, and their team at Publish Authority for their encouragement and professionalism. And, without L.D. and Dana Swift encouraging me to seek a publisher, the manuscript for *West Point* would remain, to this day, in a drawer.

There were many who helped to make this novel a reality: my invaluable first readers, including L.D. and Dana Swift, Mike Herbert, Greg Graves, Steve Foust, Trae Wolfe, John Barrett, Sandy Lyons, Travis Rush, and Marlie Ball Echavarri, I want to thank Sandy Lyons and Renee Carter for their proofing skills, my son Michael for his skill with the photos required for this project, and my son, Jason, for his ability to think outside the box in the telling of this story.

ABOUT THE AUTHOR

Following two years of college at New Mexico Military Institute in Roswell, New Mexico, J.M. Patton attended the United States Military Academy at West Point with the Class of 1973. A shoulder injury and an unsuccessful surgery yielded a medical discharge at the end of his second year at West Point. His departure from West Point was devastating to him, but he continued his education and earned a degree in mathematics at Baylor University. After successful years with a large U.S. computer company, his career evolved to various officer positions in finance, banking, and securities. He then embarked on a career change when given the opportunity to teach high school history and mathematics in a small New Mexico rural community. Here, along with his teaching responsibilities, he initiated and coached a six-man football team. In 2007, the New Mexico Military Institute asked him to return and join their faculty as an Assistant Professor of Mathematics. After retiring in 2014, with all his endeavors and professional achievements, he counts himself truly blessed to have had the opportunity to influence students' lives for eighteen great years. He is currently working on completion of the trilogy, A Full Measure.

Post note: Five years after his shoulder injury at West Point, the Houston Medical Center through the VA hospital performed a nine-hour "Let's-see-what-we-might-do-to-fix-this-shoulder" surgery, which has served him well since.

More on the author's website at JMPattonAuthor.com.

f facebook.com/J.M.Patton.Author

A NOTE OF THANKS

Thank you for reading

If you enjoyed *West Point*, we invite you to review it online and encourage your friends and family to read it as well.

Publish Authority

CPSIA information can be obtained
at www.ICGtesting.com
Printed in the USA
LVHW011155150920
666055LV00006B/716